APACHE SHADOW

Barlow was startled by the appearance of a second Apache, who was sliding down the embankment not twenty feet to his left. Barlow fired; the broncho kept sliding, and when he hit the bottom of the ravine, he fell. But Barlow's elation was short-lived; the Apache rolled over and began shooting. A bullet kicked dirt into Barlow's face as he desperately rolled away from the rim of the embankment. He felt the searing burn of a bullet on the inside of his left arm, just above the elbow. Lying on his back, he tested the arm, flexed the fingers of his left arm. Everything was still working. The bullet had just grazed the skin.

He didn't hear the third Apache's attack, or even see it. He just felt it coming, some primeval instinct kicking in to warn him of danger, and he rolled again, onto his belly, and once more blazed away with both pistols. The broncho stumbled, got off one wild shot before dropping his rifle, and then fell sprawling, almost on top of Barlow. Barlow swung a leg around and prodded the broncho with a bootheel. There was no response. The Apache was dead.

APACHE SHADOW

Jason Manning

A SIGNET BOOK

SIGNET
Published by New American Library, a division of
Penguin Group (USA) Inc., 375 Hudson Street,
New York, New York 10014, USA
Penguin Group (Canada), 10 Alcorn Avenue, Toronto,
Ontario M4V 3B2, Canada (a division of Pearson Penguin Canada Inc.)
Penguin Books Ltd., 80 Strand, London WC2R 0RL, England
Penguin Ireland, 25 St. Stephen's Green, Dublin 2,
Ireland (a division of Penguin Books Ltd.)
Penguin Group (Australia), 250 Camberwell Road, Camberwell, Victoria 3124,
Australia (a division of Pearson Australia Group Pty. Ltd.)
Penguin Books India Pvt. Ltd., 11 Community Centre, Panchsheel Park,
New Delhi - 110 017, India
Penguin Group (NZ), cnr Airborne and Rosedale Roads, Albany,
Auckland 1310, New Zealand (a division of Pearson New Zealand Ltd.)
Penguin Books (South Africa) (Pty.) Ltd., 24 Sturdee Avenue,
Rosebank, Johannesburg 2196, South Africa

Penguin Books Ltd., Registered Offices:
80 Strand, London WC2R 0RL, England

First published by Signet, an imprint of New American Library,
a division of Penguin Group (USA) Inc.

First Printing, March 2005
10 9 8 7 6 5 4 3 2 1

 REGISTERED TRADEMARK—MARCA REGISTRADA

Printed in the United States of America

Chapter 1

His name was Coughlin. Born in Texas, he'd spent four years fighting Yankees during the recent War for Southern Independence. But before that, he'd lived on the Texas frontier and had been fighting bandits and Comanche raiders from the age of ten. In fact, fighting and killing was all that Coughlin knew, which was why he excelled at his present occupation: scalp-hunter.

Coughlin had no idea how many men he had killed in his lifetime. He'd never been one to count his victims. The tally didn't matter to him. He'd killed on the Texas frontier and on the battlefields back east to stay alive. Now he killed to make a profit. He derived no particular pleasure from it. He was not consumed by a hatred for the Apache, as it seemed so many others were, especially the Mexicans. It was a hatred fed by fear, he'd decided. The feud between Mexican and Apache stretched back for generations, and it seemed to Coughlin that no Mexican would rest easy unless and until every last Apache was dead. That applied even to the ones who were trying to live in peace north of the border, the ones who resided on the reservations set aside for them by the United States government. The four Apaches in the canyon below were Coyoteros—and they were of the peaceful variety. But since the Mexicans were the ones offering the bounty on Apache scalps, and they made no distinction between peaceful Apaches or renegades, Coughlin didn't either.

He was a big, bearded man, grim and weathered as he sat cross-legged on the rim, in the scant shade offered by a stand of ocotillo. He wore a tunic of butternut gray—more than just a memento from the war, it was his lucky shirt; he'd survived Shiloh and Chickamauga and Franklin in the shirt without a scratch. Buckskin trousers and a battered, wide-brimmed hat completed his attire. A .50 caliber Sharps buffalo gun lay across his lap. He needed such a weapon, because he preferred to do his killing from a distance. It was safer that way—especially when you were dealing with Apaches, peaceful or not.

Faded blue eyes, narrowed into slits against the glare of the desert sun, scanned the opposite slope of the canyon. Somewhere over there were his two associates, Skaggs and the Mexican. They had orders not to shoot until he did. He was pretty sure they wouldn't, even though they'd been hunkered down for more than two hours and Skaggs wasn't long on patience. But Skaggs had been around Coughlin long enough to know you didn't cross the Texan if you cared at all about your health and well-being.

Coughlin wanted to wait until the four Apaches reached the water hole, which he could see from his vantage point. He'd found the water hole just today, and careful scouting of the canyon provided evidence that Apaches often visited. Of the four, one was a woman, one a child. One of the two men was young, probably not yet twenty years of age; the other was twice as old. They would be wary approaching the water hole. But once they reached it, they'd let their guard down a bit. At least Coughlin could hope that would be the case. He'd learned to wait until the moment he had the advantage. He didn't fight fair. Only people who had something to prove fought fair.

It was a shame, he mused, that the Apaches were traveling on foot—he and his associates augmented the scalp bounties they earned by selling any weapons or mounts appropriated from their victims. Coughlin had no idea why the Apaches were traveling through the canyon—where they had come from or where they were going was no concern of his. It was likely that they lived in a cowah somewhere nearby, apart, for whatever reason, from the several Coyotero che-wa-kis, or villages, located in these hills.

When they reached the water hole, the woman and child knelt to drink. The young man took a quick look around and followed suit. The older man slowly and carefully surveyed the canyon walls. He looked right at Coughlin's hiding place, but the distance was too great, and the scalphunter too skilled at blending into the environment. The older Apache finally knelt at the edge of the water, laying down the rifle he'd been carrying.

Coughlin raised his own rifle, drew a bead, and fired without hesitation.

The bullet struck right between the Apache's shoulder blades, and the impact hurled him facedown into the water hole. Across the way, Skaggs and the Mexican began shooting. The young man died next. The woman grabbed the older man's rifle and got off a few shots in Coughlin's direction; she knew, in a general sense, where the first shot had come from, and since she was Apache, she was going to die fighting. Coughlin admired her for that. He reloaded the Sharps, oblivious to the bullets burning the air in his vicinity. He was drawing a bead on the child when the

woman went down, shot dead by either Skaggs or the
Mexican, and she fell sideways just as Coughlin
squeezed the trigger. His bullet, meant for the child,
struck her instead. The child—Coughlin couldn't tell
if it was boy or girl, and didn't care—had been standing, frozen in shock and fear, ankle-deep in the water
hole. Now, suddenly, the young one bolted and, before
Coughlin could reload, disappeared around a bend in
the canyon beyond the water hole.

Muttering a curse, Coughlin finished loading the
Sharps and then quartered down the slope, moving
with a lithe grace that was surprising for someone so
big. He was sure the older Apache was dead, having
fired the shot himself, but he wasn't going to count
on Skaggs and the Mexican being crack shots, so when
he got down to the canyon bottom, he approached
the bodies with caution. His cohorts were making a
headlong descent of the other slope, and as they came
closer, Skaggs let out a whoop that echoed down the
still-as-death canyon. Coughlin grimaced. As far as he
was concerned, scalphunting was serious business, but
Skaggs thought of it as sport. An attitude like that
tended to make a man careless, and in this country a
careless man was a dead man, sooner or later.

"Hot damn!" exclaimed Skaggs, delighted. "That
was too damn easy!"

Coughlin looked at the Mexican. The Mexican
never said much, and neither did his expression. He
gazed at the dead Apaches without a glimmer of
emotion.

"Don't just stand there," said Coughlin. "Go get
the kid."

The Mexican gave him a blank look, then, with a
curt nod, started off up-canyon at a lope.

"I swear," muttered Coughlin, once the Mexican

was out of earshot, "I think that one has Apache blood in his veins."

"Mebbe we should take his scalp someday," Skaggs said and giggled.

"Yeah, why don't you try someday?" said Coughlin dryly. "I'd like to see you try."

Skaggs was picking up the Apaches' rifles. "We'll get fifty pesos apiece for these repeaters down on the border," he said gleefully.

"Almost as much as we'll get for these scalps," said Coughlin, in disgust. The Mexican government was paying twenty-five pesos for every male scalp, ten pesos for every female and child.

"It's enough," said Skaggs. "Enough to buy some mescal and a Mex woman."

Coughlin looked askance at his partner. That was all Skaggs cared about—getting drunk and having a woman. For his part, Coughlin wanted more. He wanted enough money to set himself up for life in some Mexican town. But the money they got for killing these Apaches wouldn't go far. A night or two in a border town and they'd be stone broke again. Still, Coughlin was philosophical about it—there were limited opportunities for an ex-Confederate with only one bankable skill.

A single gunshot rang out from up-canyon. It was the Mexican, taking care of the kid. Coughlin drew a knife from its belt sheath and went to work, starting with the older man. Grabbing a handful of the dead Apache's hair, he made a circular incision around the top of the skull, starting at the hairline. The scalp came off the dead man's head with a wet popping sound. Coughlin put the scalp in a pouch slung over one shoulder—a pouch stained black with the blood of previous victims. He took the young man's topknot and was working on the woman when the Mexican returned, the limp body of the child under one arm. Coughlin nodded at the Mexican. He didn't know much about the man, and was suspicious of his lineage, but it couldn't be denied that the Mexican was almost as efficient at killing as he was. He just wasn't sure that the Mexican could be trusted—and he never turned his back on the man. The profit turned on scalp-hunting was usually pretty slim, especially when cut three ways. Coughlin had occasionally contemplated getting rid of his associates, and he had to assume that the thought had crossed the Mexican's mind too. Skaggs, on the other hand, was too stupid to consider it, and too scared of Coughlin to try something like that. The Mexican didn't appear to be afraid of anything.

"Skaggs," said Coughlin, as he finished scalping the woman, "go fetch the horses."

Looking skyward, Coughlin squinted at the buzzards already circling in the hot updrafts rising out of the canyon. It didn't take them long to find death, and they served as a signpost for anyone who might be in the vicinity. Coughlin wanted to put as much distance between himself and the water hole as quickly as possible. Other Apaches weren't the only potential danger. There was the United States Army to worry about. He and his colleagues had just killed four Coyotero Apaches—and for all Coughlin knew, they'd done the deed on land that was part of the Coyotero reservation. This was something the blue bellies would frown upon, since they were trying to avoid another war with the Apaches. What the Mexican government would happily pay him for, the Yankees would hang him for.

Which was why he was more than a little annoyed

when Skaggs showed up with only two horses and their pack mule in tow.

"What the hell is wrong with you?" he snapped. "My horse, too, damn it."

Skaggs looked worried. "Your horse is dead, Coughlin."

"What are you talking about?"

"Bullet in the skull."

Coughlin recalled how the Apache woman had grabbed up a rifle and fired several rounds at the canyon rim where he'd been laying in wait. His horse had been well-hidden and on the back side of the rimrock. That she'd killed it had to be a fluke. Ricochet, possibly. Coughlin cut loose with a long string of epithets. Just his luck that something like this would happen. But he'd learned to adapt quickly—a skill learned the hard way on a half dozen battlefields, where almost nothing went the way the goddamned officers planned it.

"I'm taking your horse, Skaggs," he said, in a tone of voice that made it plain he would brook no objections. "You ride the pack mule."

"I don't wanna ride no mule, Coughlin," whined Skaggs.

Coughlin scowled. "I don't care what you want. You weigh in at half of what I do. The mule can carry you and the provisions too. Besides, it won't be for long. We'll pick up the first horse we see, and then we'll make tracks for the border."

"There is a rancho," muttered the Mexican. He was pointing due east.

"Hey, that's right," said Skaggs. "Spread run by a feller named Barton. No, Barlow. Yeah, that's it." Skaggs was pleased with himself for remembering. "Barlow, that's his name."

"I don't care what his name is," rasped Coughlin, exasperated. He went to Skaggs' horse and climbed into the saddle. "Long as he doesn't mind parting with a horse."

"What if he *does* mind?" asked Skaggs.

Coughlin glowered at him. "What do *you* think?"

They rode away from the water hole with Coughlin in the lead, and Skaggs, cursing as he kicked the mule into motion, bringing up the rear.

Chapter 2

It had been the same every morning for more than a year—Joshua Barlow would step out of the small adobe house that he called home to stand in the slanting morning sunlight on the porch and gaze across the sagebrush flats to the Mogollon Mountains, blue and jagged in the distance, and feel a great contentment sweep over him. The smell of the sage mixed with the wood smoke that rose from the chimney of the house and of the larger adobe structure across a stretch of hardpack that served as a bunkhouse for the ten men who worked for him. The horses in the corrals were stirring, galvanized by the rising of the sun. Farther out, he could see a handful of the hundreds of cattle that grazed on land belonging to him. To him and Oulay, the Chiricahua Apache woman who had become his wife. Part of that contentment was pride of ownership. But more than that was the fact that he'd been blessed, this past year, with Oulay's love. *That* was what made everything worthwhile. Compared to that, nothing else much mattered. And as long as he had her at his side, it really didn't matter if he owned a thousand cattle or none at all.

Until now he hadn't fully understood why his father, a Northerner and a high-ranking officer in the federal army, had chosen to live in Georgia, where, in the years leading up to the Civil War, so many of his neighbors had despised him and everything he represented. Timothy Barlow had fallen in love with a Southern belle—Joshua's mother—and had gladly endured the contempt and hatred of Southern natives to spend his life with her on the plantation she'd inherited from her father. In doing so, Timothy Barlow had become a reluctant slaveholder, a situation that alienated many Northerners. But no sacrifice had been too great for him. As Timothy Barlow's son, Joshua had sacrificed too, growing up an outcast, spurned by most of the other Southern-born children he knew; and sometimes, as young and self-centered people are prone to do, he'd even resented his parents for putting him in such an untenable position.

It had been for love, of course—and these days Joshua knew a love just as strong. Like his father, he was willing to risk anything, endure any situation, for that love. His one regret was that he hadn't been afforded an opportunity to tell them that he comprehended—and respected—the depth of love they'd shared and forgave them for any discomfort it had caused him in his childhood. But not too many months ago he'd received word from an attorney in Georgia that his father had died of natural causes, and that his mother had passed away only a few weeks later—of a broken heart, said some. It was a heavy blow—one Joshua wasn't sure he could have endured without Oulay's abiding love providing him with solace. And that was why his mother and father had been willing to face all the scorn heaped upon them— because when a man and a woman shared a love such as theirs, and like the one Joshua shared with Oulay, they didn't need anyone or anything else. Joshua didn't need the land or the cattle that now belonged to him, at least not for himself. He stayed and worked and toiled and sweated to build something for Oulay and for the children he hoped they would have one day.

This land—and many of those cattle—had once belonged to someone else, a rancher named John Ward. Ward was dead now, killed by Apaches. So were Ward's children, a son and a daughter. In those days Barlow had been a lieutenant in the United States cavalry, trying desperately to prevent an Apache war that Ward, and many others, had desired. That war had come, and many had died. But now peace—albeit an uneasy peace—reigned. Many of the Chiricahuas, including Oulay's father, the great chief Cochise, were renegades hiding in mountain strongholds in Mexico. Most of the other Apache bands had made their peace with the Pinda Lickoyi—the white man—and lived now on reserves set aside by the United States government for their use in perpetuity. Barlow was no longer in the army; he'd given up his commission under circumstances that had put him at risk of court-martial. He'd served, reluctantly, as chief of Apache scouts during the failed campaign to capture Cochise and his people before they could cross the border. During that campaign he had seen lives squandered, friends lost. Oulay had almost been lost to him, as well, kidnapped by a Netdahe, an Apache renegade named Kiannatah. But she had been restored to Barlow—thanks in no small part to an old half-breed scout known as Short Britches.

That was all behind Barlow now, though. Most folks expected the uneasy peace between white man and red to come to a bloody end, and soon. Barlow tried not to think about it. When he *did* think about it, he vowed to himself that he would not get involved.

Across the way, several of the cowboys who lived

in the bunkhouse were coming out onto their porch
to smoke the first cigarette of the day or to wash up
at the water basin on a trestle table near the door.
Most of the men who worked for him were vaqueros.
Barlow thought they were a good, reliable bunch.
They worked hard, were loyal to him, and he, in turn,
trusted them. But the man he trusted most of all—
Short Britches—did not live in the bunkhouse. He
spent his days and nights roaming the desert, patrol-
ling the perimeter of the ranch, looking for trouble.
There was something comforting about the idea of the
old scout riding the line. No one knew the country,
and the people who roamed across it, better than
Short Britches.

Barlow was turning to go back inside when Rodrigo,
posted on the roof of the adobe bunkhouse, stood up
and let out a whistle. Ever since the Netdahe named
Kiannatah had attacked, killing three vaqueros and
abducting Oulay, a lookout was posted around the
clock. Rodrigo was pointing to the west. Barlow
peered in that direction. For a moment he didn't see
anything. Then the horsemen appeared, coming up out
of a depression in the ground, about a quarter mile
away and heading straight for the ranch buildings.

With a grimace, Barlow stepped inside the adobe.
His rifle was leaning against the wall right by the door.
Oulay was busy cooking breakfast, but she wasn't so
preoccupied that she didn't notice when he picked up
the long gun.

"Is something wrong?" she asked.

"No," he said, speaking in her tongue. With the
help of Short Britches, he'd learned enough Apache
in the past year to communicate with her, and that,
in turn, had facilitated her learning a little English.
But she'd had more difficulty with his lingo than he'd

had with hers, so they spoke, for the most part, in Apache.

She looked at him with those dark eyes, so filled with wisdom for one so young, and he realized that he was going to have to provide her with more information. He didn't want to worry her, but on the other hand he understood her desire to stay informed—after all, she was the one who'd been kidnapped by an Avowed Killer, and it was really nothing short of a miracle that she had survived the experience.

"A few riders coming," he said. "Just being careful." In other words, it was probably nothing to worry about. He could never tell, by her expression alone, whether she was worried or not. She was Apache, after all, and a certain degree of stoicism had been inculcated in her from an early age.

Giving her a reassuring smile, he stepped outside. By now, the vaqueros at the bunkhouse had armed themselves too. The riders were close enough for him to determine that they weren't Indians. Not that this meant Barlow would lower his guard.

The vaqueros stood by, watching him. There was nothing he needed to tell them. They knew, as he did, that in this country any stranger was a potential enemy, and they would follow his lead without question.

As the horsemen drew near, Barlow sized them up. Two Anglos and a Mexican, they looked like a rough lot. The big, bearded man in the lead wore buckskins and an old Confederate tunic. Barlow knew that after the war many men had come west, turning their backs on shattered lives, hoping to make a new beginning. Some had met with success, and some were trouble. This one looked like he fell into the latter category. He gazed at the armed vaqueros arrayed, in deceptively casual poses, across the front of the bunkhouse, then angled his horse toward Barlow.

"Howdy," he said, fixing his sun-faded blue eyes on Barlow. "You the big augur around here?"

"This is my place."

Coughlin nodded in the direction of Skaggs, astride the pack mule. "We need a horse. Got one?"

"I've got horses, but none to spare."

"We've got rifles to trade, a few other things."

Skaggs held up one of the rifles they had taken from the dead Apaches.

"Got plenty of rifles too," said Barlow.

"Yeah. I noticed." Coughlin glanced across the hard-pack at the vaqueros.

"What do you have there?" Barlow nodded at the bloodstained, fly-specked pouch slung over Coughlin's saddle horn.

Coughlin's eyes narrowed even more. "Now is that any of your business?"

"Maybe not," said Barlow. "You can water your animals. Then I suggest you ride on."

Oulay picked that moment to emerge from the adobe. She stood in the doorway, behind Barlow. Coughlin and his two associates stared at her, and Barlow didn't like the look in their eyes. He raised the rifle just a little. It was enough to get Coughlin's attention.

"So you won't trade us a horse, then," said Coughlin.

"No."

Coughlin gave him a long, appraising look. Then, with a curt nod, he spurred his horse into motion, and led his two associates away from the ranch buildings. Barlow watched them until they were several hundred yards away. Only then did he lower the rifle and turn to look at Oulay. She was watching him, not the departing strangers.

"Don't worry," he said.

"I don't. I'm not afraid."

He knew that she wasn't. He was afraid, though. Always afraid that he might lose her again—and that the next time he wouldn't get her back.

This time of year there was plenty of work to be done on the range, but Barlow let the vaqueros handle it and stayed close to home. He knew what was contained in the pouch that the big bearded man was carrying. Scalps. Apache scalps, undoubtedly. And he didn't like the way the strangers had looked at Oulay.

That afternoon Short Britches rode in. The old scout dismounted at the water trough and let his horse, a shaggy mountain mustang, drink its fill. Barlow crossed the hardpack to join him.

"Trouble's coming," said Short Britches, with no more emotion than he would show in remarking on the weather.

"It's already been here. Three men. Scalphunters."

"That explains it," said Short Britches, looking out across the desert plain in the direction from whence he'd come.

"Explains what?"

"Coyotero bronchos. About a dozen of them. Coming this way, in a hurry."

Barlow took a closer look at the old scout's horse—and noticed that it had been run hard. The animal didn't look like much, but Barlow had never known of a horse with more stamina or spirit. In the mustang's case—as with its owner—looks could be deceiving. Short Britches was a scrawny, grizzled man of indeterminate age, his body bent by age. His clothing

looked like castoffs, including the battered stovepipe
hat atop his head, incongruous headgear for this country. The old scout looked like a man who deserved
one's pity, and certainly not a person who could in-
spire fear or respect. But Short Britches was the most
dangerous man Barlow had ever met.

"How long before they get here?" he asked.

"Couple hours. They're trailing three riders. I don't
know why."

"I do," said Barlow, grimly. "Those three are
scalphunters."

Short Britches gravely pondered this news for a moment. "What did you do?"

"They needed a horse. I told them no and sent them
on their way."

The old scout just looked at him.

"You think I shouldn't have let them go."

The other shrugged. "I know why you did. But the
Coyoteros probably won't."

And he did know—knew that Barlow wanted nothing more than to stay out of the trouble that always
seemed to be brewing between Apache and Pinda
Lickoyi. Barlow had sensed that Short Britches
thought it wasn't a very practical goal. And though he
would never have admitted it to anyone, Barlow was
afraid the scout was right. Now it seemed that events
were conspiring to prove that this was so. Barlow had
a certain reputation among the Apaches as one of the
few white men who could be trusted to keep his word
and to treat the Indian fairly. But not all Apaches
trusted him. He could not guarantee that the Coyotero
war party would believe that he had not aided and
abetted the trio of scalphunters they were tracking.
They might not even bother asking. Barlow felt
trapped by circumstances beyond his control into a
course of action he didn't want to pursue.

"Okay," he said gruffly. "Maybe I should have done something more. But I can't go after them now."

"No, we can't," allowed Short Britches. "We must wait for the Coyoteros."

Barlow nodded. The last thing he wanted was a fight with the Apaches. But he would fight them if it was necessary—if it was the only way he could protect what was his.

"Better go round up as many of the men as you can," he told the old scout. "And get back here as *quick* as you can."

Short Britches stripped his saddle from the mountain mustang. The animal was not only worn-out but waterlogged now. He turned the mustang loose in the corral. Shaking out a lariat, he tossed a loop over the head of one of the other horses in the enclosure. In minutes he had the fresh mount saddled and was riding out. Barlow returned to the adobe. He had to tell Oulay that they were faced with the prospect of even more trouble today. And a war party of Apache bronchos with their blood up was just about the worst kind of trouble you could find.

Chapter 3

When the Coyotero war party arrived, Barlow was ready for them.

Short Britches had brought most of the vaqueros in off the range. Some were stationed in and around the ranch buildings, on the rooftops or behind shuttered windows, all of them heavily armed. The rest were mounted and waiting behind a low rise just east of the ranch buildings, out of sight of the approaching Apaches. If shooting started, their job was to ride in and whisk Oulay away, while Barlow and the others held the Coyoteros at bay as long as possible.

Barlow had not had many dealings with the Coyoteros, but Short Britches recognized the man who led the bronchos.

"It is Valerio," he told Barlow, as they rode stirrup to stirrup out to meet the Apaches, who had paused, in a line, some distance from the ranch buildings. "He is like Cochise among the Chiricahua. The big jefe."

"Is that good or bad?"

Short Britches shrugged. "He is a reasonable man. But he is still an Apache, and if he is here, then this is no small matter."

As they approached the line of Apaches, Barlow

was struck by their appearance. Even though he had
seen more than his share of Apache warriors, they
never failed to impress him. It was as though they had
been chiseled out of the desert, out of the rock and
the heat and the sand and the wind. They were dark,
grim, lean, indomitable. Most wore white himpers and
the n-deh b'ken—knee-high desert moccasins. Some
wore bandoleros filled with shells for rifle and pistol
across their chests. Man for man, they were more than
a match for the best-trained, best-equipped soldiers.
Barlow had no illusions about his chances of survival
if the Apaches attacked.

He and Short Britches checked their horses no more
than twenty feet from the Apache line. In the center
of that line, one of the bronchos urged his pony forward. Upon closer scrutiny, Barlow saw that this man
was older than his companions, though clearly no less
strong and vigorous. He assumed this was Valerio; he
glanced at Short Britches for confirmation, and the
old scout nodded.

"Valerio, you are welcome in my home," said Barlow, praying that his knowledge of the Apache tongue
would be sufficient, considering the importance of
the moment.

"Four of my people are dead," said Valerio gravely,
"murdered by white men who have passed this way.
Were they too welcomed in your home?"

"No," replied Barlow. "They passed through, heading south."

"They asked for fresh horses," said Short Britches.
"But the padrone did not give them what they
wanted."

Valerio spared the old scout the merest of glances;
he didn't seem too impressed. "Who were these
men?" he asked.

"I had never seen them before," replied Barlow. "I do not know their names. But I'm pretty sure they were scalphunters."

"And you let them pass," said Valerio, his gaze piercing, accusatory.

"Yes. I shouldn't have. But at the time I just . . . I didn't want any trouble."

"But now we are here, and you have changed your mind," said the Coyotero jefe dryly.

Barlow grimaced. He was not without pride, and he bristled at being chastised by Valerio, but tried not to let it show. "Yes, something like that."

"If you do not want trouble, you are in the wrong place," said Valerio. "You live between The People and the White Eyes. You live on what was once Apache land. Trouble is bound to come your way, and if you seek to escape it, you should leave this place."

"This is my home. I will stay here."

"You are lucky to be a white man. You can say that. The Apache cannot. We have agreed to live in peace on land that the White Father chose for us. It is not the land we would have chosen for ourselves. But we accepted our fate. All we asked was to be left alone. Still, our people are murdered."

"I will go after the scalphunters," said Barlow. "I will bring them to justice. You have my word on it. I was wrong to let them go. I'll make it right."

"No," snapped Valerio, gesturing at the bronchos. "*We* will make it right."

Barlow felt a sense of urgency rising up within him, because he suddenly saw where all of this could lead. He'd seen it happen before—a war that could engulf the entire territory arising from a single small incident. The first Apache war—the one in which he had been a reluctant participant—had started with the killing of a few of John Ward's cattle, an act Ward had blamed on Cochise and the Chiricahua Apaches. Ward's animosity had led him to declare his own personal war against the Apaches, blinding him to reason and, ultimately, leading to his death and the deaths of many of the vaqueros who'd worked for him. Those deaths, in turn, had led to a full-fledged military campaign against Cochise, which, in turn, had brought the Bedonkohe Apaches into the fray. Many more men had perished, including some Barlow had called friend.

"You must listen to me," he told Valerio. "You have every right to seek revenge for what's happened. Those scalphunters *should* be punished, but if *you* kill them, then many whites will demand that the army take action against you. They'll say that the Apaches are on a rampage and that their lives are at risk, and the government will have to do something."

"What would you have us do?" asked Valerio.

"I'll go after the scalphunters. I'll catch them and take them to the army at Fort Union. They'll be punished."

"How do we know that the yellow-legs will punish them?"

"The army doesn't want another war with the Apaches, and men like those scalphunters are a danger to the peace. The army will want to make an example of them, to discourage others who might be thinking about trying to collect the Mexican bounty."

It was impossible for Barlow to tell if he was making any headway with Valerio; the Coyotero leader's face might have been carved from stone for all the emotion it betrayed.

"I know who you are," said Valerio, after a moment reflecting on Barlow's words. "Cochise trusted you. You have taken his daughter as your woman, with his blessing. They say you were a friend to the Chiricahuas. But now the Chiricahuas have been driven from

their villages and live like outcasts in the Cima Silkq.
It does not seem as though it did Cochise any good
to trust you."

"Then ride with me. I ask only that, when we find
the men you're after, you will let me try to do things
my way. If I fail, then you can do it your way."

Valerio gazed at Barlow a moment, and Barlow
sensed that the Coyotero jefe was sizing him up,
weighing his words. Finally, Valerio nodded. "We will
ride with you."

Relieved, Barlow asked for one hour to prepare for
the journey and invited the Coyotero bronchos to
draw water from his well for their horses. But Valerio
declined the offer to approach the ranch buildings. *He
doesn't trust me*, mused Barlow, as he turned his horse
to ride back to the adobes, Short Britches beside him,
but then, why should he? I am Pinda Lickoyi.

Short Britches waited until they were halfway to the
ranch buildings before speaking. "You're taking a big
chance," he observed.

"I'm between pillar and post," sighed Barlow. "If I
let them go, and they kill those scalphunters, we could
find ourselves in the middle of another war. And they
won't go home until they know justice has been
done."

"Some of those bronchos aren't as reasonable as
Valerio," said the old scout. "They're angry at all
white men. They'd just as soon kill you. And Valerio
might let them. There's no way to be sure about him."

"I'll be okay," said Barlow, hoping he sounded
more confident on that score than he actually felt. "I
need you and the rest of the men to stay close to
home until this business is resolved."

"The others will watch out for Oulay. I will ride
with you."

Barlow smiled. "Think you can protect me from a dozen bronchos?"

"Of course."

Barlow wasn't sure if the old scout was joking or not. "I'd feel better if you were with Oulay."

Short Britches looked at him—and knew that Barlow was thinking back to the time when the renegade named Kiannatah had killed three vaqueros before abducting Oulay. It was something, mused the scout, that would probably haunt the padrone for the rest of his days. And the fear that it might happen again was one that Barlow seemed powerless to put to rest. To tell him that the vaqueros would protect Oulay with their lives wouldn't do any good, or that she would be no safer if he stayed behind. He had been the one—with the help of an army sergeant and a few White Mountain Apaches—who'd rescued Oulay from the Netdahe broncho. Ever since then, without actually coming out and admitting it, Barlow seemed to think he was the only one who could be counted on to keep Oulay from harm.

"She will be safe only if you are successful," said Short Britches. "If I ride with you, you will have a better chance of succeeding. So, to protect her, I must go with you."

Barlow shook his head. "Well, I guess there's not much point in arguing with you. Even if I insisted that you stay, you'd just mount up and ride after me as soon as I was over the first hill."

Short Britches thought it over, and nodded gravely. "That's true," he said.

Barlow suppressed a smile and urged the horse beneath him into a quicker gait. He had a big task ahead—explaining to Oulay why he was loading his guns and riding off with a band of Coyotero bronchos in pursuit of the scalphunters. He knew what her response would be. She wouldn't want him to go, but would say nothing along those lines. And she would worry about him every waking moment during his absence. All he could do to fix that was to get the job done—and return home—as quickly as possible.

Chapter 4

When the scalphunter named Coughlin awoke the next morning, the sun had not yet risen. The sky in the east was lightening, but overhead some of the brighter stars were still visible. For a moment Coughlin wondered what had awakened him—usually it was the sun that roused him from his slumbers. Skaggs was supposed to be on watch, but he was asleep; all Coughlin could see of him was a mound on the rim on the draw. The Mexican was rolled up in his blankets, sleeping. The horses were quiet on the picket line yonder. The fire was crackling warmly. Coughlin, still groggy from a heavy sleep, frowned as he rose on one elbow. The fire? How could that be if . . . ?

And then he saw Barlow, sitting on his heels not more than a dozen feet away, on the other side of the campfire. Coughlin's reaction was violent. He threw aside his blankets, groped for the .50 caliber rifle that usually lay right beside him. The rifle was gone. He grabbed for the pistol in the gun belt that was rolled up under his saddle, which had served as his pillow the night before. The pistol was still there—his fingers brushed it—but he didn't draw the gun, because in that instant he realized that Barlow was holding a Navy Colt, aimed, almost nonchalantly, in his general direction. Gathering his wits about him, Coughlin jumped to a few conclusions. Barlow had to have ridden through the night to catch up with him and his associates. The only reason he would do that, as far as Coughlin could figure, was to make trouble. And the Navy Colt seemed to vouch for that.

"What the hell is this about?" asked Coughlin.

"Sit up slow," advised Barlow. "Don't make any sudden moves."

"Why?" sneered the scalphunter. "You gonna plug me with that smoke maker of yours?"

"I might. Or maybe my friend will."

Coughlin looked around. The night shadows were still heavy on the ground in the sandy draw where he and Skaggs and the Mexican had made camp. He didn't see anyone else.

"Your friend?"

"That's right. He carries a rifle like this one." Barlow nodded at Coughlin's .50 caliber leadslinger, which now lay at his feet. "And he's a damned good shot. In fact, he's a better shot at long range than he is close up. With me, it's just the reverse."

"I think you're bluffing," said Coughlin. "I think you come all by yourself. Question is, why? I'm thinkin' it's on account of your wife being an Apache. Guess that makes you an Apache lover. And you know what's in that pouch?"

Barlow didn't look at the scalp pouch, hanging by its strap from the pommel of Coughlin's saddle. "Yeah, I know what's in there," he said coldly. "You murdered four Coyoteros. A whole family. And I suspect you'll hang for it too."

"Hang?" Coughlin snorted. "Hang for killin' Apache vermin? It'll be a cold day in hell."

"Well, we'll see. I'm taking you into Fort Union,

turning you over to the army. I don't think they'll take kindly to what you've done."

"You're not taking me anywhere," snarled Coughlin.

"Don't try anything," warned Barlow, tightening his grip on the Navy Colt.

"Go to hell."

The scalphunter reached for the pistol under his saddle, trying to roll away from Barlow at the same time. The Navy Colt boomed once, and Coughlin felt a searing pain in his arm. The gunshot roused Skaggs and the Mexican—the former coming up out of his blankets like a scalded cat. Skaggs barely got to his feet before another shot rang out. He didn't hear this one, because a .50 caliber slug had already punched a hole in his forehead and blown away the back of his skull in a fine pink mist. Dead on his feet, his corpse pitched forward and landed facedown in the fire. Barlow was on his feet too, swinging the Navy Colt in the direction of the Mexican, who was reaching for his own weapons. The Mexican saw that Barlow had the drop on him, and froze. Keeping the Mexican covered, Barlow stepped around the fire and kicked the pistol out of Coughlin's hand. Coughlin was writhing, gripping his bullet-shattered shoulder with the other hand.

"You son of a bitch," he snarled.

Barlow let loose a shrill whistle.

"You best kill me now, you bastard," rasped Coughlin, " 'cause I'm gonna kill you. Then I'm gonna kill that Apache squaw of yours, and take her scalp. But not before I—"

Barlow bent down and planted the Navy Colt's barrel right between Coughlin's eyes. "You want to die here and now? That's fine by me. You just keep talking."

Coughlin saw the look in Barlow's eyes—and shut up.

"Holy Mother of God," murmured the Mexican.

Coughlin looked at him, then followed his gaze—and Barlow had the satisfaction of seeing all the color drain from the scalphunter's face as he spotted the Coyotero Apaches, mounted on their ponies, encircling the camp. Short Britches was with them. The old scout dismounted, joined Barlow, and gazed dispassionately at his handiwork—the corpse that lay half in the fire. The stench of burned flesh made Barlow's stomach roll. Short Britches didn't even seem to notice. He went around the fire and grabbed Skaggs by the ankles and pulled him out of the fire. Then he rolled the body over. Skaggs' hair was still on fire. Indifferent to the grotesque condition of the corpse, Short Britches checked the dead man's pockets. He looked quite pleased as he fished a half twist of tobacco out of a pocket. He pulled a piece off with his teeth and, satisfied, stood up. Coughlin watched all this with mounting horror, and by the end of it, he was staring at Short Britches as though he were staring at the devil himself. He'd seen atrocities during the war—plenty of examples of man's capacity for barbarous conduct. But he'd never seen anything quite as cold-blooded. Of course, he didn't consider his own cruel and grisly conduct as a scalphunter in the same category: Apaches, after all, were more like animals than humans, and he didn't see much difference in taking an Apache scalp and cutting off a wolf's ears for bounty.

And on the subject of Apaches—Coughlin looked warily at the grim faces of the bronchos.

"They're Coyoteros," said Barlow. "They've come to avenge the deaths of four of their own. They want to kill you. I'll let you make the choice. I either haul you to Fort Union, or I'll leave you in their care."

Coughlin realized then that he was done for. But he was a survivor, and even if, as he deemed likely, he would die at the hands of the United States Army just as surely as he would die at the hands of these Coyoteros, at least he would live a few days, weeks, and maybe even months longer if his fate rested in the hands of the yellow-legs. It would rankle to be killed by Yankee soldiers, but that was preferable to being put to death by Apaches. He knew what Apaches could do to an enemy. He'd heard stories of the way they liked to torture their captives. The longer an enemy survived their cruel attentions, the more honor the Apaches derived from his death. Coughlin thought dangling from the end of a Yankee rope was better than being skinned alive or being staked out over an anthill, or having his private parts . . . He shuddered involuntarily.

"Take me to Fort Union then," he said bleakly.

Barlow turned to the Apaches. He half expected some of the young Coyotero bronchos to fall on the scalphunters and kill them on the spot. It all depended on Valerio, and the degree of respect the Apache warriors had for him. By the looks on some of the bronchos' faces, they wanted to avenge the Coyotero dead here and now. Valerio, as usual, was unreadable.

"I will take them to Fort Union," he told the jefe, speaking in the Apache tongue, "and turn them over to the army. You have my word on it."

Valerio pointed to the scalp pouch. "And those— we will have them."

"I need to keep them for a while. As evidence to prove the accusations I'll make against these men."

Valerio nodded. "We will ride with you to the fort."

Barlow didn't want their company, but saw the futility of arguing the point. He and Short Britches bound Coughlin and the Mexican—and then Barlow wrapped Coughlin's shoulder with a rough dressing to stem the bleeding. As he and Short Britches got their prisoners mounted, the old scout took the opportunity to make an observation.

"Some people won't be happy to see you riding with Apache bronchos."

The thought had already occurred to Barlow. Like his predecessor, John Ward, he had a contract to provide the United States Army, which maintained several posts in the area, with beef. Without that contract, the ranch would not long survive as a going concern. He was already faced with a certain amount of animosity from his own kind because he lived under the same roof with an Apache woman. His father, long a friend of the Cherokees, had been branded an Indian lover when he'd spoken out against the removal of that tribe from its Georgia homeland to the Indian Territory, and now Barlow was the object of the same sort of contempt. Barlow's view was that there wasn't much he could do about it. He had fallen in love with an Apache maiden. He could no more have prevented that than he could prevent Valerio and the Coyotero bronchos from accompanying him to Fort Union. He didn't blame them—they wanted to make certain that the scalphunters would be punished for their crimes. Only then would they go home. Only then would another war be averted.

They left the body of Skaggs to the desert scavengers, and were on their way south by west as the sun finally climbed above the edge of the world. Barlow led the way, with the prisoners behind him, guarded by the ever watchful Short Britches, and the Coyoteros trailed along behind.

Chapter 5

Major Geoffrey Cronin, U.S. Army, was sitting behind his desk in the Fort Union headquarters, brooding as he stared at the territorial map that was hanging on the wall. He remembered those grand old days when, as one of the most dashing cavalry officers in the Union Army, he'd studied other maps—those of countryside over which monumental battles against Confederate forces would be waged. The vast majority of his peers were grateful for the fact that the war was over. They were inclined to view war as something terrible. Cronin did not entirely share that view. He had graduated from West Point just months before the first battle at Manassas, but his marks had not been high enough to warrant a good posting. He'd been an indifferent student at the military academy, at least where book learning was concerned, excelling instead in horsemanship and swordsmanship— attributes not highly prized in the peacetime army. But when war broke out, Cronin had been given an opportunity to shine. And like fellow West Pointer George Armstrong Custer, he'd quickly earned for himself a reputation as a gallant, dashing cavalryman, courageous and daring in battle, beloved by the men who followed him. He rose swiftly through the ranks as his battle honors grew—Second Manassas, Chancellorsville, Gettysburg.

But then the conflict had ended and the War Department, as it had with Custer, decided that the best place for Cronin was the frontier. Cronin had thought so too. Now that the Southern rebellion had been crushed, the republic would once again look westward, expanding and growing in that direction as it fulfilled its manifest destiny, which meant potential conflict with the natives and more opportunities for a man like Geoffrey Cronin to shine. And so it had been with great expectations that he had accepted the posting as commander officer at Fort Union.

Now, though, after several months at Union, he felt differently about his prospects. The "Apache problem" that people had been talking about back east didn't seem to be much of a problem, after all. The renegades were in hiding down in Mexico, and so far had not seen fit to launch raids into the United States. The peaceful Indians were residing on their reservations. Cronin's job was to keep the peace—to make sure the peaceful Apaches stayed on their reservations, and that they were left alone by whites. He felt more like a warden than a warrior. And he wasn't happy about it. Not happy at all. He'd been shuffled off into this dusty hellhole and promptly forgotten. At the age of twenty-nine, he faced the likelihood that his career was over, and he was seriously considering giving up his commission. There was a war going on south of the border. Conservatives in Mexico had negotiated with Napoléon III to create a Mexican empire, and Napoléon had persuaded an Austrian archduke named Ferdinand Maximilian to accept the crown. Maximilian and his wife, Carlota, had arrived in Mexico in 1864, only to find most of the population up in arms and supportive of Benito Juárez. Maximilian's reign depended almost entirely on French arms, and for a time, Napoléon III had sunk men and material into Maximilian's effort to hold on to his empire. Now, though, it seemed that Napoléon III had lost his enthusiasm for the endeavor, and Maximilian had issued a call for mercenaries to replace the French troops, who were being withdrawn gradually. Some veterans of the Civil War—both Union and Confederate—had answered that summons. Cronin was considering doing likewise, though he didn't particularly care whether Maximilian or Juárez ruled Mexico. But the emperor was offering more than glory—he had plenty of gold, which he had taken from the Mexican people, and was now offering to men who would fight for him. While he figured that Maximilian was doomed, Cronin thought it possible that he might be given the chance to participate in a battle or two, and take some of that gold off the emperor's hands, before the inevitable happened. Compared to rotting away in this outpost, the plan had a lot to recommend it.

He heard the tattoo of bootheels in the wide hallway beyond the door, then the rapping of knuckles on the door itself, just before the door creaked open on its hinges and Sergeant Yard poked his head into the room.

"Major?"

"What is it, Sergeant?"

"I think you better come see this, Major."

Cronin glanced out the window. Through the grimy panes of glass, he could see men running across the parade ground. There was some sort of commotion out there, and probably had been for a while, but he'd been wrapped up in his reverie about Mexico and hadn't noticed. Until now.

He stood up. "What is it, Yard?"

"Lookout reports a group of Indians coming in, sir."

"Apaches?"

"Most likely sir. Only . . . only there are some white men with 'em, sir."

"Not a war party, then," said Cronin, disappointed.

"I don't know, sir. I don't think so."

Annoyed, Cronin grabbed his hat and gauntlets off the corner of the desk and with long strides crossed the room. Brushing past the sergeant, he said, "Next time you knock on my door, Yard, try to know more than you did this time."

Yard watched the major stride down the long hallway, and since Cronin's back was to him, he indulged himself with a look of pure hatred. "Yes, sir," he said, and followed, making sure his face was devoid of emotion as he followed Cronin outside.

The sun was high in the sky, and its heat was like a hammer, but Cronin was impervious to heat, or any of the elements, for that matter. Physical discomfort was of little consequence to him. He threw a quick look around. Many of the men of the garrison were hastening toward the gate, and there was a congregation of blue uniforms on the east wall. He bent his steps in that direction, but there was no urgency in his stride; he assumed there was nothing to this alarm. The worst enemy of the troops at Fort Union these days was boredom, so any arrival, no matter how innocuous, might be greeted like the Second Coming. As he climbed up to the east wall, he noticed that Lieutenant Symonds, the officer of the day, was looking through field glasses. Cronin looked out across the desert plain and saw the group of riders; they were close enough now so that field glasses were superfluous—he could tell that most of the horsemen were riders, and by their garb, he took them for Apaches. But in front of the Indians were several white men. He couldn't tell for sure about the one wearing the battered stovepipe hat, though . . . .

Belatedly aware of the commanding officer's arrival, Symonds lowered the field glasses. "What are your orders, sir?"

"Well, Lieutenant," sighed Cronin, "what say we take a chance and open the gate? There are only about a dozen of them, so if they mean to do us harm we ought to be able to hold our own, don't you think?"

The men who heard this exchanged glances. They were well aware that Major Cronin had nothing but contempt—usually ill-concealed—for them. He spoke often of the brave men who had served with him in the war, and though he hadn't come right out and said it, he obviously thought the soldiers who were posted at Fort Union were of an inferior stripe. Like most officers from back east, Cronin no doubt believed that troops who served on the frontier were the flotsam and jetsam of the United States Army, the undesirables who were shuffled off into the middle of this godforsaken country and good riddance.

"Yes, sir," said Symonds, a chill in his voice. The major's contempt extended also to officers who had not had the good fortune to fight in the war too—and he fell into that category.

He called down to the sentries to open the gate. Cronin left the wall, and Symonds followed. The major placed himself in the middle of the gateway, as though (thought Symonds) he was a modern Hector on the bridge, perfectly capable of holding the breach against any and all comers, most of all a dozen well-armed Apache bronchos.

The rider in the lead—a white man—turned to speak to his companions, who checked their horses, and then proceeded alone to approach the gate. He stopped his horse a few feet away from Cronin, and did not dismount.

"Who are you?" asked Cronin.

"The name's Barlow. Joshua Barlow. I'm here to see Major Trotter."

"Trotter has been reassigned. I'm in command here now. Major Geoffrey Cronin—at your service, Mr. Barlow." Cronin leaned his head a bit to one side so that he could see past the mounted man. "Who are your friends?"

"One of 'em's Valerio, chief of the Coyoteros."

Cronin raised an eyebrow. "Is that so? And to what do we owe the honor?"

"We're delivering some prisoners to you, Major." Barlow twisted in the saddle, made a motion, and the rider wearing the stovepipe hat escorted Coughlin and the Mexican closer, while the Coyoteros remained where they were, warily watching the soldiers arrayed on the wall above the gate.

"Prisoners? Whose prisoners?"

"Mine," said Barlow. "These two"—he gestured at Coughlin and the Mexican—"are scalphunters." He took the scalp pouch that was hanging from his saddle horn and let it drop into the dust at Cronin's feet. "And here's the evidence. A few days ago they murdered four Coyoteros on the reservation."

Cronin looked at the bloodstained pouch a moment, then lifted his gaze to Barlow. "Now I remember. Barlow. I've heard about you. What's your involvement in all this?"

"Just trying to . . . avoid more problems, Major."

"I was wondering who would be riding with Apaches. I guess I shouldn't be surprised to find it's you, sir. After all, from what I've been told, you've made it a habit to take the Indian side in things."

"Not taking anybody's side. But these two broke

the law and threatened the peace, so the way I see it,
their punishment is your responsibility."

"Thank you for pointing out my duty to me, Mr.
Barlow."

Barlow glanced grimly at Short Britches. To find
Major Trotter replaced—especially by this man—was
a stroke of bad luck. Having served with Trotter, Barlow knew him as an honest, forthright officer with a
by-the-book approach to his job and precious little
ego to contend with. Trotter would have been happy
to render justice unto the scalphunters. Barlow wasn't
sure the same could be said for Major Cronin.

The major turned to Lieutenant Symond. "Take
those two into custody, Lieutenant," he said, without
enthusiasm.

"Yes, sir!" Symonds looked around at the troopers
who had gathered to watch the proceedings, and called
out two names. These men stepped forward, and took
charge of Coughlin and the Mexican. The former
turned in his saddle for one last glower in Barlow's
direction.

"We'll meet again," he snarled.

"I doubt it," said Barlow.

"Lock them in the guardhouse," Symonds told the
troopers, "and then notify the surgeon that one of
them is wounded."

"Is there anything else I can do for you today?"
Cronin asked Barlow.

"That about does it." Barlow turned to Valerio,
spoke to him briefly in Apache.

Valerio gave a curt nod, and barked an order to his
bronchos. They turned their ponies and rode away to
the north. Barlow spared Fort Union one last look. It
had been his post once, and he thought about the
acquaintances he had made here. Most of them were
dead now. He was eager to put the place—and all the

memories it held—behind him. So he nodded to Cronin and kicked his horse into motion. Short Britches followed. Cronin watched them go. When he turned to enter the fort, he was annoyed to find the congregation of troopers blocking his path.

"Lieutenant Symonds, find these men something to do. Sergeant Yard?"

"Yes, sir."

Cronin pointed at the scalp pouch. "Bring that along."

"Yes, sir."

Yard picked up the pouch and fell in behind the major, who started across the parade ground, making for the headquarters building. When they reached the porch, Cronin stopped, turned, and looked at the pouch.

"Don't bring that in here," he said.

"No, sir. What, um, does the major want me to do with it?"

Cronin had already made up his mind. "After nightfall, Sergeant, you will ride an hour in any direction you choose, and then bury that pouch. After which you will forget you ever saw it. Is that clear?"

Yard was perplexed; he had no idea what the major was doing, but he *did* know that it wasn't his place to understand. "Yes, sir," he said.

"Good." Cronin took another look around the stockade, an expression of disgust on his face, shook his head, and went inside.

Chapter 6

Coughlin spent a week in the Fort Union brig with the Mexican. Thanks to the ministrations of the outpost's surgeon—less than gentle but thorough treatment—he recovered from a slight infection and an accompanying high fever. He wondered why they were bothering to fix him up, since he fully expected to be hanged or shot for his offenses. So when, on the morning of his eighth day of captivity, a lieutenant arrived to inform him that the commanding officer wished to see him, he assumed he was about to be officially informed of the charges that faced him and the fate that lay in store for him. Shackled hand and foot, he was marched across the parade ground in sunlight that was blinding to a man who'd just spent a week in the suffocating dark of the guardhouse.

When he was ushered into Cronin's office, the major was busy at his desk with dispatches. The lieutenant put Coughlin in a chair facing the desk, then stood at attention behind the chair until the major glanced up.

"Wait outside, Lieutenant."

The lieutenant withdrew and Cronin turned his attention back to the papers on the desk for a moment. Coughlin thought that was pretty cold-blooded, since he was waiting to be condemned. He noticed a pistol on the desk, and for a second or two thought about going for it; he was going to die anyway, so what did it matter if he killed one more son of a bitch?

"I wouldn't do it, if I were you," said Cronin, without looking up.

Coughlin sat very still, surprised. Leaning back in his chair, Cronin laced his fingers together and stared at the prisoner with hooded eyes.

"The surgeon tells me you're going to recover from your wound. I had decided to keep you in the brig until I was sure you would survive."

"Afraid I'd cheat the hangman?" sneered Coughlin.

"Not that it mattered much to me. The thing is, I have no intention of putting you on trial. I'm going to release you and your associate."

"What?" Coughlin sat forward, certain that he hadn't heard right.

"There are, of course, a couple of conditions. . . ."

"You're lettin' me go?"

"Are you hard of hearing or just slow?"

Coughlin scowled. "Take these irons off me and then say that, you goddamned Yankee."

Cronin was unruffled. "I learned a very valuable lesson on the battlefield: to adapt to constantly changing circumstances and to turn them, whenever possible, to my advantage." He glanced at Coughlin's butternut gray tunic. "I had hoped you learned that lesson too."

"Just get to the point," said Coughlin. "Why aren't you gonna hang me?"

"Because you're of more use to me alive."

"How am I of use to you?"

"You kill Apaches for money. If those Coyoteros had, in turn, killed you, my purpose would have been served. Unfortunately, Barlow interfered. His mistake is that he assumed I want to prevent a war. The contrary is true. So I'm going to let you go about your business. Whether you kill more Apaches, or they kill you, is no concern of mine."

Coughlin was beginning to understand. "You think you're smart, don't you? You think you're better than me too. But you're not. Yeah, I kill for money. But you kill for glory. It's just sport to you."

"Don't try to antagonize me. I could change my mind." Cronin opened a desk drawer. Then he stood, picked up the pistol, and stuck it in his belt before circling the desk to stand over Coughlin. Opening his hand, he revealed a skeleton key. Coughlin figured it fit the shackles he wore. "So what do you say?" asked the major. "Do you want to live a while longer or not?"

"Cut me loose."

Cronin unlocked the shackles. When he was done, he called out for Sergeant Yard, who entered the office immediately. Coughlin turned in the chair, and saw that the Mexican was standing, still shackled, in the wide hallway behind the noncom, guarded by two troopers. Cronin tossed the key to the sergeant, who freed the Mexican.

"Sergeant Yard will escort you to the gate," Cronin told the scalphunters. "I will not provide you with cavalry horses. But there's a town, of sorts, not far to the east of this post. Maybe you'll find what you need there."

"What about guns?" asked Coughlin.

"Fend for yourself."

"And the scalps that bastard Barlow took from me. What about them?"

"Gone," said Cronin. "Go collect some more."

Coughlin snorted. "No guns, no horses. You might as well sign our death warrants."

Cronin shrugged. "As I said, whether you live or die doesn't matter, not in the grander scheme of things."

Coughlin had the urge to tell Cronin what he could do with his grander scheme, but decided not to waste his breath. With one last baleful glare at the major, he walked out of the office, rubbing his wrists. Yard hesitated, looking to Cronin for confirmation—and received it in the form of a curt nod. Then he too left the room, closing the door softly. Satisfied with himself, Cronin sat down behind his desk and gazed at the territorial map, this time with a hopeful expression on his face. Mexico and Maximilian could wait just a while longer.

Somebody with a droll sense of humor had named the town Paradise Gulch, but it was certainly no paradise, and not really much of a town. It had sprung up out of the sand and rock and cactus not long after Fort Union was established—a tent town populated by individuals who tried to make a living by catering to the needs, whims, and desires of the soldiers posted at the fort. That meant Paradise Gulch had a good many card sharps, whiskey peddlers, cutthroats, and ladies of easy virtue. A soldier might think of it as paradise because he could get cheap liquor or a cheap woman there. But inevitably his opinion about the place would change—as soon as he'd been cheated out of his pay, or rolled by hardcases in an alley, or found himself afflicted by a disease acquired as a consequence of intimacy with one of the town's "soiled doves." Eventually, Paradise Gulch would become a ghost town. It's denizens would move on to greener pastures. There were no "respectable" citizens who wanted to make the town a permanent feature of the territorial landscape. And that meant there wasn't any law, which suited Coughlin just fine.

During the long hike from the fort to Paradise

Gulch, the scalphunter gave serious thought to the means by which he would acquire guns and horses for himself and the Mexican. He had no money to pay for these things. This left him with only two options, as far as he could tell: He could try to steal what he needed, or attempt to talk someone into giving it to him. The latter hardly seemed realistic. So when he arrived at the outskirts of the town, he'd made up his mind; he and the Mexican made their way to a livery at the north edge of the town. They went over a wall and through the back door of the adobe-and-timber stables. Once inside, Coughlin cast about for something to use as a weapon, in case anyone tried to stop them. But before he could find anything, the all too familiar sound of a hammer being cocked reached his ears. Resigned, the scalphunter just shook his head. He was having a hellacious string of bad luck.

A man emerged from the shadows of a stall up near the front of the stables. He was a paunchy, balding man with a double-barreled ten-gauge shotgun braced against a shoulder and aimed at the pair of interlopers.

"You boys are up to no good," he said. "I can smell it. Make any sudden moves and I'll kill you where you stand. Don't think I won't. Got a barrel full of buckshot for each of ya." He squinted at the Mexican. "Seen you comin'. Thought at first you was deserters. Get some of them kind through here now and again. But you"—he pointed with his chin at the Mexican—"you ain't no deserter. Never seen a bluebelly greaser."

"We're not deserters," growled Coughlin.

The man spat a stream of tobacco juice. "Then what the hell are you?"

"We're scalphunters. The army was holding us as prisoners for a spell. Then we were cut loose."

"Really." The man sounded skeptical. "Guess they was just overcome by your charm and good looks, eh?"

"Why don't you go to hell?"

"I'm there already, or haven't you noticed? I'm thinkin' you're here to steal some horses, am I right?"

"You're right," said Coughlin, too disgusted to play the man's games. "So what do you aim to do about it?"

The man lowered the shotgun a bit. "Well, I can't bring myself to shoot men who do the territory a favor by killin' Apaches. You ain't got no money at all?"

"None. Nor scalps, either. The army confiscated what we had."

"But they let you go." It didn't make any sense to the livery owner. "Goddamn bluebellies. They should be protectin' us from those redskins. Instead, they're protecting the Injuns from us."

"It was the major who set us free. Seems he wants us to keep killing Apaches."

"Now why would he want that?"

"Why don't you ask him yourself?" rasped Coughlin. "Now either fire that blunderbuss or get out of our way."

"Much as I admire your work, boys, I can't let you take my horses without payin' for 'em. This ain't no charity. I gotta make a livin', same as you."

"Fine. I'll give you my note. Soon as we collect the bounty on some more scalps, I'll see to it that you're paid back."

The livery owner grinned, flashing a mouthful of crooked yellow teeth. "You don't look like the type to go out of his way to pay off a debt. But tell you what. You head on down to the Red Door Saloon and talk to the man who runs it. His name is Hagen. You might be able to work something out with him."

"Why is that?"

"Why, just the other day I was down at the Red Door having me a shot of Hagen's snakehead whiskey. Heard him talking about a bunch of Aravaipa Apaches that have set up a village over near Camp Grant. He thought it was downright wrong that a bunch of Injuns would feel safe and sound next to an army post." The livery owner chuckled. " 'Course, Hagen hates Apaches more'n most—and that's saying something, in these parts—on account they killed his brother."

Coughlin glanced at the Mexican. He wasn't quite sure how, just yet, but he had a hunch that this man Hagen and that bunch of Aravaipa Apaches meant his luck was about to change.

Chapter 7

A week later, Coughlin was thinking back to that moment when his luck had changed for the better, as he stood on the rim of a low ridge peering through field glasses at the Apache village located less than a half mile away. Beyond the village, the sun was setting in a blaze of reddish-orange glory behind a jagged blue line of mountains. He handed the glasses to the Mexican, who stood beside him, and glanced behind him at the knot of horsemen who waited at the foot of a steep, rocky slope. Hagen was down there, with seven other men recruited in Paradise Gulch.

"I count at least thirty jacales," he told the Mexican. "Must be at least a hundred and fifty Apaches down there. That's a lot of scalps, amigo."

"Not split ten ways," muttered the Mexican, a comment that, for him, was a long-winded speech.

Coughlin shook his head. "Only a couple of those boys down there are even thinking about scalp money. Hagen and the others just want to kill Apaches. So this is what we'll do—we let them do most of the killin', and we'll do most of the scalpin'. And after it's done, we head for Mexico, where we'll finally have our pockets filled with pesos. We've hit the jackpot."

The Mexican just grunted, and returned the field glasses to Coughlin. "What about the soldiers?"

"What about 'em?" Coughlin once more scanned the desert with the field glasses. Somewhere west of the Aravaipa village was Camp Grant. According to Hagen, the outpost was garrisoned by no more than forty men commanded by a lieutenant named Summerhayes. According to Hagen, Summerhayes was an incompetent shavetail and his men were the dregs of the army, and it was the opinion of the saloonkeeper that the Camp Grant garrison posed no threat to their plans. Coughlin was of the same opinion, but not for the same reasons. "The soldiers don't matter," he continued. "By the time they figure out what's happened, you and me'll be making tracks for the border. If they bother anybody it'll be Hagen and the others. And I don't know about you, compadre, but after tomorrow, I won't care what happens to Mr. Hagen."

The Mexican nodded. He didn't care about anyone, least of all Hagen, despite the fact that the proprietor of the Red Door Saloon had provided them with horses and weapons out of his own pocket. In fact, Hagen had been willing to pay for anything they wanted after finding out about their line of work. He saw in the two scalphunters the means by which he could finally realize his dream of vengeance against the Apaches. It didn't matter to him that his brother hadn't been killed by Aravaipa—in fact, Hagen's brother had been in the employ of the Butterfield Stage Company during a period of time a couple of years earlier when that company had been beset by a series of raids that most people believed to have been perpetrated by the Bedonkohe renegade named Geronimo. A hostler at one of the stage company's way stations, the brother had been slain during one of those raids.

As far as Coughlin knew, the Aravaipa had not been involved in any attacks on white folks. They were about as peaceful a bunch as you were likely to find. This, however, wasn't enough to make Coughlin think twice about killing them. Peaceful or not, they were Apaches, and their scalps would bring just as many pesos as those of warlike renegades.

In Hagen's view, Coughlin and the Mexican were the most experienced Apache killers he was ever going to find. An astute businessman, he knew his own limitations. An attack of this magnitude, on a group the size of the Aravaipa band, was not something he could pull off by himself. And while Coughlin had never undertaken anything of this scope—an all-out assault on an Apache village—he had convinced Hagen that he was the right man to lead such a enterprise. Coughlin deemed it his best chance to finally realize his dream, to earn enough blood money so that he could settle down in Mexico and enjoy life for a spell. Hagen would have his vengeance. Major Cronin would likely have his war. And Coughlin would just sit back in some out of the way Mexican village, drinking mescal and messing with the senoritas, while the world went to hell in a handbasket.

"We better get back down there," said Coughlin.

They descended the slope and rejoined Hagen and the others.

"What's it look like?" asked the saloonkeeper.

He sounded edgy. In fact, he'd been making Coughlin nervous ever since they'd left Paradise Gulch. It had been Coughlin's experience that in this kind of enterprise, a nervous man got himself—and often everybody around him—killed.

"It looks quiet," replied the scalphunter. He started to unsaddle his horse.

"What are you doing?" asked Hagen.

"We'll camp right here. Good a place as any."

"Camp? Why not ride in and finish it now?"

"In the morning."

"Why in the morning?"

"It's the best time, for a lot of reasons."

Hagen looked at the others. "I don't cotton to the idea of sitting around here, with Apaches just over the hill."

Coughlin turned to look at him. "I know you're footing the bill here and all. But you wanted me along because I've had some experience in this kind of thing. We ride in at dawn because that'll put the sun at our backs, which gives us an advantage. And some of 'em will still be asleep. Those that aren't won't be expecting any trouble. Okay?"

Hagen nodded, reluctantly conceding that Coughlin's reasons made sense.

"And while we're at it, let me say this," added the scalphunter. "There are probably no more than twenty-five or thirty bronchos with that bunch over there. But when you start shooting, shoot anything that moves. Apache women can kill you just as quick as the men can. And the boys learn how to use the bow at an early age."

The others exchanged glances. Then one, whose name Coughlin could not recall, spoke up. "I'm not sure about killing children."

"Haven't you heard?" asked Hagen coldly. "Nits make lice. Remember, those Apache brats will grow up to be killers just like their fathers. They've got to be exterminated. All of them. Only then will this country be safe for white folk. And since the army isn't going to get the job done, it's up to us."

Coughlin scanned the faces of the other men. He didn't know much about them, or why Hagen had chosen them to come along. It was risky going into a fight with strangers, but under the circumstances he didn't have much choice. The only man here he knew he could count on was the Mexican. But the way he had it planned, that would be okay. Whether Hagen and the others lived or died tomorrow didn't matter to him. All he could think about was the rich harvest in scalps. . . .

They attacked the Aravaipa encampment just the way Coughlin had in mind—riding in on galloping horses, coming in from the east with the just-risen sun at their backs, blinding the startled Apaches, most of whom never knew that the attackers numbered only ten. Yelling like banshees, guns blazing, the white men tore through the village like a whirlwind of destruction, and Coughlin was pleased to see that none of the others seemed to have any problem gunning down the women and children right along with the men. For his part, he had pistols in both hands and the reins clenched between his teeth, and he made just about every one of his shots count. When he'd gone about a third of the way through the village, he abruptly checked his horse, and noticed that the Mexican, close by, was doing likewise. Hagen and the others kept going. Coughlin jumped down out of the saddle—a man on foot made less of a target—and put a bullet right between the shoulder blades of a young Apache woman who was fleeing for her life. She fell, dropping an infant child that she'd been cradling in her arms. Coughlin didn't waste a bullet on the baby. He stepped over the dead woman and entered the nearest jacal. An old man was standing in the middle of the lodge, gripping a knife; Coughlin gunned him down— and then saw the other three occupants, a woman and two children, huddled in the shadows. He fired three times, killing them all, then paused to reload before stepping back outside.

For a moment he surveyed the scene. Dead and dying Apaches littered the ground. Over yonder, a broncho was running at the Mexican with a tomahawk raised aloft; the Mexican whirled and put two bullets into the warrior's chest, knocking him backward. A haze of dust lay heavy in the still morning air, and Coughlin couldn't see Hagen and the others, but he could tell by the gunfire that they were on the far side of the village. It sounded to him as though the Aravaipa were fighting back now; that didn't surprise Coughlin—he and his associates had enjoyed the element of surprise, but while they might be considered "peaceful" Indians by some, the Aravaipa bronchos weren't going to stand by and watch their families being slaughtered. *Time to get to work,* thought Coughlin. Drawing his knife, he bent over the nearest corpse—the woman who had been carrying the infant child—and proceeded to take her scalp. In place of the leather pouch, confiscated by Barlow and the army, he had a gunnysack he'd picked up in Paradise Gulch. In a matter of minutes he'd taken more than thirty scalps, and the sack was almost half full, the bottom soggy and black with blood. Nearby, the Mexican was making quick work of his victims.

The gunfire on the far side of the village began to slacken. Coughlin had no way of knowing if that meant Hagen and the others had dispatched the rest of the Apaches, or if they themselves had been killed. Either way, his instincts told him it was time to make tracks. He returned to his horse, tied the gunnysack to the saddle, and mounted up. The Mexican was following his lead and doing likewise. Together they left the scene of carnage, riding south for Mexico. Cough-

lin was pleased with the way things had worked out.
Ten days ago he'd figured himself done for. Now he
was finally making for the border with enough scalps
to really fill his pockets with pesos.

Chapter 8

When the vaquero named Rodrigo rode in with the bad news, Barlow was working on the corral, where damage had recently been done to the gate by several rambunctious broncos. Even though it seemed the crisis with the Coyoteros had been settled to everyone's satisfaction, he'd still been inclined to stay as close to home—and to Oulay—as possible. He had a hunch that even if trouble had been averted it was just a temporary respite. The situation with the scalphunters had pretty well convinced him that he was just fooling himself if he thought that peace between Apaches and his own kind could be maintained. Sooner or later, all hell would break loose. And when it did he wanted to be in a position to protect the woman he loved.

Rodrigo was riding like the devil himself was giving chase—and that made Barlow put down his tools and pick up the repeater that he always kept within reach. Like all the vaqueros who worked for him, Rodrigo had spent his entire life in this country, which meant there was very little that could spook him. But he looked spooked when he reached Barlow and checked his horse, yanking on the rein leather so hard that the animal's front legs locked and the back legs skidded under him so that it seemed to be sitting down on the hardpack.

"What is it?" asked Barlow, bracing himself for bad news.

"Manolo," gasped Rodrigo. He plunged head and shoulders into the water trough, quenching his thirst and washing off the layer of pale dust that covered his face. Coming up, he elaborated. "Manolo is dead. And more than twenty cattle. Killed by Apaches!"

Barlow's gaze was bleak. "Where?"

"Five, maybe six miles to the north. Right on the river, at Black Horse Crossing."

Barlow muttered a curse. "You're sure it was Apaches?"

"Sí," said Rodrigo solemnly. "I know their handiwork, padrone. I have seen it many times. There were ten, maybe twelve unshod horses. What should we do?"

"We wait, until sundown, and the rest of the men come in. You get up on the roof with Pablo. Take your rifle with you."

"We cannot just leave Manolo out there."

"We won't," snapped Barlow crossly. He had no intention of leaving the dead vaquero for the desert's scavengers. Nor was he about to leave Oulay and the ranch unguarded, not with a dozen bronchos on the prowl.

As Rodrigo headed for the bunkhouse, where he would climb up to the roof to join Pablo as lookout, Barlow racked the repeater on his shoulder and trudged across the sun-bleached yard to the adobe house he shared with Oulay. She had noticed Rodrigo's arrival, and was awaiting him in the doorway, shading her eyes and peering curiously at her man, trying to read his expression. Barlow didn't try to hide the fact that he was troubled. Had he tried, it probably wouldn't have done any good; she was almost always able to read him like a book.

"Manolo's dead," he said curtly, and went inside. Throwing the rifle on a table, he opened a trunk and pulled out a bottle of whiskey. He didn't often drink, but today he needed one to smooth out his nerves.

She watched him intently as he took a long pull on the bottle, and wiped his mouth with a sleeve.

"Rodrigo says Apaches did it," he added.

"Poor Manolo. He was too young to die."

Barlow nodded—and took another drink. Manolo had been the youngest man on the payroll. When he'd come looking for a work a year ago, he'd sworn he was twenty, but Barlow hadn't believed him. Still, he was cousin to one of Barlow's best men and seemed to have plenty of grit, so he was signed on.

"Why would they do such a thing?" she wondered aloud, gazing out through the doorway. "You have always been fair and honest with my people."

"Maybe they figure this is still their land." Barlow thought about another swig, then reluctantly corked the bottle. He needed to keep his wits about him. "And maybe they're right."

She was silent for a moment, pensive. "You stayed here for my sake. But you didn't have to do that. I would have gone anywhere with you. I still will go anywhere."

He watched her, sympathetic, knowing that there was more that she wasn't saying, and sensing that she'd long ago resigned herself to the likelihood that she would never see her father again. Nonetheless, he held to his belief that it meant at least *something* to her to live here, in the land of her birth, where she could at least see the mountains that she'd once called home. But was that really why he'd worked so hard to make a home for them here? Barlow was beginning to wonder about his motives, especially now that his stubborn determination to stick to it was proving hazardous to Oulay's health. Maybe his reason was much more selfish. Maybe it was because he didn't like being run off. There was a pride in him that, according to his mother, had been spawned by the contempt with which his peers back in Georgia had treated him. Instead of turning away from their contempt, he'd confronted them. There had been plenty of fisticuffs as a result, and if he'd thought that he could earn the respect of those who hated him, he'd been mistaken. But at least he'd earned some self-respect. And here, now, things weren't that much different. There were those in the army who despised him—some even thought him a deserter. Many of the white civilians in the territory considered him an Indian lover and, therefore, a traitor to his race. And the many Apaches, he assumed, hated him for no other reason than he was white. Most men, he mused, would have had the sense to seek out greener pastures. But not him. Even if it meant putting the woman he loved at risk—not him.

It wasn't too late, he told himself. He could put Oulay on a horse and ride out with her, leave the territory, leave Apacheria, leave all the hate and the violence behind.

But he just couldn't do that.

"We're not going anywhere," he said bleakly. Putting the whiskey bottle down, he moved to the stove, where she always kept a pot of coffee on. He poured himself a cup. It was hot and thick and had a kick like a mule. Just the way he liked it. He sipped the coffee, then took it over to the table and sat down there, in a position from which he could look out through the open door at the approaches to the ranch. "We'll stay right here. This is our place. It doesn't belong to John Ward anymore, and it doesn't belong to the Apaches, either. It's ours, and that's how it'll stay."

She turned and gave him a patient smile. "Of course." That was all she said. She came away from the door and sat down at the table across from him. Reaching over the rifle that lay atop the table, she rested her hand on his forearm. They stayed like that, without talking, but content to be close, the rest of the afternoon, until the vaqueros began to drift in from a day's work on the range.

Barlow left eight men at the ranch to watch over Oulay, and rode out with Rodrigo and Mendez, who had been Manolo's cousin, and one other. Numbering only four, they wouldn't stand much of a chance against a dozen bronchos, but Barlow wasn't willing to leave a smaller number behind at the ranch.

It took them about an hour to reach the crossing, and every minute of that time, Barlow expected the Apaches to appear out of nowhere, which they seemed to have a knack for doing. But they arrived at the river without mishap. The sun had set, and in the darkening sky they could see a moving black spot—a spot that became distinguishable as a half dozen buzzards circling. When they got to the scene of the killing, they found that a few of the scavengers had already landed, and were starting to feed, not only on some of the dead cattle that were scattered through the sagebrush, but also on the body of the young vaquero. With a strangled cry, Mendez unsheathed his rifle and fired a few rounds as he raked big-roweled spurs across his horse's flanks, urging it into a gallop. Barlow didn't think it was very smart to do any unnecessary shooting with hostile Apaches around, but he didn't try to stop Mendez. Squawking indignantly, the

buzzards scattered, their wings making a leathery
sound. Mendez leaped out of the saddle and fell to
his knees beside Manolo and cradled the boy's body
in his arms. Silent tears streaked his coarse cheeks.
Barlow and the others were embarrassed. They hung
back and said nothing. Finally, Mendez stood up and
carried Manolo to the extra horse they'd brought
along. Barlow dismounted to help him drape the dead
man across the saddle. They covered the corpse with
a blanket, and then lashed it down with a rope.

"I'm sorry," said Barlow, when they were done. The
words didn't seem adequate, but what else was there
to say?

With a stricken expression, Mendez just nodded.

Rodrigo had ridden a tight loop around the area.
Now he returned to inform Barlow that he'd counted
sixteen dead cattle. Barlow assumed that Manolo had
been driving the cows to water when he'd been waylaid by the Apaches. At least they hadn't mutilated
the boy. He wondered why, and the only conclusion
that made sense was that they'd been in a hurry. They
were on their way to a particular destination when
they'd stumbled on Manolo and the cattle.

That destination could be the ranch.

"Let's get back," he said.

The last shreds of daylight were beginning to fade
from the western sky when, halfway back to the ranch,
they were ambushed.

The first shot brought down Rodrigo's horse. The
second knocked Mendez out of his saddle. Barlow and
the other vaquero were returning fire within a matter
of seconds, even though their assailants were well concealed in the sagebrush and cactus that covered the
flats. Though wounded, Mendez struggled to his feet
and starting blazing away with his pistol; with the
other hand he held fast to the reins of the horse that

carried Manolo's body, even as his own horse made tracks with a high-stepping trot. Barlow knew how unlikely it was that he'd be able to hit anything—even if he could see a target to shoot at—if he continued firing from the deck of a fiddle-footing horse, so he dismounted, and as the horse began to move, he used it for a moment as a shield to get closer to where Rodrigo lay, still and facedown, in the dust. The other vaquero dismounted, also, and he too used his horse as a shield, but then a bullet struck the animal in the heart and it went down quickly. The vaquero emptied his pistol and then started for his compadres, but an Apache slug hit him in the thigh and knocked him down. Barlow knelt beside Rodrigo, placed a hand on the vaquero's back—and was relieved to find that the man was still breathing. He'd been knocked cold by the fall. Barlow turned and shouted at Mendez to let go of Manolo's horse and to get down. For a moment he thought that the vaquero was going to ignore him— which meant he would surely die. But he came to his senses in time; letting go of the reins, he hit the dirt not far from where Barlow was crouched.

Now that they had no clear targets, the Apaches' fire slackened. Barlow took the opportunity to crawl over to the third vaquero, who was writhing in the dust, clutching with bloody fingers at his leg. Clawing at the seams of his shirtsleeve, Barlow pulled the stitching loose and ripped off the sleeve. This he used as a makeshift tourniquet to stem the flow of blood from the wound. The vaquero was fading in and out of consciousness as shock set in. Barlow knew that they would have to get the man back to the ranch and take the bullet out and cauterize the wound, or he would die before the night was out.

But how were they going to do that? They were pinned down.

Mendez crawled over to join him.

"Padrone, there are only a few of them, I think," said the vaquero.

"Yeah," said Barlow. That meant the rest had probably proceeded to their main target—the ranch. It was likely that the bronchos had cut the trail he and the vaqueros had made on their way out to retrieve Manolo's body. A few of the Apaches had hung back to spring the ambush. Barlow was nearly overwhelmed with frustration. Oulay was in danger—and there wasn't anything he could do to help her.

Chapter 9

There was only thing to do.

Even though the odds were stacked against his survival, Barlow figured the way out was to go after the Apaches—to crawl through the brush until he found them, and hope he could kill them before they killed him.

Mendez seemed able to read his mind. The vaquero drew a big belduque from a belt sheath. "I will go," he said grimly. "I have a score to settle with them."

"No, I'm going. You stay here with the others. In case I don't make it."

"You will make it, Padrone."

"Right." Barlow reloaded his pistol, and took the pistol from the hand of the young vaquero, who had slipped into unconsciousness, reloading it, as well, before snugging it under his belt.

"Take this." Mendez offered the knife.

Barlow accepted the offer gratefully. He told himself he'd been in a similar situation before. He and Sergeant Eckhart had been ambushed by Apaches, in a fix every bit as desperate as this one—and they'd survived. They'd survived because the Apaches had grown impatient, left their cover, and charged forward to finish the fight, allowing Barlow and the sergeant to pick them off, one by one. Barlow was impatient now, but he wasn't going to stand up and charge the Apaches. Though the sky was darkening rapidly, he would still be silhouetted if he stood above the sage and cactus, and the bronchos would surely pick him off. Dead, he would not be of much help to Oulay.

He began to crawl through the brush, trying to make no sound, going slowly, and working hard to keep his nerves in check. If he made a telltale noise or a sudden move and gave himself away, the game would be over. But it was bad enough to face a broncho when you knew where he was; when you didn't even know that much, you were in trouble. Barlow stopped every few feet to listen hard. There was nothing to hear, and he began to wonder if the Apaches were even there anymore. Sweat poured in rivulets down his face, stinging his eyes. He didn't bother wiping the sweat away; he made no unnecessary movement.

It took him a quarter of an hour to move thirty feet. And then he thought he saw something, out of the corner of an eye—a shadow moving in shadow to his left. He stopped moving—stopped breathing—and strained to see in the gathering night gloom. Had it just been his imagination? He was beginning to think that this was so—and then saw the movement again. It was one of the bronchos, moving as silently as a ghost, crouched low. The Apache was heading in the opposite direction, trying to get closer to the place where Mendez and the others were concealed. Barlow raised himself up into a crouch, waited a moment until the Apache was well past him, and then stood up and charged forward, pistols in both hands, blazing away. Muzzle flash momentarily lit up the night, and he caught a glimpse of the broncho, turning, with a shocked expression on his face—and then several of

Barlow's bullets hit him, and he went down in a bloody heap. Barlow heard a loud cracking sound, and threw himself to the ground. He'd heard that sound before—the noise a bullet made when it passed too close for comfort. It was followed immediately by the boom of a rifle. Make that two rifles, at least. Barlow rolled sideways, trying to get out from under the withering fire of the other Apaches. A pistol joined in, and Barlow figured that had to be Mendez. Then, abruptly, the shooting stopped.

Barlow lay still a moment, catching his breath and letting his nerves settle down. He'd been damned lucky. One broncho down. How many more to go? One thing was certain—he had to keep moving. Now, though, he no longer had the element of surprise on his side. Instead of moving directly toward the other Apaches, whom he believed to be further to his left, he began crawling in the same direction as before. Within moments he found himself on the rim of an embankment. Below him was a dry gulch. He wondered if he could use it as cover to get behind the bronchos. While he pondered the wisdom of this tactic, he was startled by the appearance of a second Apache, who was sliding down the embankment not twenty feet to his left. Barlow fired; the broncho kept sliding, and when he hit the bottom of the ravine, he fell. But Barlow's elation was short-lived; the Apache rolled over and began shooting. A bullet kicked dirt into Barlow's face as he desperately rolled away from the rim of the embankment. He felt the searing burn of a bullet on the inside of his left arm, just above the elbow. Lying on his back, he tested the arm, flexed the fingers of his left arm. Everything was still working. The bullet had just grazed the skin.

He didn't hear the third Apache's attack, or even see it. He just felt it coming, some primeval instinct kicking in to warn him of danger, and he rolled again, onto his belly, and once more blazed away with both pistols. The broncho stumbled, got off one wild shot before dropping his rifle, and then fell sprawling, almost on top of Barlow. Barlow swung a leg around and prodded the broncho with a bootheel. There was no response. The Apache was dead.

Barlow crawled a few feet away from the body, then paused to listen hard, wondering if another Apache would suddenly appear out of the darkness. He heard the sound of horses on the run. Scrambling to his feet, he returned to the embankment. A solitary broncho was galloping past on his pony, leading two riderless horses. Barlow raised a pistol, took aim, and squeezed the trigger. The hammer fell on an empty chamber. In the next instant the broncho was urging his pony up the embankment, and in a matter of seconds, he had disappeared into the night on the other side of the arroyo. Hunkering down in the sagebrush, Barlow waited a good five minutes. Three horses—had there been only three bronchos? He heard nothing more. Still, he would have waited longer, just to be on the safe side, except that his anxiety for Oulay's well-being overwhelmed caution. He turned and headed back for the vaqueros, taking the precaution of calling out as he got closer, to avoid being shot by Mendez.

He handed the big knife back to the vaquero. "Two dead. The other's gone. I didn't need this, but thanks anyway."

Mendez took the knife. The horse carrying the body of his cousin Manolo stood nearby; Barlow's horse and Mendez', were nowhere to be seen. Mendez used the knife to cut the rope securing the corpse to the saddle. He pulled the body, stiff with rigor mortis, down into his arms, laid it gently out on the ground, then stood and looked at Barlow.

"I will stay with them," he said, nodding at Rodrigo and the third vaquero. "You go, padrone. Bring back help."

Barlow hesitated. He didn't like leaving Mendez and the others behind. But Mendez had already sized up the situation, and thought it through, and come to the right conclusion. Barlow didn't argue. He nodded, and climbed into the saddle, spurred the horse into a gallop, and rode for the ranch.

The ranch was under attack.

Barlow heard the gunfire, crackling in the distance, from more than a mile away. Drawing nearer, he could see the muzzle flashes from the adobe house and also from the vicinity of the bunkhouse. He wasn't sure where the Apaches were, and at this point he wasn't about to hang back and wait until he knew more. All he could think about was Oulay. She was all he had. He couldn't lose her. He spurred the horse into an all-out gallop and rode straight into the melee.

It didn't take him long to figure out where the enemy was. The rifles located around the bunkhouse were turned on him, and suddenly the air around him was filled with hot lead. Still, he nearly made it. Not thirty feet from the adobe the horse beneath him shuddered, stumbled, and went down. Barlow jumped clear; as the animal's head went down, he threw his right leg over and landed on his feet, running for the door to the adobe. The door flew open and several vaqueros emerged, pistols and rifles blazing, to cover his approach. One of them was hit, and the impact threw him back into Barlow as the latter crossed the threshold; Barlow lost his balance and fell, skidding across the puncheon floor. The vaqueros piled inside. The door was slammed shut, and they scattered as

several bullets slammed into the timbers, splintering
them. Barlow looked up as Oulay fell to her knees
beside him. She looked distraught as she touched his
arm. By the light of a single lantern sitting on the
floor nearby, Barlow saw that his arm was covered
with blood. He threw the other arm around her and
pulled her close to him.

"I'm all right," he breathed, relief flooding through
him that she was unharmed. She helped him to his
feet, and he held on to her, not willing to let her go
just yet. Taking a quick look around, he saw that there
were seven vaqueros in the adobe. That was one less
than he had left behind to guard Oulay. He didn't
need to ask where the eighth man was; he had a pretty
good idea. Of the others, two were wounded, and that
included the man who had just been shot. One of his
companeros was tending to his wound, which Barlow
saw was a minor one. The other man, however, didn't
look good. He was laid out on the floor in a back
corner, covered with a blanket, and there was no color
in his sweat-streaked face. He was unconscious, his
breathing shallow. Seeing him reminded Barlow of
Rodrigo and the other vaquero, out there in the desert
with Mendez.

The Apaches were still shooting, and several vaqueros were at the adobe's windows, returning fire. Shell
casings littered the floor. One man walked up to
Barlow.

"We are happy to see you, padrone. But where are
Rodrigo and the others?"

"We were ambushed on the way back from the
crossing," explained Barlow. "Rodrigo and Pepe were
wounded. Mendez stayed behind with them."

"There is enough food and water here to last us
several days," said the vaquero. "The Apaches cannot
burn us out. Soon, I think, they will give up and go

away. When they attacked, we freed the horses from the corrals. So when they go, they will go empty-handed."

Barlow nodded. What the vaquero had said was true—they were relatively safe inside the adobe. There was just one problem. He couldn't wait several days to return to Mendez and the others. He didn't know about Rodrigo, but he was pretty certain that Pepe would be dead by then.

"No," he said, "we can't wait days—or even until morning. We've got to drive those Apaches away and then get back to Mendez."

"But how, padrone?"

"I don't know," confessed Barlow.

"It is too bad that the scout isn't here," lamented the vaquero.

Barlow nodded. He'd been thinking the same thing. Where was Short Britches? These vaqueros—especially those who had worked for John Ward—had come to expect the old scout to be there for them when trouble arose. They had an almost mystical faith in his ability to do that. And Barlow realized that his own expectations where Short Britches was concerned were unrealistically high.

Oulay brought him a cup of coffee. He sat down at the table and sipped it gratefully. She sat down across from him, gazing into his eyes. It was somewhat ludicrous, he thought—that they were sitting here, as they did most mornings to spend a few quiet moments together before he left for the day's work, with men fighting, and some of them bleeding, all around them. But there was no place at the windows for him. Besides, now that he'd ridden into this trap, he had to find a way out of it.

"Don't worry," he told her, trying to sound reassuring. "Everything will be fine."

And that, he mused, was even more ludicrous. What an odd thing to say with bullets slamming into the adobe walls of their home.

"I'm not worried. Not anymore—now that you're back." She hesitated a moment, and he could tell that she was debating whether to say something more. "I heard what you just said. I know it is none of my business—but there is one way to make the Coyoteros go away."

In spite of everything, Barlow had to smile. In Apache society, a woman left the details of warfare to the menfolk. He recalled the first time he'd laid eyes on her. He had accompanied an Indian Bureau commissioner to the village of Cochise, to speak to the Chiricahua jefe about a peace treaty. They had met around a cook fire in the cowah of Cochise, and Oulay had been one of the women who sat in the shadows at the back of the lodge, their presence tolerated only because their task was to serve the men food or drink if such was requested. But as the men conversed on weighty matters, the women would not have dreamed of making their own feelings known. Barlow valued Oulay's opinion, and always tried to make her feel as though she could speak to him about anything. She was smart, he knew, and she paid attention to everything that was going on around her. But the training she'd received as an Apache nahlin was too deeply engrained; she seldom spoke her mind, and never interfered in his business.

"I'm listening," he said.

"Find their horses," she said, leaning across the table to speak clearly, but softly, over the boom of the rifles. "They will be guarded by only one, and it is usually the youngest and least experienced among them. Run their horses off, and they will break off this fight and go in search of them. Without horses, their raid is over."

"Of course," said Barlow. "Yes, you're absolutely right."

He finished off the coffee and was about to stand up when she grabbed his hand with both of hers.

"Please," she said, speaking now in an intense whisper, "do not do this yourself. You have done enough tonight. And you have been lucky."

"I can't ask these men to do something I wouldn't do myself."

"You *would* do it. They know that. But I ask that you *don't* do it."

Barlow was startled. In the time they had been together she hadn't asked him for much—and she had *never* made this sort of request before. She had to know that it would run counter to his instinct, to everything he stood for.

"She is right, padrone," said the vaquero to whom Barlow had spoken moments before. "You have already taken too many chances. Some of us will go. I have fought the Apaches many times before. Forgive me for saying so, padrone, but I can do what needs to be done as well as you can."

"I know that," said Barlow curtly. He stared at Oulay, and she looked away, fearing—he supposed—that he would be angry with her—or, at least, very disappointed. But he did not feel either of these emotions. She had suffered hours of torment wondering if he had been slain by the Coyoteros. Was this so much to ask of him? To give her, for once, at least *some* peace of mind.

Barlow settled back down at the table and picked up his coffee. "Okay," he said.

The expression of joyful relief on her face was

worth the shame he felt in sending others out on a mission that could cost them their lives while he remained behind, relatively safe behind the walls of the adobe.

Chapter 10

The morning sun was hammering heat into the hard-pack when Barlow opened the bullet-scarred door of the adobe and cautiously stepped out. His appearance was met with silence rather than a hail of Apache lead. The Coyoteros were gone.

Two vaqueros had slipped out of the adobe hours earlier, under cover of night, and using a trapdoor built into the base of the structure's back wall. That door had been suggested by Short Britches, who had told Barlow that people who lived in Apacheria often added such a feature so that they might escape if under attack.

The vaqueros did not return until shortly before first light—and during their absence Barlow had suffered a lifetime of emotional anguish, knowing that he might never be able to forgive himself if they were killed doing what he felt he should have done himself. But they weren't killed, and when at last they returned, they told of how they'd circled wide around the ranch buildings, how they'd found the place where the Apaches had left their horses, and how they had killed the single Coyotero who stood guard over the horses before running all but two of the ponies off. These two they'd brought back to the adobe. The Apaches

immediately broke off the fight and went off in pursuit
of their horses, just as Oulay had predicted.

Now, thought Barlow, as he was joined by some of
the vaqueros, the question was whether the Coyoteros
would return. That, however, wasn't his first concern.
Three of his men were stranded in the desert some
miles away.

He told two of the vaqueros to ride out and find
some of the ranch's horses or mules. They would have
to take a wagon out to retrieve their companeros, and
the Apache ponies were not suited for the harness.
While they were gone, Barlow and the others searched
for and found the corpse of the vaquero who had been
killed at the onset of the Apache attack. They were
relieved to see that his body had not been mutilated,
and buried him in a small graveyard fifty paces away
from the ranch buildings. In this graveyard lay the
remains of three other vaqueros—the men killed by
the renegade Kiannatah on the night, long ago, when
he had kidnapped Oulay. Barlow wondered if another
grave would have to be dug for the badly wounded
man he'd left behind with Mendez the night before.

They were paying their last respects around the
mound of fresh dirt when one of the vaqueros touched
Barlow's shoulder. Barlow looked up, and followed
the man's gaze. A single horseman was coming over
the rim of the hill to the south. Even at this distance
it was easy to identify the man. He wore a battered
stovepipe hat. As Short Britches urged his horse down
the rocky slope, Barlow walked out to meet him.

"Where have you been?" he asked the old scout.
"You missed all the fun."

Short Britches surveyed the ranch buildings. "I am
sorry," he said. "I must be getting old. I did not know
that this trouble was coming. But I *do* know about
some other trouble headed this way."

Barlow's heart sank. "Now what?"

"A column of bluecoats. No more than a hour away."

"Wonder what the hell they want."

Short Britches did not respond.

"Well," said Barlow, exasperated, "I guess I'll stick around and find out. I've got two men out looking for our stock. As soon as they get back, I want you to take a wagon and as many men as you think you'll need to pick up Mendez and two others. They're three miles out, toward the river crossing. Two of 'em are hurt. Think you can find them?"

Still, Short Britches said nothing—because the question, in his opinion, was not deserving of an answer.

When the column of soldiers appeared from the south, Short Britches and his detail of three vaqueros, one mounted and the other two in a wagon pulled by a pair of ranch horses, had just disappeared into the heat haze that shimmered above the surface of the desert to the west. The rest of the vaqueros were lounging about in any strip of shade they could find. As far as Barlow was concerned, they deserved a day of rest and recuperation. Repairing the damage done during the battle with the Coyoteros, and rounding up the rest of the stock, could wait until tomorrow. Though they were exhausted, and most seemed to be sleeping, they kept their weapons near at hand. The Apache threat was still a very real one. The bronchos were out there, somewhere, and as long as that was the case, no sane man could rest easy, no matter how exhausted.

On the one hand, Barlow was relieved to see the soldiers, since their presence made it much less likely that the Coyoteros would strike again. But he was wary, nonetheless. What did this visit signify? It wasn't likely that the army knew of the Coyotero raid. Not yet. Barlow figured he'd been the first one hit.

There were eighteen men in the column, dusty, bone-weary men on run-down horses that looked like they'd been pushed hard day and night. The officer at the head of the column called a halt and angled his horse across the hardpack to approach Barlow, who stood watching from the striped shade of the ramada that fronted the adobe house. As the officer drew near, Barlow was pleasantly surprised to see that it was Charles Summerhayes, one of his messmates from his days as a lieutenant with the garrison at Fort Union. He hadn't seen Summerhayes for many months, and in that time his friend had changed a great deal. Back when they'd been at Fort Union together, Summerhayes had seemed like hardly more than a boy then, still wet behind the ears, and scarcely mature enough for the burden of responsibility carried by a commissioned officer in the United States Army. Barlow had shared quarters with Charles and two other lieutenants, Hammond and Trotter, and of his three roommates, Summerhayes had been, in Barlow's opinion, the least likely to succeed. And yet both Hammond and Trotter were dead, both slain in action against the Apaches—and here was Summerhayes, looking like the veteran of desert warfare that he was. You could look into his face and see that he'd been to hell and back.

Reaching the adobe, Summerhayes dismounted, wincing at the stiffness in his joints caused by long hours in the saddle. As he turned, Barlow stepped forward with hand extended.

"Hello, Charles. It's been a long time."

"Joshua." Summerhayes stripped the leather gauntlet from his right hand and shook Barlow's hand.

"You're looking well." He took a long look around the ranch. "Looks like you were hit hard."

Barlow nodded. "A Coyotero war party, yesterday. They left last night."

Barlow heard Oulay in the doorway behind him. Summerhayes looked at her, swept the dusty campaign hat from his head. "Morning, ma'am."

"Lieutenant Summerhayes," Barlow told her. "He and I served together."

"My pleasure, ma'am," said Summerhayes. "I've long wanted to meet the young lady for whom Joshua gave up the army."

"As I recall," said Barlow, curiosity getting the better of him, "there was a young lady in your life too, Charles."

"There was."

Something in the way he said it warned Barlow that this was a subject best left alone. At Fort Union, Summerhayes had spent much of his time pining for a woman he'd left back east. Barlow recalled that his parting words of advice to Charles had been to give up his commission so that he could go home and make the woman he loved his bride. Apparently, Summerhayes hadn't taken that advice.

"My men and horses need water," he said, changing the subject. "Mind if we use your well?"

"It's a spring, back behind the house," said Barlow. "Help yourself."

Summerhayes summoned a sergeant, gave instructions that the men should give their mounts some water and fill their canteens from the spring. Then he turned back to Barlow, and there was a grim look on his face.

"I had no idea the Coyoteros were on the warpath," he said. "Looks like it's all going to hell now. Beg your pardon, ma'am."

"What's happening?"

"I've been at Camp Grant for the past year. A couple months ago a band of Aravaipa settled down near us. They were friendly—as they always have been. Though nobody came right out and said so, I think all they wanted was protection. You know about the bounty Mexico is offering for Apache scalps?" Barlow nodded. "Living down near the border got too hot for them. Guess they thought they were safer." Summerhayes looked away, and his tone was bitter. "They were wrong. Three weeks ago some white men attacked the Aravaipa village. They killed men, women, and children. And they took a good many scalps. Five of the whites were killed. A few got away. We captured two of them. Those two talked. Said their leaders were a pair of professional scalphunters. One Mexican, one white man named Coughlin."

Barlow felt a chill run down his back. "This white scalphunter. What did he look like?"

"Big man, with a beard. Wore a Confederate shirt. At least that's how he was described to me." Summerhayes cocked his head to one side as he read Barlow's expression. "You know this man?"

"I'm afraid so."

He'd never known the scalphunter's name, but Barlow was certain that the man Summerhayes had described was the same one he'd captured and turned over to Cronin at Fort Union.

"Unfortunately, Coughlin and his Mexican friend got away clean," said Summerhayes, shaking his head. "You should have seen what they did to those Apaches, Joshua. I've never seen anything more horrible in my life."

"Wasn't your fault," said Barlow, sensing the guilt that burdened his friend. "There's nothing you could have done."

"How do you know Coughlin?"

Barlow had been dreading the question. "He and his associates killed four Coyoteros, then swung by here looking for fresh horses. Valerio and some of his men were hot on their trail. I took Coughlin and the Mexican into custody—the third scalphunter was killed—and turned them over to Major Cronin."

"Cronin!" Summerhayes was surprised. "Cronin had them? Then how . . . ?"

"I'd like to know how, myself," said Barlow. He had a pretty good idea, already. But he wasn't ready to give voice to his suspicions. Not until he knew more.

"I'm here on the major's orders," said Summerhayes. "Received a dispatch from Fort Union nine days ago, ordering me to proceed there at once, and on the way to swing by here and bring you along."

"What does Cronin want with me?"

"Not him. General Howard."

"Who?"

"General Oliver Howard. You've heard of him."

Barlow nodded. He knew a little about Howard—a man who had graduated from West Point several years before him, and who had fought with distinction during the war, serving as one of the better corps commanders in the Army of the Potomac.

"What's Howard doing out here?"

"He's in command of this district now."

Barlow wondered what the head of the military district could want with him. Had the issue of his unorthodox departure—some would call it desertion—from the United States Army come up again? He'd hoped that was all behind him now. Whatever Howard's reason for wanting to see him, Barlow had a hunch he wasn't going to like it.

"I know what you're thinking," said Summerhayes.

"But you might as well come with me. General Howard is not a man to cross swords with. If you don't come along, he'll just send another detail—and the next time they'll probably have orders to bring you back in irons."

Barlow grimaced. He knew Summerhayes was right. Ignoring the general's summons was not an option.

"All right," he said. "I'll go. On one condition. You leave some of your men here to help my vaqueros in case those Coyoteros decide to come back for seconds."

"I can do that."

"And I sent a wagon out to bring in some wounded men. I won't leave until I find out how they're faring."

Summerhayes shrugged. "Suits me."

"Fine. Come on in. Get some coffee and some grub."

"Thanks. My men . . ."

"Your men will be fed," said Oulay. "Come in, Lieutenant."

She preceded them into the adobe. Summerhayes hung back a moment, taking a long look around, and when his gaze came to rest on Barlow, there was a wistful smile on his face.

"You've got a nice set up here, Joshua."

"I just hope I can hold on to it," said Barlow, and led the way inside.

Chapter 11

Oliver Otis Howard tried to start every day with a few minutes of Scripture reading—a habit he had learned from his mother, a sternly pious woman who had instilled in her son the importance of faith and morality in life. This was a lesson Howard had tried to put into practice in all of his endeavors. Educated at Bowdoin College, he'd seriously considered becoming a minister. But following his graduation from West Point, he'd served for several years at the military academy as a mathematics professor. Shortly before the outbreak of war, he'd been intent on leaving the army and devoting the rest of his life to the service of the Lord. His devotion to country, however, had forced him to postpone this move. He'd commanded troops at First Manassas, and then at Fair Oaks during the Peninsular Campaign—where a severe wound had resulted in the amputation of his right arm. Despite this, he was right back in the fray at Second Manassas and Fredericksburg. At Chancellorsville, his XI Corps was routed by Stonewall Jackson. At Gettysburg, his command was driven back, with heavy losses, at Cemetery Ridge. These reverses, however, could not detract from his obvious talents as a warrior and leader of men. In the last months of the war he was transferred to the West, where he commanded the Army of the Tennessee in the Atlanta campaign, and he became one of William Tecumseh Sherman's most trusted and reliable lieutenants during the March to the Sea.

Through four years of the horrors of war, Howard's faith had sustained him—and he expected the men under his command to be sustained by it as well; he insisted that his troops regularly attend prayer meetings. When the war was over, he seemed the best possible choice for a task that would require a man of unshakeable moral convictions—he was President Andrew Johnson's first choice to head the new Freedman's Bureau, which was supposed to assist the South's freed slaves. In hindsight, Howard wasn't sure he'd been the best man for the job; although he had fought with an evangelist's fervor and fearlessness to help the former slaves to survive in a new South that was every bit as hostile to them as the old, he sorely lacked the diplomatic skills necessary to deal with Southern whites. In short order he'd become one of the most despised representatives of Yankee Reconstruction. He had no respect for or mercy on slaveholders and ex-Confederates, and his outspoken advocacy of black suffrage and his support of the notion that land should be confiscated and redistributed among the freedmen made him few friends—and a whole host of enemies.

The federal government had shied away from the idea of land redistribution, but a Constitutional amendment guaranteeing the rights of black men to vote had, finally, been approved by Congress. In Howard's opinion, though, he hadn't done enough. And so he had helped found an all-black college in the District of Columbia—and even though he knew that hubris was a sin, he was secretly quite proud of the fact that the institution had been named Howard University in his honor.

In spite of all the trouble he'd had with white Southerners, they had at least been Christians—even though, in his mind, they didn't always act in a Christian manner. Now the army had sent him to the frontier to deal with the Apaches, and many of his friends back east, God-fearing and decent people all, thought of the Apaches as barbaric heathens of the worst sort. Worth exterminating, but hardly worth saving. Howard wasn't so sure about that. His mother had believed that no human beings were so far gone that they couldn't be saved. Still, he had to remind himself that he was still a soldier, not a missionary; his job wasn't to save the souls of the Apaches, but rather to keep the peace in the territory. He'd been given monumentally difficult tasks before. He had a sense that this one would be the most difficult of all.

He sighed, and closed the book, and sat there for a moment, ramrod straight in a chair, looking out the window of the quarters that Major Cronin had given over to him. From this vantage point he could see the Fort Union parade ground. It was early, and in the gray light of dawn, he could see that the garrison was beginning to stir. Howard absently touched the empty right sleeve of his tunic. When he was troubled, he had the odd sensation of aching in an arm that he had lost years ago. He thought it possible that this sensation was God's way of reminding him that, though he'd faced much adversity in his life, his faith was strong enough to see him through.

Putting the Bible aside, Howard stood, blew out the candle that had provided him with the illumination he had needed for reading, and stepped through a door into a wide hallway. A single sentry snapped to attention.

"Send someone for Major Cronin," said Howard. "I want to see him as soon as possible."

"Yes, sir!"

The soldier went to the outer door of the headquarters building, opened it, and spoke to someone outside. Howard crossed the hall to the commandant's office.

A quarter of an hour later, when Cronin arrived, Howard was standing behind the desk, gazing up at the territorial map.

"Good morning, sir," said Cronin. "I trust you slept well."

"Yes." Howard was completely indifferent to creature comforts, and wasted no time on the subject. "Has this fellow Barlow arrived yet?"

"Yes, sir. He rode in with Lieutenant Summerhayes several hours ago."

There was something Howard detected in the major's voice—something he couldn't quite identify. But he felt confident that it signified strong feelings on Cronin's part about the civilian named Barlow.

"What do you think of him?" asked the general.

"I don't have an opinion, to be honest, General."

Howard smiled. When people told him they were being honest, it was a pretty safe bet that they were lying about something.

"But I can tell you what other people say about him," continued Cronin.

"That would be hearsay."

"Yes, sir. But out here rumors and reputations count for a lot."

"I see. The Orientals give as much credence to myth as they do to facts, and their civilizations are well advanced, while they consider us Yankees, who are loath to believe anything that we can't confirm with our own eyes, to be barbarians."

Cronin was perplexed; he had no idea what the general was trying to say—if anything.

"What *do* they say about him?" asked Howard, turning again to the map, which put his back to Cronin.

"That he's an Apache lover, sir. He's got an Apache woman, and that alone will make you plenty of enemies. Some say he deserted the army to warn Cochise of danger, and to be with this woman—who, by the way, is Cochise's daughter, I believe. I'm not prepared to say he's a deserter. My predecessor didn't seem to think so. He *did* say, however, that there was bad blood between Barlow and *his* predecessor, Colonel Lyman, who died in a campaign against the Apaches. On that campaign, Barlow served as chief of scouts and then was put in charge of a detachment that was assigned the task of preventing Cochise and his Chiricahuas from escaping across the border into Mexico. Barlow failed to accomplish that. After which he resigned his commission and took up raising cattle."

Howard was silent for a moment, and Cronin assumed he was pondering this information. Finally, the general said, "It doesn't really matter, at present, what the whites around here think of him. The important question is, what does *Cochise* think of him?"

"By all accounts, they are friends."

"If so, then he will serve my purposes nicely. Be good enough to bring him to see me at once, Major."

"Yes, sir." Cronin was about to leave when he thought of something and turned back. "General, I trust you'll see fit to confide in me about the purpose of your visit. In a situation such as this—one that is so potentially dangerous—it would help if I . . . if *everyone* was fully informed."

Howard faced the major, and a perfunctory smile moved the thick mahogany brown beard that covered the lower half of his face. "We know each other well, Major. We fought together on several battlefields. So I think you know that I keep my subordinates as informed as they need to be to carry out their duties."

"Yes, sir." Cronin left the office, simmering. Yes, he had served with Howard, and he remembered him well. Howard was a stickler in matters of protocol, but wasn't always orthodox when it came to methods. And there was always that air of superiority about him—the same air that Cronin associated with other Bible-thumpers. It was as though such people expected others to respect—and certainly not to question—them, since they were always in the right.

There had been more than a few generals in the Union Army who had frowned upon Cronin and his methods. Their disapproval went beyond the usual competition between the various arms—it wasn't just criticism that a cavalry officer might expect from an infantryman. He knew that some had questioned his apparent disregard for the lives of his men; they had pointed to the fact that his command suffered a very high casualty rate. A few had gone so far as to suggest that Geoffrey Cronin was quite willing to sacrifice his men if it meant more glory for him. That he often achieved spectacular success on the battlefield was probably the only thing that had saved him.

Cronin didn't know if General Howard had been one of his critics during the war. But he had a feeling their approach to the Apache problem would be very different. And that didn't bode well.

Neither did the presence of Joshua Barlow. As he trudged across the parade ground, Cronin fretted over what Barlow might say to the general about the scalphunters. He'd let Coughlin and the Mexican go—and they'd proceeded to do exactly what he'd hoped they would. The attack on the Aravaipa village was just the sort of thing that would get all the bands of the Apaches worked up and shouting for war. But the arrival of General Howard was a complication—a potentially dangerous one for him.

Chapter 12

He found Barlow with Lieutenant Summerhayes outside the mess hall; they were about to go inside and
have breakfast. He told Barlow that Howard wanted
to see him at once. Barlow reluctantly accompanied
him back across the parade ground. They walked together in silence—until they'd reached the foot of the
steps leading up to the porch of the headquarters
building. There Cronin stopped, while Barlow continued on. The major grabbed his arm.

"I want to talk to you about those two scalphunters
you brought in," said Cronin.

Barlow looked at the hand on his arm. "Let go."

Cronin let go. "I let them go."

"That explains how they showed up at the Aravaipa
village," said Barlow dryly.

"There wasn't enough evidence to hold them."

"Evidence. What do you call the scalps they had
on them?"

"Those scalps disappeared."

"That's convenient."

"I don't think I like your tone, mister."

"I don't think I like you, Major."

"If I were you, I'd be careful making any accusations."

Barlow met Cronin's hooded gaze with a steely one of his own for a moment. Then, without another word, he turned his back on the major, crossed the porch, and entered the headquarters building. Cronin followed him. An orderly ushered Barlow into the office where General Howard was waiting. As Cronin was crossing the threshold into the office, however, Howard told him to wait outside. With a grimace, Cronin complied. For a few moments he nervously paced the wide hallway. But when he became aware of the looks being given him by the orderly and the sentry at the door, he left the building.

"Good morning, Mr. Barlow," said Howard. "Please be seated. Would you like some coffee? I'll have the orderly bring you some."

"No, thanks." Barlow slacked in a chair facing the desk, behind which the general remained standing. "I just want to get this over with, General, so that I can go home."

"I hear you've had some trouble with Apaches."

Barlow nodded. "We were attacked. A couple of my vaqueros were killed, a couple more wounded."

"I'm sorry to hear that. We've had reports of outbreaks in various parts of the territory in recent weeks."

"I'm not surprised. News travels fast out here. And bad news travels faster. You'll have a war on your hands now, after the massacre of the Aravaipa."

"I hope not," said Howard solemnly. "I've seen more than enough of the suffering and strife that war can cause."

Barlow was silent for a moment, studying the general. Howard seemed sincere. All good soldiers knew the full value of peace.

"Well," said Barlow, "I think maybe they should have sent you out here sooner, General."

"Perhaps." Howard finally sat down behind the desk. "I'm told you're an Indian lover, Mr. Barlow. Is that true?"

"I've killed too many Apaches to qualify. If there's any difference between me and some others in these parts, it's that I see Apaches as humans. Some are better than others. That applies to all races."

"Fear and ignorance breed loathing," murmured Howard. "This is a brutal land. It shouldn't come as a surprise that the Apache can be brutal in his turn."

"I've seen brutality on both sides."

"I'm sure that's true. So what is it that you want, Mr. Barlow?"

"What do I want?" The question caught him by surprise. "I just want to be left alone. By the Apaches—and by you. If you'll pardon me for saying so." Howard's thick beard moved so that Barlow thought he might be smiling.

"What you're saying is, you want peace."

"Of course."

"Good. So do I. That's why I need your help."

"My help," echoed Barlow, suspiciously.

"Let me see if I can explain. There are a number of separate bands of Apaches—isn't that so? There is no one leader or chief."

"No, there isn't."

"So who would you say is the most widely respected of the Apache leaders?"

Barlow didn't even have to think about it. "Cochise."

"Who is in the Sierra Madre Mountains of Mexico at present, with the rest of his people, the Chiricahuas."

"Right. But not because they *want* to be there."

Howard nodded. "I want you to accompany me to

the Sierra Madre, Mr. Barlow. I want to talk, face-to-face—man to man—with Cochise. If I can persuade him to stay off the warpath, then I think this current situation that we find ourselves in will be . . . manageable."

Barlow stared at him. "You've got to be kidding."

"On the contrary. I've never been more serious."

"You can't just ride into the Sierra Madre, General. You try that, with or without an army behind you, you won't live long enough to see Cochise."

"I'm willing to take the risk—for peace."

Barlow scoffed. "Well, I'm sure as hell not."

"You're married to his daughter?"

"What does that have to do with anything?"

"Then he must trust you."

"Maybe once. I doubt he trusts any white man, anymore."

"Is Cochise a man of integrity?"

"I've never met a man with more."

"Then he will at least listen to what you have to say. And if I'm with you, then there's a chance he might listen to me as well."

"So I'm supposed to vouch for you—a man I only met five minutes ago."

"You're a good judge of character. You would have to be, to have survived for so long in this country. What do your instincts tell you about me?"

"That you're sincere." Barlow shook his head. "But that doesn't matter. It's suicide to go into the Sierra Madre."

Howard gazed across the desk at him a moment—and changed tack. "What would happen if Cochise and the Chiricahuas go on the warpath?"

"I know where you're going with this," said Barlow, realizing that the general was trying to outflank him.

"All the other bands would go to war, for certain. But I don't think you're seeing the situation clearly, General. It's too late. There's *going* to be a war."

"It's never too late," said Howard stubbornly. "I'm going to find Cochise and talk to him. The question is, will you help me?"

Barlow thought it over. Like Howard had suggested, he was listening to his instincts, and those instincts were telling him that the general was also a man of integrity. He was honest, straightforward, determined— the kind of man Cochise would respect. If there was anyone who could persuade Cochise to keep the peace, it was this man.

"I have responsibilities, General," he said at last.

Howard nodded. "Of course. Your ranch. Your men. And most of all, your wife."

"Exactly."

"I give you my word that, for as long as you are away, assisting me, a full company of soldiers will remain at your ranch. Would that serve to ease your mind?"

"Considerably," admitted Barlow.

"Then you will ride with me."

"I will," sighed Barlow. He couldn't help thinking that it was the craziest thing he'd ever agreed to do. And also that it would be the last.

"Then we will leave in one week's time. I must send a wire to the War Department, and the War Department, in turn, will have to communicate with the Mexican government."

"Which government is that? The government of Maximilian, or of Juárez?"

"Yes, well—that's a complication we may have to deal with. To be frank, I would just as soon cross over into Mexico without informing anyone."

"That makes two of us."

"But the War Department insists that Mexico be fully informed about my mission. So we will depart in one week, arrive at the border approximately one week later. Does that suit you?"

"Sure." Barlow stood up to go.

"One more thing," said Howard. "A couple of the men who conducted the raid against the Aravaipa are in custody. I want to assure you that they will be punished to the fullest extent of the law."

"That's fine," said Barlow, "though it won't make a damn bit of difference to most Apaches."

"The guilty must pay for their crimes."

"Some of the guilty. I think some of the men who are responsible for the massacre got away. I *know* at least one did."

"Do you know this man's identity?"

"Yes," said Barlow harshly. And then, with Major Cronin's name on his lips, he changed his mind. "Me. Because I had a couple of scalphunters in my hands, General, and I could have turned them over to the Coyoteros. I should have. Maybe if I had, none of this would've happened."

"What did you do with them?"

"Maybe someday I'll tell you," said Barlow. "Now, if you'll excuse me, I'd like to go home." *I have to tell my wife that I'm leaving again—and that this time I can't guarantee I'll be coming back.*

As he left the headquarters building, Barlow expected to be confronted by Cronin. But the major was nowhere to be seen. It was just as well. He had decided, on the spur of the moment, that he would deal with Cronin himself. He wasn't sure how or when. That way, maybe he could wash away some of the blood that was on his own hands. Or maybe not. Either way, at least one more guilty party would pay.

Chapter 13

The border town had a name—Santo Domingo—but there was nothing to distinguish it from the other border towns Barlow had seen. It was a dingy collection of adobe huts with a single rutted street and a zocalo, or square, that had a well in the center, and a few scrawny trees around the well providing scant shade from the punishing sun. The street was populated with pigs and stray dogs and half-naked children, and the people of the town stood in the doorways or the windows of their huts and watched with an impassive attentiveness as Barlow and General Howard rode in on weary horses. They made their way to the well, and dismounted. Barlow dropped the bucket and cranked it back up again, resting it on the lip of the well to let their mounts and the single packhorse drink. Two women who had been on their way to the well for water, clay ollas balanced on their shoulders, stopped in their tracks a stone's throw away and just stood there, watching the two gringos warily.

"Not much of a welcome," remarked Howard.

"They don't trust strangers," said Barlow. "They've been given good reason not to."

"It appears we're early for our rendezvous."

Barlow nodded, dipping his hand into the half-empty bucket and splashing a little water on his dust-caked face. They were supposed to be met here at Santo Domingo by a military detail, which was to provide them with safe passage. Barlow didn't think much of the idea, figuring it would be safer for them to travel alone than with soldiers, since the latter might draw the attention of rebel forces. But according to Howard, Washington still recognized the government of Emperor Maximilian, and Mexico had to be notified of the general's mission to avoid the possibility of an "incident," and the Mexican government had insisted on the escort.

There was a small church on the north side of the square, and opposite that was a cantina. Once the horses had slaked their thirst, Barlow and Howard headed in that direction. The interior of the cantina was dark, but Barlow didn't mind; there wouldn't be much to see, save the dirt on the floor and the flies on the walls. A small, balding man with a buccaneer's mustache was behind the bar, which consisted of warped planks laid across several barrels. The only other occupant was either passed out or asleep at a table in the corner. The bartender asked them what they wanted.

"What will you have?" Barlow asked Howard.

"I don't touch strong spirits," said the general.

Barlow put some hard money on the bar and ordered pulque. The bartender produced a bowl filled to overflowing with the milky beverage, made from fermenting fresh sap from the agave. Barlow carried it to a table and sat down with his back to the wall so that he could face the doorway. Howard sat in a chair facing him. Although saddle-weary, the general still sat ramrod-straight, not permitting his spine to touch the back of the chair. Though he'd only been traveling with Howard for a few days, Barlow thought he had a pretty good read on the man. The general was no spring chicken, and the trail they had traveled had been a hard one for him, but he was no complainer, and he wasn't about to reveal, even to Barlow, that he was bone-tired. He didn't cut himself any slack, and Barlow surmised that as a commander he would drive his men hard. Barlow had wondered if the trek to the Sierra Madre would turn out to be one during which he'd have to spend much of his time looking out for the general. But Howard was tough as old leather. And even with one arm he was clearly the kind of man you'd want backing you in the event of trouble. In fact, in trail-grimed civilian clothes, his beard no longer meticulously groomed, he looked like a tough customer. And that, mused Barlow, was what you wanted to look like on the border. In this country, if you showed any sort of weakness, there were plenty of two-legged predators who would tear you to pieces.

Santa Domingo looked peaceful and harmless enough, yet Barlow didn't let his guard down. He knew that appearances could be deceiving.

"How long are we going to wait?" he asked Howard, after sipping the potent pulque. "There's no telling when—or even if—that escort will get here."

"I know," said Howard. "Considering the distances involved, I'd be very surprised if a message wasn't delayed, or lost altogether. I would say a couple of days, at the most." He threw a look around the cantina. "I'm guessing there is a shortage of suitable accommodations in this town."

"We don't want to stay here anyway," said Barlow. "If we have to hang around, it'll be better to camp a little ways out."

Howard noticed that, like the other citizens of Santo Domingo, the bartender was staring at them. "Perhaps we should let it be known why we're here, just to put these people at ease, if nothing else."

"Not a good idea," said Barlow.

Howard looked at him. "You don't trust anyone, do you?"

Barlow thought about it. "Not really."

Of course, that wasn't entirely true. He trusted Oulay. And missed her. She had insisted on coming with him, using as the principal foundation of her argument that it might be her one chance to see her father, Cochise, again. That wasn't altogether untrue, but the real reason was that, after listening to him explain the mission upon which he was about to embark, she'd decided that the odds were stacked against his coming back alive. And since life would have no meaning for her once he was dead, she wanted to go with him—wanted to *die* with him. While he understood her motives, and sympathized, he couldn't let her come along, and used as the principal foundation of *his* argument that it was going to be enough of a challenge to keep himself alive without his having to worry about her safety.

He'd had second thoughts about going. Plenty of them. But the more he thought about it, the more convinced he'd become that this was the only way to prevent an all-out Apache war. The Aravaipa massacre had a few of the bands, like the Coyoteros, on the warpath. That was bad enough. But if Cochise went to war all the Apaches would follow him. Not just the Chiricahuas, either. Cochise was the one leader around whom all the bands, which usually did not get along, could unite. And Barlow shuddered to think what would happen if the entire Apache nation rose up against the Pinda Lickoyi. The outcome of such a war was not in doubt; the United States was too powerful. The Chi-hinne could not prevail. But they would inflict so much death and cause such widespread destruction that the United States would prosecute the war until every last Apache was dead or in chains. And along the way, many people would die. This was exactly what General Howard was risking his life to prevent, and Barlow had decided he had to lend assistance.

When Barlow had finished the pulque, they left the cantina, mounted their horses, and rode west out of town. Barlow found a good campsite a mile and a half later—a hollow surrounded by barren hillocks, with a stream nearby, and also a rock outcropping, which would provide them with a defensible position if attacked.

"This will do," he said.

"Yes, yes, this is fine," said Howard dubiously. "But if the escort arrives in Santo Domingo, how will they know to find us here?"

"They'll be told where we are."

"By whom?"

"The people of the village. Somebody will track us, just to see if we're gone for good. They won't bother us here. We probably won't even see 'em. But they'll know, and they'll tell the soldiers, if asked."

"Well," said Howard, his tone of voice indicating that he wasn't entirely convinced, "I'll trust you know what you're doing. You know this country, and these people, better than I do."

Barlow dug a hole and built a small, smokeless fire in the middle of it, with which he cooked a supper of beans and biscuits and brewed some coffee. Then he covered the fire with dirt. They didn't picket the horses, but rather kept the saddles, cinches loosened, on their mounts, and the reins tied around their left wrists. Barlow kept the packhorse ground hitched.

They ate supper as the sun went down. By its dying light Howard read a little Scripture. After a while he closed the Bible and looked across at Barlow, who was stretched out on his blankets, gazing up at the stars.

"Are you a religious man, Mr. Barlow?"

Coming out of the blue that way, the question caught Barlow by surprise. "Well, I . . . I don't know. I guess not. I don't go to church."

"Do you pray often?"

"Not really, no." Barlow sat up. "My mother and father took me to a church a few times when I was a child. But then they stopped."

"Why did they stop?"

"My father was Timothy Barlow. He was an army officer, and a Unionist. He was instrumental in putting down the nullifiers in South Carolina. And he was a friend to the Cherokees in Georgia."

Howard nodded. "Yes, I've heard of him. I regret that I was never afforded an opportunity to meet him in person."

"My mother was Southern, and they lived in Georgia, even though they weren't made to feel welcome there. They concluded that our presence in the congregation was too disruptive. From that time on, every Sunday, my mother would read to me from the Good Book."

"Nothing wrong with that," said Howard. "You don't have to be a member of a church to become close to God."

"My father wasn't religious. Not in the conventional sense of the word. And I don't think I am, either."

"Well," said Howard, "you're young. Young people often stray from the path. But as they get older, and the travails of life beset them at every turn, they often seek solace in God's word. It can work wonders."

"So can a fast horse and a loaded gun."

Howard chuckled. "That's true. But when all else fails . . . You must forgive me. From an early age I wanted to be a minister. And yet I made soldiering a career. And every time I find myself on the verge of giving up my commission, and devoting the rest of my days to the Lord's service, I'm called upon by my country."

"My father had the same problem. Though it wasn't serving the Lord that he wanted, of course."

"The plans we make usually go awry, don't they? I think it's because God has His own plan for our lives. Sometimes His plan is quite different from the one we choose. All we can do is take comfort in knowing that everything that happens to us is for a reason. But—excuse an old man's ramblings. Why don't you get some rest? I'll take the first watch."

Barlow nodded. He wasn't buying Howard's "old man" routine; in the time they'd spent on the trail together, he'd learned that the general was someone he could depend on. So he rolled up in his blankets, turned on his side, and went to sleep, secure in the knowledge that the old warhorse would be an alert lookout.

They spent the next two days waiting for the escort. It didn't come. With each passing hour, Barlow became more impatient. They weren't accomplishing anything sitting here. He wanted to press on for the Sierra Madre. Wanted to find Cochise, introduce him to Howard, let them have their talk, and then get home to Oulay, where he belonged. He knew that, logically, she was quite safe; Howard had promised a company of troopers to watch over her, and the general had delivered. Best of all, that detachment was under the command of Charles Summerhayes. And Short Britches had promised to stick close to the ranch, as well. Oulay was probably the best protected person in the territory. But logic could not combat Barlow's feeling that, in this time of danger and uncertainty, his place was by her side.

He didn't give voice to his impatience. He wasn't going to badger Howard. There was no need to, anyway; he was certain that the general knew where he stood. Besides, Howard had said he would wait a couple of days for the escort to arrive—and he was obviously a man who did what he said he'd do. And at the end of the second day, he told Barlow that he was through with waiting There were any number of possible explanations for the failure of the escort to show up. Time was of the essence. They would depart for the Sierra Madre at first light.

It had become routine for Howard to take the first watch and Barlow the second, so it was Barlow who sat just below the rim of the hollow as the first light of dawn streaked the eastern sky. He was about to stir himself, and go down into the camp to awaken the sleeping general, when he noticed a splotch of darkness against the lightening sky. It took him only a few seconds to recognize it as smoke. A lot of smoke, rising up from the general vicinity of Santo Domingo.

He watched the smoke for a moment, sensing that it meant trouble and pondering what to do about that. Then he went down to the camp. He was tightening the cinch of his saddle when Howard stirred in his blankets, and sat up. One glance at Barlow and he knew something was amiss. He was on his feet in an instance.

"What is it? What's the matter?"

"Something's wrong in the village. I'm going to go take a look."

"Is that wise?"

Barlow didn't answer. Some made a habit of steering well clear of anything that looked like trouble. But in the event it came his way, he wanted to know more about it.

"Stay here," he told Howard. "I'll be back as soon as I can."

He climbed into the saddle, and was about to turn his horse in the direction of the smoke when he noticed that Howard was heading for his own mount.

"What are you doing, General?"

"First rule of combat, Mr. Barlow," said Howard gruffly. "Never divide your forces in the face of an enemy of unknown strength and disposition. I'm coming with you."

Barlow grimaced, but didn't waste time with an argument. "Suit yourself," he said.

Towing the packhorse, they headed east, where now even more smoke was rising in an ominous black plume from Santa Domingo.

Chapter 14

Barlow had concluded that Santo Domingo was being raided, and as they drew closer and heard an occasional gunshot, this seemed to be confirmed. The question was, who were the raiders? Apaches? Bandoleros? Dismounting on the backside of a low hillock, he and Howard crept to the rim and peered over. What they saw shocked them both. The raiders wore the uniforms of Mexican dragoons. It was a very distinctive uniform—the short green tunics and the brass helmets gleaming in the bright morning sun and adorned with black horsehair plumes were unique to the dragoons. There could be no mistake. Nor could Barlow and Howard mistake what they were doing to the inhabitants of the village. Santo Domingo was in chaos. The dragoons were roaming through the adobes, some on horseback, others afoot, kicking in doors, entering the homes, and dragging the people out into the street. The villagers were being herded together, and if any tried to run they were pursued and cut down by saber or pistol shot. Men, women, and children—it didn't matter to the dragoons.

"Good God," breathed Howard. "What are they doing? Barlow, why is this happening?"

Barlow felt sick to his stomach. "I don't know."

"We must do something," said the general.

Barlow calculated that there were at least twenty dragoons in the village. "Nothing we *can* do," he muttered.

Mesmerized by the horror of the scene, he belatedly realized that the general was no longer beside him. He rolled over on his side and looked back down the slope of the hillock—to see Howard once more in the saddle.

"Hey!" he shouted. "What the hell are you doing?"

"I will not just sit by and watch that . . . that butchery."

He kicked his horse up the slope and galloped right past Barlow's position, so close that Barlow had to roll out of the way of the animal's hooves. He knew that Howard wasn't trying to run him over, but rather wanted to throw him off balance long enough to ride clear; the general figured that, given half a chance, Barlow would try to stop him.

Cursing, Barlow half ran, half slid down the slope to his own horse, leaped into the saddle, and set off after Howard. The general had already been spotted, and a pair of dragoons were riding out to meet him. Barlow got to him just as they did. One had a pistol aimed at Howard. The other carried a lance, and he looked like he was inclined to run the general through. Barlow inserted himself between the lancer and Howard and grabbed the lance. The lancer shouted angrily at him and tried to jerk the weapon free. Barlow held on, and laid a hand on the pistol at his side, noticing out of the corner of his eye that the second dragoon was swinging the pistol in his direction.

"No," said Barlow, firmly. "This man is a general in the United States Army. He is here at the invitation of Emperor Maximilian."

In this place, at this time, it seemed an outlandish

claim, and Barlow didn't expect the dragoons to believe him—especially since Howard was clad in trail-
worn civilian clothes. He could only hope that his
proclamation would give the two dragoons pause.

Howard caught on. "I am General Oliver Howard,"
he said, with all the dignity he could muster, "and I
demand to see your commanding officer. At once!"

The dragoons exchanged glances. A third horseman
approached from the village. This one was clearly an
officer.

"What is going on?" he asked, and his gaze swung
from the dragoons to Howard to Barlow. "Who are
you?"

"Joshua Barlow. This is General Howard, of the
United States Army."

The scowl on the officer's face disappeared in an
instant, replaced by a broad, affable grin. "General
Howard! Of course. I am Captain Emilio Cordova, at
your service, sir. Welcome to Mexico."

"Captain, what is the meaning of this?" Howard
gestured toward the village. "What in God's name is
going on here? How can you stand by and allow your
men to . . . to commit such outrages?"

Cordova shrugged. He looked sheepish. "I have my
orders, General."

"Orders? From whom?"

Cordova pointed, and for the first time Barlow noticed a man sitting in the striped shade of a ramada
at the near edge of the village, adjacent to the first
adobe. He wore a blue uniform adorned with more
braid than Barlow had ever seen on one officer. The
way he sat there, arrogant, insouciant, idly watching
the tumult and violence in the street, rubbed Barlow
the wrong way.

"Colonel Villiers," said Cordova—and Barlow
thought he heard the faintest hint of contempt in the

Mexican officer's voice. "He is convinced that every village in this part of the country harbors a Juárista. Pardon me, General—a partisan of the rebel Benito Juárez."

"Since when do you take your orders from a French colonel, Captain?" asked Barlow.

"Since France saw fit to install His Highness, the Emperor Maximilian, upon his throne."

"This must stop," said Howard. He was infuriated, red-faced and trembling with pent-up rage, and Barlow was afraid he would do something reckless and get them both killed. "I'll have a word with your French colonel." He spurred his horse forward. Captain Cordova moved his mount out of the way, and Barlow got the distinct impression the Mexican officer was relishing the confrontation that was about to occur.

Howard wasted no time in urging his horse forward, seemingly oblivious to the Mexican dragoons who had been on the verge of killing him only moments before, and who still watched him with dark, unfriendly eyes. Barlow and Cordova followed, and the dragoons brought up the rear. Howard rode right up to the ramada and placed himself and his horse squarely in front of the French colonel. Villiers looked up at him with hooded eyes.

"You are blocking my view," he said.

"If you are in charge here, I demand that you stop this at once."

Unruffled, Villiers glanced at Cordova. "Who is this man?"

"He claims to be General Oliver Howard, Colonel," said Cordova, "the man we were sent here to meet."

"I see." Villiers turned his attention back to Howard. He did not bother to stand. "I am here as an observer, General. Captain Cordova is in command."

Cordova's expression darkened. "Since that is so," he said curtly, "I will do as you ask, General."

Villiers shot him a hard look.

At that instant, a dragoon emerged from a nearby adobe, roughly dragging a boy of about twelve along with him. A woman followed, begging the soldier to release her son. The dragoon seemed not to hear, and the woman lunged at him. With a curse, the dragoon savagely threw the boy to the ground and twisted around. The woman lost her grip on him and fell at his feet, and the dragoon took the opportunity to kick her as hard as he could. Seeing this, the boy leaped to his feet and hurled himself at the soldier with such fury that the man staggered. Recovering quickly, the dragoon knocked the boy down. Cursing louder now, he drew his saber, clearly intent on running the boy through.

He didn't get the chance. Barlow was already on the move. He gave no thought to the risks involved as he kicked his horse forward and guided the responsive animal straight into the dragoon. The soldier fell sideways, dropping the saber and scrambling to avoid being trampled by the snorting, wild-eyed horse. As Barlow swung out of the saddle, the boy scrambled to his feet again and ran to his mother's side. She lay curled up in a ball, clutching at her midsection. Barlow started toward them, then whirled as Howard shouted a warning. A mounted dragoon was galloping up Santo Domingo's street, saber raised, heading straight for Barlow. The latter didn't have time to draw his pistol—instinctively he made a desperate dive, right across the path of the oncoming horse and forced the dragoon to swing the saber across his body. Missing his mark, the dragoon checked his horse. Barlow got to his feet—just in time to be struck by the first dragoon, who barreled right into him and drove him backward. Falling, Barlow hit the back of his head so hard that he nearly passed out. He threw the dragoon off and rolled away. Out of the corner of his eye, he saw that the mounted dragoon was turning his horse, preparing to make another charge. This time, though, Barlow had a few precious seconds to spare—and his hand dropped to the pistol at his side.

Cordova's voice pierced the ringing in Barlow's ears, as the captain shouted a curt order that brought the mounted dragoon up short. The other one, though, didn't seem to hear. Or if he did, he didn't care whether he disobeyed his commanding officer or not. His blood was up, and with a snarl of rage, he got up and started toward Barlow again. Barlow figured only one thing would stop him—he drew the pistol and aimed it at the man's head. The dragoon stopped, the barrel of the Colt only inches away.

Everything seemed to come to a complete halt. Barlow didn't take his eyes off the dragoon in front of him, but he realized that the commotion in the street had all but ceased. The other soldiers had stopped what they were doing; their attention was fastened on the confrontation between their compadre and the gringo.

"Captain Cordova," said Barlow, pleased that his voice was quite calm and steady, "tell your man to stand down. I don't want to have to kill him."

Cordova rode forward, putting his horse between Barlow and the dragoon. He snapped a curt order to the latter and then turned his attention to Barlow. "Please lower your weapon, senor. There has been enough killing today."

Barlow complied, and Cordova issued more orders to the dragoons. Scanning the street, it occurred to

Barlow that his altercation with the Mexican soldiers had served as a diversion, capturing the attention of Cordova's men long enough for the people of the village to make themselves scarce. But that hadn't happened soon enough for the several campesinos who lay dead in the dust of the street. He turned away from the sight, and helped to her feet the woman who had been trying to save her son from the dragoon. She was young and pretty, though her face was pale and smeared with dirt and drawn taut with pain.

"Are you badly hurt?" he asked.

She shook her head, giving him a wan smile of gratitude.

Cordova rode up. "My apologies, senora. My man says that your son told him his father—your husband—is a Juárista. I am not trying to make excuses for his behavior. But he says that is why he acted the way he did."

She just looked at the captain, with that impassive, unreadable expression that all campesinos—at least those who wanted to stay alive—learned early on to produce on demand.

"Is it true, senora? About your husband?"

"I have not seen my husband in years," she said, with an edge of defiance in her voice. "I do not know what he is doing. I do not even know if he is alive or dead."

Cordova touched the visor of his helmet. "Again, my apologies." He turned his horse away.

Barlow went to retrieve his own horse, which was standing nearby, and led it back to the ramada, where General Howard, still under the watchful eye of the two dragoons, was waiting for him. Cordova was there, as well, and Villiers hadn't moved.

"If these are the tactics you employ," Howard was

saying to the Frenchman, "then it's small wonder that you are losing the war against the men you call rebels."

"Did not your side do the same thing in your own civil war?" asked Villiers.

Howard grimaced. "If you are referring to General Sherman's March to the Sea, I was there, sir, and I can assure you, the rape and murder of civilians was not condoned."

"What about confiscation?"

"What about it?"

"You know as well as I, General, that one of the most effective ways to put down a rebellion is to deny the rebels the support of the people. Without that support, the rebels cannot survive. It is from the people that they get their provisions. It is the people who hide them from the authorities. It is the people who spy for them. The people are the roots of the vine, and if you tear up the roots, the vine withers and dies. This is what I have tried to teach Captain Cordova. And it is a lesson I learned from studying the American Civil War. Your war, General."

"Your men killed innocent people in cold blood."

"They killed people, yes. But how do you know they were innocent?"

"How do you know they weren't?"

Villiers shrugged. "If so, it is too bad. In war, innocent people sometimes lose their lives. Especially in a war in which the enemy is a coward, disguising himself as one of the innocents until your back is turned—and then he drives a dagger into your heart."

Barlow could tell that Howard was on the verge of losing control, so he stepped forward. "General, remember why we're here. What's done is done."

Howard glared at him. "So I should just forget what I've seen here today? Impossible. I am a soldier, sir, and what I have seen is a stain upon the honor of all soldiers everywhere."

Barlow shook his head. He didn't see any point in remarking on his own experiences where soldiers doing dishonorable things was concerned.

"Please, gentlemen," said Cordova, "let's put this behind us, shall we? General, we are here to provide you with safe escort to your destination. I think the sooner we are on our way, the better."

"No," snapped Howard, truculently. "I will not go anywhere with this . . . this man." He made a dismissive gesture in the direction of Villiers.

Villiers gave a short, derisive laugh. "That's fine with me," he said. "I did not travel halfway around the world to safeguard some old fool who thinks he can simply walk into the stronghold of the Apaches and come back alive. No. There is a war to be fought. Captain, collect your men. We have done enough here."

"I should say so," muttered Howard.

As Cordova rode off down the street to round up the dragoons, Howard dismounted and turned to face Barlow.

"We will stay here until I'm sure they're not coming back," said the general.

"Whatever you say."

"You were right, Mr. Barlow. I should have listened to you. Now I will rely on you alone to get me to Cochise."

Barlow didn't say anything. The likelihood of getting Howard to the Sierra Madre—much less getting him out again—appeared to be increasingly remote.

Chapter 15

After Villiers and the dragoons had gone, Barlow and Howard lingered for a couple of hours in Santo Domingo. They sat in the striped shade of the ramada, where the French colonel had earlier been taking his ease. At first they'd demonstrated a desire to help the campesinos care for their dead, but the people of Santo Domingo had quietly but firmly declined their assistance. So now all they could do was sit and watch. Listening to the wail of women grieving over the fallen innocents, Howard shook his head, his anger and outrage still at the boiling point.

"That Napoléon III has as much gall as his famous predecessor," growled the general, "but not even Bonaparte would be so arrogant as to think he could simply install a man like Maximilian on a throne and force the people of this country to bend themselves to his will. And for this"—he made a sweeping gesture that encompassed the tragedy that had recently visited the village—"the French must be made to answer."

"If it's any consolation," said Barlow, "the Mexicans have been doing this to each other since the days of Santa Anna."

Howard glared at him. "I didn't think you would take up for the likes of that Villiers fellow."

"Not taking up for him. But I've heard all about what's been going on down here from the vaqueros who work for me. There probably isn't a family down here that hasn't suffered in some way similar to what we've just witnessed at some point in the past thirty years."

As though to drive home his point, the young woman and the boy who had been targeted by the dragoons emerged from their adobe at that moment and brought Barlow and Howard a plate of tortillas, another of beans, and a clay jug of water.

"I can't eat," said Howard. "I have no appetite. But thank them for me, will you?"

Barlow thanked them. He was starving. That always seemed to happen to him after a brush with death. The woman and her son lingered, watching as he rolled up a tortilla, dipped the end of it into the beans, and began to eat.

"It is I who should thank you," said the young woman. "You saved my son's life."

"De nada," said Barlow. He glanced, curious, at the boy. "What is your name?"

"Manuel."

"Manuel, why did you tell the soldier about your father being a Juárista? Didn't you realize what might happen to you?"

"I do not care what happens to me," said Manuel, vehemently. "I hate the French. And I spit on the soldiers who do their bidding."

"Manuel," said the woman, her tone one of gentle scolding.

"You're very brave," observed Barlow. "But next time, think of the tears your mother would cry if anything happened to you."

Manuel looked at his mother, suddenly crestfallen, and for a moment Barlow thought the boy would begin to weep.

"I am sorry, Mama," he said.

She bent down and kissed the top of his head. "Wait for me inside, Manuel," she said, with a voice full of infinite love and forgiveness.

He ran into the adobe. She turned and smiled at Barlow. "Thank you again, senor. Manuel is a good boy. But he is headstrong, and proud. His father was . . . is the same way."

"So *is* he a Juárista, your husband?"

"I do not know. As I told the captain, he has been gone for several years now. When he left, he would not tell me where he was going or how long he would be away." She looked away, struggling to maintain her composure, and Barlow could tell that she was leaving much unsaid—particularly the fact that, in her heart, she knew her man was never coming back.

"I have no money," she said suddenly. "I have no way to repay the kindness you have shown us."

"Don't want payment," said Barlow.

"If you are staying, you are welcome to stay in our home. It is not much but . . ."

"We're not staying. But thanks just the same."

"Oh." She seemed genuinely sorry to hear that they were soon to depart, and Barlow figured it was because she was afraid—afraid that the soldiers would return, that her son was still in danger. Barlow thought it was probably futile to try to impress upon her that neither he nor Howard could protect her. In his mind, he hadn't saved her or her son. That had been done by Cordova. If the captain hadn't intervened, they'd all be lying dead in the Santo Domingo dirt.

As she turned away, he said, "What is your name, senora?"

"Angeline," she replied. The question took her by surprise. "Angeline Cabreras."

He nodded his thanks. She smiled and disappeared into the adobe.

"One wonders," said Howard bleakly, "how a woman alone can survive for long in this country."

Barlow didn't respond. His attention was focused on the street of Santo Domingo—because suddenly there was nobody on it. The campesinos of the village had vanished as if by magic. Wary, he looked around, knowing there had to be a reason for this phenomenon. And there it was—a solitary horseman, emerging from the brasada.

Captain Cordova.

"My God," breathed Howard. "They're coming back."

"I don't think so." Barlow stood up, left the shade of the ramada, and walked out to meet the dragoon officer.

Cordova was all smiles, as though they were the best of friends. As though what had happened earlier had never happened.

"Senor, I am glad I found you still here."

"How come?"

"I suggested to Colonel Villiers that I return, and offer my services to you and the general. After all, my orders were to escort the two of you to the Sierra Madre. My responsibility is to see you safely there, and as a soldier, I take my responsibilities very seriously."

"I think we'd be better off traveling without you, Captain. Nothing personal."

"If you are afraid my uniform will attract unwanted

attention from the Juáristas, you need not concern yourself. They would attack you even if I did not accompany you. But if it would make you feel more at ease, I am willing to wear civilian clothes."

Howard stepped forward. "Were we to agree to this, and we were stopped by Juáristas, I would not hesitate to divulge to them your true identity, Captain. I will not be branded a spy."

"I understand, General. And I accept the risk."

"I don't like it, General," said Barlow. "And frankly, I don't want to be associated in any way with the Mexican government—since the government is responsible for the bounty on Apache scalps. And that's the source of all our troubles."

"The bounty," said Cordova, "was a decision made by the emperor's ministers and advisers. I do not approve of it, myself."

"Well," said Barlow dryly, "that makes me feel a lot better."

Seeing that he wasn't going to get anywhere with Barlow, Cordova turned to Howard. "General, it is far more likely that you will meet other army detachments. My presence will ensure that you'll have no difficulties with them. I strongly urge you to consider my offer. Your safety is my only concern in this matter."

Howard thought it over. Then he glanced at a frowning Barlow. "Well, he did save your life. I guess that should count for something."

Barlow just shook his head. He was grateful to the captain for intervening in his scrape with the two dragoons. But gratitude only went so far.

"Only as far as the mountains, then," he said. "He doesn't go any farther than that."

"Believe me, senor," said Cordova fervently, "I have no desire to commit suicide by entering the stronghold of the Apaches. Once the mountains are within sight, I will take my leave, with my duty done and my conscience clear."

"So you think we're committing suicide by going into the mountains," said Howard.

"If you come out alive, it will be a miracle, General."

Amused, Howard looked again at Barlow. "Well, at least you two agree on something."

Chapter 16

When the bronchos appeared, rising up from the rocks that littered the steep slopes of the canyon, Barlow was surprised to feel a sense of great relief. For the better part of three weeks, he had been living on the edge, wondering what would happen when they finally arrived at their destination—wondering whether the Apaches would kill them immediately. He was inclined to think that this would be the case. But he couldn't be absolutely sure, and not knowing was the worst part of it all.

Now they would find out.

They had departed Santo Domingo twelve days earlier, and the journey from the border to the Sierra Madre Mountains had been relatively uneventful. Captain Cordova proved to be good company. And as they did not meet any Juáristas, he didn't turn out to be a liability. By the time they parted company, at a small village called Dolorosa, Barlow was almost sorry to see the captain go. He'd had time enough to conclude that Cordova was a man of his word, a gentleman, a true soldier. That didn't entirely exonerate him, in Barlow's mind, for having stood by while his dragoons terrorized Santo Domingo and killed innocent campesinos. But Barlow had learned a lot more from the captain about the military and political situation in Mexico. He'd learned, for instance, that men like Villiers held the power of life and death over Mexican officers. One word from Villiers, and Cordova would have faced a swift court-martial and execution. He'd learned too that Cordova was genuine in his hatred for the French—and the emperor. The captain did not like the Juáristas, either—he thought that most of them used the rebellion against Maximilian as an excuse to murder, rape, and plunder. He conceded hat Benito Juárez was probably sincere in his concern for the well-being of the country and its people. But most of his followers were no better than criminals. The captain's father had been an officer loyal to Santa Anna, and Barlow got the impression that Cordova would have preferred a Mexican republic with a military man as *el presidente*.

As for the Apaches, Cordova believed that they would be—as they had been for as long as anyone could remember—a thorn in the side of the Mexican people for many years to come. Sooner or later, though, they would be wiped out. This was inevitable; there was no place for them. The hatred, on both sides—Mexican and Apache—ran too deep. There had been too much blood for there ever to be a lasting peace.

In parting, he wished Barlow and Howard well— and then informed them that he was going straight to the little *iglesia* in Dolorosa, where he would light a candle and pray for their souls. The general thanked him.

They had proceeded immediately into the mountains, and on the first day had seen no sign of Apaches. Barlow hadn't expected that to last—and here they were, on the second day, three of them. At least there were three that he could see. The rocky

slopes of the canyon might have concealed a hundred
bronchos. Barlow remembered the old saying: You
didn't see an Apache until he was in the process of
killing you.

He didn't expect them to recognize him immediately, and then to welcome him with open arms. Even
if he were recognized at once, he couldn't be at all
sure that he'd be welcomed. Not all the Apaches in
the Sierra Madre Mountains were Chiricahuas, and
even some of the Chiricahua had never liked him. But
there were plenty of Bedonkohe hiding out up here
in the Cima Silkq. The Bedonkohe had gone to war
against the Pinda Lickoyi on behalf of the Chiricahua
several years ago, and for that, they had become outcasts, unable to return to their homeland. And also in
these mountains were the Netdahe, the Avowed Killers, the renegades who came from all the bands and
owed their allegiance to none. They were led by the
one called Geronimo. And Barlow wondered if,
among the Netdahe in the Cima Silkq, the one named
Kiannatah still lived.

Rather, Barlow's hopes were all hinged on the
possibility—slight though it was—that any Apache he
happened across would not be in a hurry to kill two
White Eyes. That they might be curious as to why
two of the Pinda Lickoyi had ventured alone into the
Apache stronghold. After all, they could always kill
the white men later.

He was fairly sure that this was why he and Howard
weren't already dead. He had a moment or two of
grace. If he said the right thing, he and the general
might live. If he didn't . . .

"I am Barlow," he said, speaking in the Apache
tongue. "I have come to see Cochise, to tell him of
his daughter, Oulay."

It wasn't true, of course—that wasn't why he was

there. But he wasn't sure that the truth would be quite so compelling. If these bronchos were Chiricahua, they would probably know his name even if they didn't know him by sight. He was, after all, the Pinda Lick-oyi, who had taken as his woman the daughter of Cochise, and that had caused quite a stir among the Chiricahua. Many were the young bucks who had actively sought Oulay's favor. They had been stunned and angered when Cochise had allowed Barlow to take her away. In fact, it was quite possible that at least one of these three men had been a suitor of Oulay's. And while that man would resent Barlow, and might even feel compelled to kill him, the fact that he was son-in-law of Cochise would, hopefully, cause him to refrain from such action.

The bronchos edged cautiously closer. Howard looked at Barlow, ready to follow his lead. The general didn't appear to be at all rattled. It was a brave man indeed, Barlow knew, who could maintain his composure when confronted by Apache bronchos. There was something elemental about these warriors, something that engendered fear in the most stalwart of men, just as a tornado or a rattlesnake coiled to strike would engender fear. That fear was nothing to be ashamed of. What counted was how you dealt with it.

Moving slowly, very slowly, Barlow used his left hand to unbuckle his gun belt, and then he let it drop to the ground. To render oneself helpless in the face of this kind of danger wasn't easy, but he had to convince the bronchos that he'd come in peace. He could only hope that General Howard had nerve enough to do likewise.

He did—and the bronchos seemed to relax a bit. One looked at his comrades, and nodded.

"He is telling the truth. He is the one who took Oulay. I remember him."

"It could be a trick," said the second, more belligerent than the others.

"We have watched them all day," said the first broncho. "They are alone. I say we take them to Cochise. What harm could come of that?"

They looked at the third broncho, and Barlow sensed that, for whatever reason, his life depended on what this man said.

The third man nodded. "I agree. We can kill them anytime we want. We will take them."

Vastly relieved, Barlow glanced at Howard, who was watching him, trying to read his expression for some clue as to what his fate would be.

"So are we going to live?" asked the general.

"For the time being," replied Barlow. "Just don't try anything."

"A little late for trying anything," said Howard dryly, "since I've just surrendered my weapons."

While one broncho stood watch over them, a second gathered up their guns, and the third disappeared, to return a few moments later with three unshod mountain mustangs. Once mounted, one of the bronchos—the one who had made the decision to take them to Cochise—rode up alongside Barlow and used his headband to blindfold his prisoner. One of the other Apaches did the same thing to Howard. Barlow wasn't concerned. He understood the reasoning behind the blindfold. They were about to take two White Eyes to the hideout of the Chiricahua, and they didn't want their prisoners, once freed, to find their way back— with a column of soldiers in tow, for instance. The one who had blindfolded Barlow took the reins to his prisoner's horse and led the way. The second broncho took charge of Howard. The third Apache brought up the rear as they proceeded single file up the canyon. *So far so good,* thought Barlow. They were going to reach Cochise alive. The next problem would be to get out of those mountains alive.

They rode for several hours, and by the position of the sun's heat on his body, Barlow calculated that they were heading primarily westward, though their route twisted and turned considerably. He could also tell that they were climbing higher into the mountains. Of course, this knowledge was useless—he couldn't have retraced the route they took that day even if his life depended on it. But he had no problem with the blindfold, since it could mean the difference between life and death, even though it was unnerving to travel without the benefit of sight, especially when one was at the mercy of Apache bronchos.

When, at last, they reached their destination, and the blindfold was removed, Barlow saw before him an Apache che-wa-ki on a high plateau surrounded by rugged peaks—not unlike the hideout in the Mogollon Mountains in which he had once found Cochise and his people, following the outbreak of trouble that, in the end, had forced the Chiricahuas to seek sanctuary in Mexico. And while the long history of animosity between Apache and Mexican might have led some to wonder at the wisdom of such a choice, Barlow knew what the Sierra Madre Mountains meant to all Apaches. For generations these mountains had been a refuge, and few Mexicans were foolish enough to venture into them. Long ago, the Mexican government had tried to root the Apaches out of the Sierra Madre; they had sent their best commanders and most veteran troops into the mountains for that purpose. Each expedition had resulted in disaster. For their part, the Apaches believed that the Sierra Madres—they called the mountains the Cima Silkq—had been set aside by the Great Spirit for them, and that the Great Spirit and the ghosts of their ancestors watched over them and kept them from harm as long as they remained here.

The che-wa-ki was a large one, consisting of dozens of jacales constructed of dirt, clay, stones and sticks. The men, women, and children who had gathered to watch the arrival of the two white men looked none the worse for the fact that they were exiles from their homeland. But then, the Apaches were a resilient people. Barlow knew them well enough to look beyond the stoic facade, however. He knew, for instance, that under normal circumstances, and contrary to the perception of them—shared by most whites—they were a solemn bunch, that Apaches were good-natured and friendly, able to cheerfully accept the trials and tribulations of life. This attribute was usually hidden from strangers, but Barlow sensed that there was no joy here, even beneath the surface. No happiness, and no hope, either. Physically, the Apaches were more durable than most. Emotionally, though, they were vulnerable. And the past years, living like hunted animals, with no place to go, and no prospects for the future, had taken a heavy toll on them. Barlow was glad he had refused to allow Oulay to accompany him. These were her people, and what she would have seen behind their eyes and in their hearts would have upset her greatly.

The escort of bronchos dismounted in the center of the village, and bade Barlow and Howard to do the same. Barlow glanced at Howard, and noticed that the general was studying the people that surrounded him with keen interest. He wondered if Howard was going to judge the Chiricahuas by their appearance. At first blush they seemed unthreatening—dark, wiry, dirty, most of them short of stature, clad in plain, undecorated garb no better than one would see worn by poor campesinos. They did not cut grand, warlike figures like the Comanches or the Cheyenne. But Barlow, like others who truly knew the Chi-hinne, would not have hesitated to state, if asked whether he preferred to battle a dozen Comanche warriors or a single Apache broncho, that he would choose to confront the former over the latter any day of the week. Would the old soldier realize this? Or would he be wondering why he'd come all this way, risking so much, just to keep these people, who did not look as though they posed any sort of threat at all, from going to war against the United States?

And then the crowd parted, and a man Barlow knew well—a man he respected as much as any other—stepped forward. It was Cochise, leader of the Chiricahua, and the one in whose hands rested the fate of the two Pinda Lickoyi who had ventured into his realm. Taller than most of his kind, and broader in the shoulders, Cochise *looked* every inch a warrior. He had a commanding presence. Howard looked at him, then at Barlow, and the expression on his face spoke volumes. *You don't have to tell me who this one is,* it said.

Cochise hardly seemed to notice Howard; his attention was entirely focused on Barlow. He strode forward and extended a hand of friendship. Barlow took it gratefully.

"My daughter," asked the Chiricahua jefe, "is she well?"

"She is well. She sends her love and respect."

Cochise was visibly moved. "I think often of her," he said wistfully.

"She misses you too. She wanted to come with me, but I would not let her."

Cochise nodded. "The trail is a long and dangerous one. You were right to make her stay behind."

"One day I will bring her," said Barlow, and he meant it as a vow. "When the trail is less dangerous."

"That day will be long in coming, I fear." Cochise finally acknowledged Howard's presence. "Why have *you* come all this way?" he asked Barlow.

"To bring *this* man to you. He is a chief among the Pinda Lickoyi warriors. He asks to speak with you."

"About what?"

"War," said Barlow, "and peace."

Though Barlow and Cochise spoke in the Apache tongue, and Howard did not understand a word of what was passing between them, he snapped to attention and saluted the Chiricauhua jefe. The gesture startled Barlow, but he quickly realized that it was a smart thing to do. For one thing, it left no doubt in anyone's mind that, despite Howard's trail-stained civilian clothes, he was a officer. And that being the case, it was a sign of respect proffered to Cochise.

"Is he to be trusted?" Cochise asked Barlow.

"Yes," said Barlow, without hesitation, honored to know that Cochise relied on his judgment in such an important matter.

Cochise nodded. "Then come," he said, gesturing toward his jacal. "We will talk."

Chapter 17

Though he felt a little guilty about it, Barlow could not overcome a profound indifference to the conversation that General Howard had with Cochise, a conversation that went on for hours. He was, of course, glad to see that the two men hit it off; it was soon clear that each man saw in the other someone of integrity, someone whose words they could trust. That was all well and good—but Barlow had to wonder if, in the long run, that would make any difference. After all, honest and trustworthy men on both sides had attempted to forge a peace between the United States and the Apaches—and all their efforts had availed them nothing. The mistrust and hatred remained. The blood continued to spill. There was no question that these two old warriors, Cochise and Howard, desired peace above all else. Yet there were many other men, red and white, who, for various reasons, wanted and worked for war. Being a realist, Barlow had to assume that the latter would have their way in the future, just as they had in the past.

Howard told Cochise of the troubles north of the border, holding nothing back. He blamed not the Coyoteros but rather the scalphunters—and the Mexican government, which had offered the scalp bounty.

Nonetheless, the Coyoteros were attacking white ranches, white travelers, and the white stagecoach line that ran through the territory. And it was the duty of the United States Army to protect the people and their interests. As much as Howard hated to think of it, much blood would be shed. And inevitably, the Coyoteros would be defeated. What Howard hoped to do, as he explained to the attentive Chiricahua leader, was to prevent more violence and bloodshed. This was why he had come to the Cima Silkq, to speak to Cochise, to be the one to explain the events now occurring in the United States—and to urge Cochise to do everything in his power to keep the Chiricahuas from entering the fray. To do so, argued Howard, would only bring more hardship to Cochise's people.

Cochise complimented Howard for his bravery, and acknowledged that he believed that Howard was speaking truly, from his heart. It took a man who had the courage of his convictions to risk everything in coming to the Cima Silkq, as Howard had done. And Cochise also acknowledged that the general's prediction with respect to the outcome of the hostilities between the United States and the Coyoteros was no doubt accurate. It would avail the Chiricahua people nothing to become involved in that struggle.

And yet, continued Cochise, his people had suffered much hardship in past years—so much that some of them wanted only to strike back at their enemies. In the eyes of these people, the enemy was not only the Nakai-Ye—the Mexican—but also the Pinda Lickoyi, the White Eyes. When they learned that their brothers, the Coyoteros, were on the warpath against those enemies, they would want to join the fight. He went on to explain to Howard at some length about his standing as jefe. Just because he was the leader of the Chiricahua did not mean that he could issue orders

and expect the bronchos to obey them, in the way that
Howard would issue orders to his bluecoat soldiers.
The Apache broncho was always his own man, and
was always allowed to follow his own heart. If he followed the leadership of Cochise, it was because he
chose to do so. Cochise could speak to his people, and
urge them not to go to war. But he could make no
guarantees to Howard.

The general said he understood; all he hoped for
was that Cochise would make his best effort. If the
Chiricahua did not go to war, then many of the other
Apache bands would think twice before siding with
the Coyoteros. And then fewer people would have to
die before peace was restored to the territory.

Stressing again that he was making no guarantees,
Cochise surmised that most of the Chiricahuas would
listen to his advice and keep the peace. But he had
no influence whatsoever over the other bands, and
modestly doubted that the course of action he and his
people followed would determine the course followed
by the Bedonkohe, the Mescalero, the Mimbreno.
And then he told Howard that there was another
group of Apaches who would jump at any chance to
fight. These were the Netdahe, the Avowed Killers.
They were led by a man called Geronimo. They were
not many in number, but they could do great damage.
They were hiding out in the Cima Silkq, and occasionally they would venture down into the desert, to strike
at the Nakai-Ye. Cochise hated them. Not only because their actions ran counter to his efforts to keep
the peace. And not just because their raiding made
life more difficult for the Chiricahua, since their victims did not distinguish between a Netdahe renegade
and any other Apache. But also because one of them,
the one called Kiannatah, had killed in cold blood an
old friend, Nachita.

Hearing the name of Kiannatah made Barlow sit up and take notice. He asked Cochise when and how this had come to be.

"It happened," said Cochise gravely, "after you took Oulay away to safety. We were on our way here, nearly to the border, when Kiannatah showed up among us. He killed two of our men. He asked about Oulay. I told him only that she was no longer with us. In order to escape with his life, he took Nachita as a hostage, promising to let him go unharmed. Instead, he murdered Nachita."

Barlow nodded, deciding on the spot that it wouldn't do anyone any good if he told Cochise that Kiannatah had found Oulay after all. That the Netdahe had kidnapped his daughter and, but for the courage of Short Britches, a handful of White Mountain Apaches, and a cavalry sergeant named Farrow, might have succeeded in making off with her.

"So as far as you know, Kiannatah remains here, in these mountains?" asked Barlow.

Cochise nodded. "I have not seen him with my own eyes. He knows that because of what he did to my friend I would kill him if I *do* see him."

Barlow let the matter drop. As long as Kiannatah lived, Oulay was in danger. But he knew he didn't stand a chance of finding the Netdahe broncho in the Sierra Madre. Besides, at the moment Oulay was in far graver danger from other sources—especially if Kiannatah remained in hiding in the Cima Silkq. His best course of action was to return to her side as quickly as possible.

For that reason, Barlow hoped that the meeting between Howard and Cochise would soon come to an end. The general had gotten what he'd come from— assurances from the Chiricahua chief that he would do everything in his power to keep his people out of

the Indian war brewing north of the border. He should
have known better, though. Cochise insisted that they
remain the night as his guests, and it would have been
rude to decline that invitation.

They left the Chiricahua che-wa-ki at first light the
following day. Cochise gave Barlow some gifts to carry
to Oulay. He also provided them with an escort of a
half dozen bronchos. They would, said Cochise, see
Barlow and Howard safely out of the Cima Silkq. Of
course, the two men would have to be blindfolded,
added the jefe apologetically. This was not because he
did not trust Barlow and Howard. But if it was discovered that they'd visited the Chiricahua stronghold,
they might be made prisoner by the Nakai-Ye soldiers,
who could, conceivably, torture them into divulging
the route they'd taken.

This was highly unlikely, thought Barlow. Still, he
was glad that neither he nor Howard had mentioned
the fact that the Mexican government knew of their
mission into the Sierra Madre Mountains. This was
knowledge that would only cause Cochise needless
anxiety. He assured Cochise that both he and the general appreciated the wisdom of using the blindfolds.

"My great hope," said Cochise, in parting, "is that
one day before I die I may see my daughter again."

"She shares that hope, as do I," said Barlow, moved
by the powerful emotion hidden within the jefe's wistfully spoken words.

As they rode away from the stronghold, Barlow's
spirits were high for the first time in weeks. Finally he
could allow himself to entertain the notion that he
and Howard were going to pull off the impossible.
That they were actually going to survive a journey
into the Cima Silkq. And that he was going to see
Oulay again. Wouldn't she be surprised when he
showed up, alive and well!

*   *   *

The evening of the day that saw the departure of Barlow and Howard from the Chiricahua stronghold, Cochise was in his jacal when a man entered to inform him of Geronimo's arrival.

"Bring him to me," said Cochise, with a grimace.

A moment later the leader of the Avowed Killers entered the jacal. Geronimo was tall and lanky. His broad, deeply lined face had a cruel cast, made more so by the wide knife slit of a mouth. His features were those of a man who did not show himself, or anyone else, any mercy whatsoever. Cochise feared no man, not even Geronimo. But he feared what this man represented—the total destruction of the Apache people. Even so, he understood the attraction that Geronimo held for many Apaches. Many young warriors—even among the Chiricahua band—held him in reverence, seeing him as something more than a rebel and an outlaw. They knew Geronimo could not lead them to victory. The odds against the Chi-hinne were too great, and only a fool believed that The People would eventually triumph over their enemies. So Geronimo could never be the savior of his kind. Rather, he was viewed as the savior of Apache honor. Under his leadership, at least the Apaches would go down fighting, never to be forgotten—and feared—by the Pinda Lickoyi and the Nakai-Ye. Other leaders were willing to buy time at the cost of Apache honor. Cochise knew that there were rumblings in the ranks of the Chiricahua bronchos about him in this regard.

Cochise beckoned for Geronimo to sit at the jacal's fire. The outlaw broncho did so. He threw a furtive look around the jacal, and Cochise surmised that he was wary of a trap. A man without honor, mused the Chiricahua jefe, expected other men to be without honor, as well.

"There were white men here," said Geronimo flatly. "I have come to find out if Cochise has signed *another* treaty paper."

There was more than a trace of sarcasm in his voice. Cochise bit down on his anger, realizing that the implication here was that he was a coward, kowtowing to the wishes of the Pinda Lickoyi.

"I have not signed another treaty paper," replied Cochise coldly. "When I signed one years ago I gave my word to live in peace with the white man. I keep my word, so there is no need for another treaty paper."

"The white man has not kept *his* word. He has broken that treaty paper you signed."

"Yes," conceded Cochise. "But then, I am not a white man."

Geronimo nodded. He looked around again, and Cochise thought that perhaps the Netdahe leader was hoping for some tiswin, or some food. But Cochise was in no mood to play the good host. In his opinion, it was enough that he even allowed Geronimo in his jacal.

"Who were these white men who dared come into the Cima Silkq?" asked Geronimo. "What did they want?"

"Who they are and why they came is my concern. But I will tell you this. They are brave men who came here knowing they might be killed. And yet they came in hopes of saving lives."

"Pinda Lickoyi lives."

"And Chiricahua lives. The Coyoteros have gone to war against them north of the border."

Geronimo gazed at Cochise for a moment with hooded eyes. "You tell me only what you wish me to know. Perhaps Cochise hopes the Netdahe will now leave the Cima Silkq and go north to join the Coyoteros in their fight against the Pinda Lickoyi. Perhaps he hopes that we all be killed."

"You *will* be killed," replied Cochise, "because of the path you have chosen. But contrary to what you may believe, I don't care what happens to the Netdahe. Except for one of you. The one called Kiannatah. I owe it to an old friend to kill that one myself."

Geronimo smiled—a faintly derisive smile. "Cochise has courage. But I fear he would be no match for Kiannatah."

"Send him to me, and we will see about that."

"The suggestion is an interesting one."

"I am sure you thought of it before," said Cochise dryly. "You must have thought that if Kiannatah killed me, you would then be able to recruit many more Chiricahua men to your cause. I stand in your way. As long as I live, you cannot rally all the Chihinne to battle against our enemies."

"At least Cochise still recognizes them as the enemy."

"I know who my enemies are. I have Pinda Lickoyi enemies. I have Nakai-Ye enemies. And I have Apache enemies. But I will tell you this. The Coyoteros have gone to war because of the actions of scalphunters who killed many Aravaipa who wanted only to live in peace. The scalphunters were Pinda Lickoyi, it is true. But the ones to blame are the Nakai-Ye, who have placed a bounty on our heads. The Nakai-Ye are our worst enemies."

Geronimo shrugged. "Perhaps." Abruptly, he stood. "I go now."

Cochise stood as well. He refused to look up to the likes of the Netdahe leader. He wanted to know what Geronimo intended to do; he hoped that the Avowed Killers would be unable to resist the temptation to go north and join the Coyoteros in their fight. But he didn't ask Geronimo, well aware that he could not rely on the Netdahe leader to tell him the truth.

Geronimo started out of the jacal—at the threshold he paused and turned back to Cochise. Once again there was an unpleasant smile on his cruel face.

"You do not believe this is so, but sometimes I have visions. I have seen the future. One day all the Chi-hinne will rise up against their enemies. We will die, yes. But we will die with honor, and in such a way that the Nakai-Ye and the Pinda Lickoyi will never forget us. In that way, at least, we will go on forever. And when the children of our enemies speak of the Chi-hinne they will do so with dread in their voices. And when they say a name, it will be my name, not yours. All of these things, I admit, give me satisfaction."

With a curt nod, he slipped out into the night.

Chapter 18

Kiannatah was bored.

Sitting cross-legged on a sandy hillock above the jacal that had been his home these past few years, he gazed out across the rugged countenance of the Sierra Madre—and brooded. Though it was the middle of the day, and the summer sun hammered his broad shoulders, he was impervious to discomfort. Long ago he had learned to embrace hunger, thirst, and pain. These things reminded him of his purpose in life: to suffer and to make others suffer, in turn.

Many years ago, in the Nakai-Ye village called Dolorosa, which, located at the base of the Cima Silkq, was less than a day's ride away from his jacal, Kiannatah had watched his entire family massacred by the Mexicans. The Nakai-Ye had invited his band to come to Dolorosa, pretending to offer friendship. Kiannatah had been but a boy then. Somehow he had escaped with his life. And ever since that terrible day he had lived for vengeance.

He had lost count of the Nakai-Ye and Pinda Lickoyi he had slain since then. No matter how many he killed, the thirst for revenge never left him. It seemed clear to him that killing the enemy was the only course left to all Apaches, and he had nothing but contempt for most of his kind, since they were inclined to live in "peace" with the Mexican and the white man. Even the other Netdahe chose not to wage a vigorous war against the enemies of The People, preferring instead to occasionally raid Mexican villages like Dolorosa— and usually when they wanted whiskey or mule meat or women. They killed, yes, but usually only when a Nakai-Ye stood between them and the loot they sought. Geronimo himself—the one man Kiannatah looked up to, a man whom he had believed was a kindred spirit, since Geronimo too had seen his entire family butchered before his very eyes—now appeared content to waste his life away in these remote and barren heights.

At that moment, the Mexican girl emerged from the jacal below. Shading her eyes with one hand, holding an earthen jug in the other, she paused just outside the jacal and looked all around. Looking for him. Not because she missed him, or was concerned for his welfare. But rather because she feared him. Kiannatah watched her, unmoving. She did not see him, even though he sat in plain sight, perhaps a hundred yards from the jacal. He was expert in the Apache technique called enthlay-sit-daou; he had learned how to blend into his surroundings so completely that people could look right at him and not see him. Finally, the Mexican girl gave up and ventured down to the spring located near the jacal. Kiannatah watched as she knelt down and filled the earthen jug with water. Then she balanced the jug on one shoulder and hurried back to the jacal. At the entrance she paused, looked over her shoulder, and once more scanned the countryside, before vanishing inside like a mouse into its hole.

Seeing her, Kiannatah had to deal with a measure of self-contempt. He did not love her. In fact, he did not care for her at all. How could he care for her?

She was Nakai-Ye. Over a year ago, during a raid on a Mexican village, he had been about to kill her when a sudden urge to take her captive had gripped him. He couldn't explain that change of heart to himself, except to lay the blame for it on Oulay, daughter of Cochise.

Growing up, Kiannatah had vowed that he would never take a wife. Never have children. A family was a liability for an Avowed Killer. Concern for loved ones weakened a warrior, sometimes fatally. And then he had seen Oulay, and desired her. But Cochise had done the unthinkable. The Chiricahua leader had allowed Oulay to live with a white man—and even worse, a yellow-leg soldier. Kiannatah had abducted Oulay, intending to bring her to the Cima Silkq, to force her to love him, and to stay with him always. But some of the soldier's friends had foiled that plan. Not long after that, Kiannatah had spared the life of the Mexican girl. He had brought her back to the Cima Silkq. He hadn't tried to force her to love him; he didn't want her love. But he had forced her to stay with him. She wasn't Oulay, of course, but she sufficed as the object of his sexual desires, and as someone to take care of the jacal that was his home. But even though he told himself that he could do without the Mexican girl, he still felt contempt for what he perceived to be a personal weakness, and he'd concluded that dreams of being with Oulay had made him, somehow, less inclined to live out his days alone—the way, in his mind, a true Netdahe should.

The Mexican girl was perhaps sixteen years of age now. In the first days of her captivity she had tried to escape a couple of times. He had always caught her, and beat her severely, and when he left on subsequent raids, he would always tie her up so that she couldn't flee even if she was still of a mind to do so. Although he spoke only a little of her tongue, he knew enough Spanish to understand from her that she would no longer, now, be welcomed home, since she had spent so much time with an Apache broncho, and her people would naturally assume that he'd had his way with her. In the eyes of her family and friends, this made her fatally damaged goods. Kiannatah was unmoved; it really didn't matter how her family would treat her, since she would never see them again.

Kiannatah yawned. Soon, he thought, it would be time to conduct another raid against the Nakai-Ye. He considered paying a visit to Geronimo, to argue for just such a course of action. The Netdahe leader lived nearby, but while his jacal was but a few miles away as the crow flew, it would take a half day to negotiate the maze of canyons to reach it. Most of the other Netdahe remained in close proximity to their leader. Yet while he considered himself an Avowed Killer—indeed, he thought of himself as a better Netdahe than all the others—Kiannatah had never befriended any of Geronimo's other followers. Even in the early days he had kept himself apart. This might not have been the wisest course, since Geronimo had come to favor him, and at one point had even said that Kiannatah was the closest thing to a son that he had. This had engendered a good deal of jealousy and, sometimes, outright animosity toward Kiannatah among the other Netdahe bronchos. Ironically, he was an outcast even from a band of outcasts.

It wasn't that Kiannatah thought he needed Geronimo's permission to conduct another raid. But he preferred to ride with at least two or three other Netdahe. Even though they did not like him, most of the other Netdahe would accompany him on a raid, because they knew that, like Geronimo, Kiannatah was a brilliant tactician who was assured of success.

Kiannatah had made up his mind to leave his place on the hillock and descend to the jacal when he was struck by the sudden and absolute conviction that he was being watched.

He peered at the jacal for a moment, but the Mexican girl was nowhere to be seen. Then he carefully scanned the rimrock all around. Nothing. Still, he was sure that there was someone out there. His instincts seldom led him astray. Who could it be? Another Apache, certainly. No Nakai-Ye or Pinda Lickoyi could get so close without betraying himself. Besides, neither the Mexicans nor the whites dared venture into the Cima Silkq these days. But just because it was an Apache did not mean there was no danger. Kiannatah did not trust his own people. Most were afraid of him. Some hated him. And there was one in particular who wanted nothing more than to see him dead—Cochise.

Deciding swiftly on a course of action, Kiannatah rose and proceeded down the slope to the jacal, acting for all the world like nothing was wrong. But once inside, he moved quickly to the back of the jacal and, dropping to one knee, dug down into the hard-packed dirt until he found the knotted end of a rope. The Mexican girl, squatting by the cookfire in the center of the jacal, watched him, wide-eyed. Pulling on the rope, Kiannatah lifted a small trapdoor made of rough-hewn cedar planking. Below was a narrow tunnel. Before dropping down into the tunnel, he gave the Mexican girl a fierce glance.

"Stay inside," he snapped, in his own tongue, "and be quiet."

She nodded, having picked up enough Apache during her year of captivity to understand clearly. Looking at her, Kiannatah saw the hate shimmering in her eyes. He was going out to, quite possibly, die—and she was fervently hoping for that result.

Once in the tunnel, Kiannatah crawled swiftly to its terminus, some twenty yards east of the jacal. He emerged through another dirt-covered trapdoor, in a spot surrounded by boulders and blocked from view in every direction. Slipping through a pair of boulders tilted one against the other, Kiannatah circled to the north, using the rough contours of the terrain to remain hidden from anyone who might be lurking on the rimrock. He couldn't know for certain where the intruder was located, but he did know that the best vantage point from which to get a clear view of the jacal and its surroundings was to the north.

He was right. The intruder was on the northern rimrock. But it wasn't an enemy. At least Kiannatah didn't think so.

Geronimo was sitting cross-legged in the shade of a huge catclaw, rifle across his lap. He could not see the jacal from this location. And even though Kiannatah approached from behind him, moving as silently as a ghost, Geronimo somehow knew he was near.

"Good," said the Netdahe leader, without turning around. "I am glad you are here. I was growing weary of waiting."

Kiannatah lowered his rifle. Circling Geronimo, he sat on his heels facing his mentor. He didn't ask why Geronimo was playing this game—why he hadn't simply approached the jacal openly. That was the way of the Netdahe leader; he was constantly testing others, especially those who rode with him. Knowing this did not temper Kiannatah's annoyance, however.

"Why are you here?"

Geronimo was surprised by the curtness of the question. "I bring you good news, Kiannatah. Valerio and his Coyoteros have gone to war against the Pinda Lickoyi."

Kiannatah's eyes were suddenly bright with interest. "And you are going north to join them."

Geronimo shook his head. "No. But I tell you this because I thought *you* would want to go."

"Why does Geronimo choose not to?"

"The time is not right."

Kiannatah made a dismissive gesture. There was scorn in his voice. "What does that mean?"

Geronimo watched the young Netdahe warily. He had seldom seen Kiannatah like this, so openly defiant. "One day all of the bands will rise up against the white man. Then the men will turn to me to lead them in one final battle against our enemies."

"So with you, now, it is not enough to kill our enemies. It is fame you seek."

Geronimo checked his anger. "I will die fighting, the same as you, Kiannatah. But for my death to count for something, I will choose the time and place."

Kiannatah thought it over. He realized that, as far as Geronimo was concerned, he had become a liability ever since his killing of Nachita, friend to Cochise. Perhaps this was Geronimo's way of getting rid of him. He quickly considered his options. He could refuse to go, and dash the Netdahe leader's hopes. But there was an even better way.

"I am not so particular," he said dryly. "I will go north, and join the Coyoteros. I grow weary too—weary of hiding in these mountains like an animal. I am an Apache, and whenever there is a chance to strike the enemies of my people, I will go there."

Geronimo stood up. The Netdahe leader was very grave. "Even your own people are your enemies, Kiannatah," he said.

He turned his back and walked away. It was a risky

thing to do, because there was no telling how Kiannatah might react. But he was, after all, Geronimo—and he had to demonstrate that he wasn't afraid of this man. Even though that wasn't precisely true.

Watching Geronimo walk away, Kiannatah smiled coldly. He had learned many things from the Netdahe leader. He had been an attentive pupil in the ways of war. Now he would put all that he had learned to the test. And best of all, he would return alive, dashing Geronimo's hopes.

On his way back to the jacal, Kiannatah debated what to do about the Mexican girl. Before, he had never been gone more than a few days. But this time he would not return for a very long time. As far as he could tell, there were only two choices: He could set her free or he could kill her.

Reaching the jacal, he set the rifle down just outside the doorway and drew his knife before crossing the threshold.

Chapter 19

Even though it seemed like the world was going to hell in a handbasket, Barlow had two months of relative peace and quiet on his ranch with Oulay, during which time he tried very hard to convince himself that there was at least a slim possibility that the current Apache troubles would not visit him and his again. Of course, he knew that wasn't going to be the case. And so it was with more resignation than resentment that one day he heard the news from Short Britches that a small detail of soldiers was on its way. With a fatalist's sigh, he asked the old scout if he recognized any of the men.

"One of them is your friend, the lieutenant," said Short Britches. "And there is one who does not wear a uniform. But it is easy to see that he is a soldier."

"It isn't General Howard?"

Short Britches shook his head. "This one has a yellow beard. And both arms."

Barlow didn't bother asking if the soldiers had seen Short Britches. They wouldn't have, unless the old scout had wanted them to.

Short Britches watched Barlow closely. He saw how the padrone cast a despondent look around the ranch.

"Every time the soldiers come," remarked the scout, "you end up going away, even though you never *want* to go. This time, maybe you should go away before they get here. I will tell them you won't be back for a long time, and then they will go."

"You mean I should run," said Barlow.

"You are too proud. I have always thought so. I have always thought that pride would be the death of you."

"Maybe," said Barlow glumly.

Short Britches glanced beyond Barlow, and for the first time that he could remember, Barlow thought he saw a glimmer of sympathy in the scout's sun-faded eyes. He turned to see Oulay standing at the doorway of their adobe home—and could hardly bring himself to look at her, because the expression on her face made plain the fact that she knew, and dreaded, what was coming.

"I'll go tell the lookout."

It was a job he could have given Short Britches, except that he did not want to bear witness to any more of the suffering reflected in the eyes of the woman he loved.

The detail arrived a couple of hours later. The only man among them that Barlow recognized was Lieutenant Summerhayes. The man with the blond beard looked to be about forty years of age, and was clad in a canvas hunting outfit and a pith helmet. He was tall, spare, and sinewy. Most striking of all, however, was his choice in mounts. Instead of a horse, he rode a mule. But Short Britches was right—a single glance and you could tell he was a soldier. His bearing was military. This was a man accustomed to command. His was a stocky, durable build, and while it was clear these men had traveled a long way in a short time, he looked none the worse for the ordeal. The same could not be said of the four troopers who accompanied him and Summerhayes.

"Hello, Joshua," said Summerhayes, as the soldiers checked their weary mounts in front of the adobe. "I've brought you another general."

"Just what I wanted, Charles. Thanks."

"General George Crook, Mr. Joshua Barlow."

Crook swung down from the saddle and stuck a hand out. "A pleasure to meet you, Mr. Barlow. I've heard a lot about you from General Howard. He thinks a lot of you."

"The last time I saw him," said Barlow, "I asked him to forget I even existed."

Crook smiled. "I understand."

"Do you?" Barlow gestured halfheartedly at the adobe's door. "Come on in."

Crook accepted the invitation, while Summerhayes tarried outside long enough to tell the troopers to water the horses, and where they could find the spring. Barlow introduced Crook to Oulay, and then the three men sat down at the table while Oulay provided them with cups of coffee.

"How's the war going?" asked Barlow.

"Not well," replied Crook gruffly. "Which, I gather, is why General Howard sent for me."

"I see."

"It seems the thinking was that, with Cochise and Geronimo apparently being content to remain down in Mexico, this Coyotero chief named Valerio would be easy enough to handle," said Crook. "Apparently, that hasn't been the case."

"Valerio's not to be underestimated."

"General Crook has earned his reputation as the army's best Indian fighter," said Summerhayes.

"Is that right?"

Summerhayes gave him a funny look. Barlow's ambivalence struck him as odd. "Oh, yeah. Like you, Joshua, he graduated from the military academy at West Point. . . ."

"At the bottom of my class, I should add," said Crook wryly.

"And he was posted to California," continued Summerhayes. "He led successful campaigns against the Shoshones and the Nez Perce. During the war he fought at Second Manassas and Chickamauga, and breveted major general of volunteers. He commanded the Army of West Virginia during the Shenandoah campaign, serving under Phil Sheridan. And then, after Lee surrendered, he was posted to Oregon to subdue the Paiute. And now, at General Howard's request, President Grant has sent him down here to end the fighting between whites and Apaches once and for all."

"Well," said Barlow, "you've done your homework, Charles."

"I've followed the general's career for some time," admitted Summerhayes, with unabashed admiration. "In my opinion, he is the best Indian fighter in the army."

Crook looked mildly amused by the lieutenant's enthusiasm, but said nothing.

"You might find the Apaches a harder nut to crack than the Paiutes, General," said Barlow.

"I've done my homework too, Mr. Barlow. Read all I could find about the Apaches, including the field reports from officers who have served in the territory for the past twenty years, along with written accounts by traders who frequented the Santa Fe Trail. Having done that, I'm inclined to agree with you. I know I have my work cut out for me."

Barlow nodded. "It's good that you're not going to

underestimate them. I've seen a lot of good men killed needlessly because their commanders did just that."

Crook leaned forward. "I may be an Indian fighter, Mr. Barlow. But I'm not an Indian hater. The first thing I learned when I got to California, fresh out of West Point, was that the Indians seemed to have a valid reason for being at war with us. The Senate rejected no less than eighteen treaties that had been negotiated with the tribes out there. You know what that left them with? Nothing. No rights whatsoever. We promised that they could keep at least a portion of their homeland. But in most cases, they didn't get to keep any of it. So they struck back. And being an officer in the United States Army, I had to fight them. It was a difficult decision. But the only option was to quit the army, and I wasn't prepared to do that."

Barlow tried to conceal his concern. "Why are you here?"

"My task is to put down the Coyoteros. Now I fully understand why they've gone on the warpath—it has to do with that damned scalp bounty put up by the Mexican government, which resulted in that massacre of the Aravaipa. I know all this, but it doesn't change anything. The Coyoteros have to stop their raids. I would prefer to do that as quickly, and with as little blood shed, as possible. In previous campaigns against other tribes I've discovered that using native scouts can facilitate matters greatly. I would like to do that again here. Now I understand that it's been done before, to a degree. You were once made chief of scouts, with a number of White Mountain Apaches under your command—isn't that so?"

Barlow was about to speak when Short Britches walked in. The scout's intrusion startled him. It wasn't like the half-breed to interrupt when he knew that Barlow was engaged in business. But he stood there, just inside the door, looking unapologetic. For a moment no one said anything—Barlow and Crook and Summerhayes all stared at Short Britches, and he looked right back at them.

"Who is this man?" asked Crook, finally.

"He works for me," said Barlow.

"That coffee smells good," said Short Britches. "Mind if I have some?"

"Help yourself," said Barlow, curious to know what the scout was up to. He turned to Crook. "It's okay. You can talk freely in front of him. He's to be trusted."

"He's a good man," agreed Summerhayes.

Crook peered speculatively at Short Britches as the scout stood while Oulay poured coffee into the cup he was holding. "Part Apache?"

"I don't know," confessed Barlow. "I never asked. What about it, old man?"

"Me? I have a little bit of everything in me, I think."

His coffee cup filled, Short Britches wandered over to a chair in the corner of the room and sat down, appearing to be much more interested in the java than in what the three men at the table were talking about.

"There were six White Mountain scouts," said Barlow. "Most of them were killed. The rest went home. Using Apaches for scouting is probably a good idea, but I don't know where you'll find enough willing to do the job. Just because the Mescaleros and the Mimbrenos and the Bedonkohes aren't on the warpath doesn't mean they're feeling too friendly towards white people these days. They know what happened to the Aravaipa too."

"That's why I'm hoping you'll help me, Mr. Barlow," said Crook. "From everything I've been told, the Apaches trust you more than they do any other

white man. Maybe you can talk some of them into
helping."

"And if I did, then what?"

"Then I would hope you'd consent to serve as my
chief of scouts in this campaign."

Barlow's lips thinned. He glanced angrily at Summerhayes, who looked sheepishly away. Barlow didn't
blame Crook for asking the question, but he thought
that at least Charles, or maybe General Howard,
would have talked Crook out of making the offer.
Both of them ought to have known how he would
react.

"Absolutely not," he said.

Crook paused, choosing his words carefully. "I
haven't been in the Arizona Territory for very long,
but I'm guessing there are plenty of people around
here who would just as soon have a war with the
Apaches, and be done with it. But you're not one of
them." He glanced around the adobe's interior. "You
have a nice place here. You've made a good start for
yourself. Surely you place a high value on peace."

"He's done plenty to keep the peace," said Short
Britches, over the rim of his coffee cup. "More than
his share, if you ask me."

"Of course," said Crook. "Brokering a meeting between General Howard and Cochise—that alone was
a remarkable achievement, and one that will save un-
told lives."

"Then how come you people won't leave him
alone?" asked the old scout.

"That's enough," said Barlow quietly.

"I don't think so. They're going to try to talk you
into it. And you might let them. I've seen it happen
before. I'm just saying what needs to be said."

"I already said no."

"But they're still sitting here, aren't they? They're not done with you yet."

Barlow turned to look at the old scout. "What's gotten into you?"

"The fact is, General," said Short Britches, addressing Crook, who had been watching the exchange with intense interest, "you're asking the wrong person anyway. I could find plenty of scouts for you. And I'll lead them for you too. We can take care of the Coyoteros in no time at all."

Crook's gray eyes brightened. He turned to Summerhayes. "You know this man. Is what he says the case?"

The lieutenant nodded. "I'll vouch for him. Besides, Joshua here has trusted him with the one thing he cares most about. That about says everything you need to know."

Crook glanced at Barlow, then at Oulay, and finally back at Short Britches. There were some things that weren't being said, but he didn't need them to be spelled out. Besides, his instincts told him that Joshua Barlow wasn't a man who was going to change his mind. Not this time. He'd said no. Turned the offer down flat.

"Fine," he said. He wasn't one to agonize over a decision that had to be made. "There is no time to lose. I want at least twenty-five scouts at Camp Bowie in a fortnight. I intend to ride with five full companies into the land of the Mimbrenos and the Mescaleros. Those bands have not yet gone on the warpath, but I've heard that many of their young men are aching to do so. They must be persuaded to remain at peace."

"How do you aim to do that?" asked Short Britches.

"By telling them the truth. I will not lie to an Indian. Too many of my kind have already done that. I will tell them that it doesn't matter who started the present troubles. They cannot be allowed to continue. I'll give them my word that they'll be protected from bad white men. But in exchange, they must protect whites from bad Indians. If bad Indians continue to raid I won't be able to protect them. I also intend to point out to them that more whites are coming. This they probably already know. But the point must be driven home that one day soon they will no longer find enough wild game to sustain themselves. They must learn to farm. As soon as the Coyoteros have been defeated, I intend to begin an irrigation project that will help them grow their crops. And then I will help them find markets for those crops. When the whites see that they intend to remain on their reservations, and have set aside their weapons for good, they will cease to fear the Apaches. And what they no longer fear they will no longer hate."

Barlow shook his head. It all sounded fine, and he didn't doubt that Crook was sincere. Perhaps the general had succeeded with the same plan with other tribes. But it wouldn't work with the Apaches. They would never become farmers.

"You don't believe this will ever come to pass," said Crook, watching Barlow, and smiling faintly.

"It's a nice dream," said Barlow.

Crook stood up. "It will work. It has to, because, if it doesn't, the Apaches will be wiped out. And I would not like to see that happen." He nodded to Oulay. "Thank you for the coffee, ma'am. Come on, Lieutenant, we'll start back at once. There's no time to waste." He glanced once more at Short Britches. "Camp Bowie. Two weeks." With that, he walked out.

Summerhayes gulped down the rest of his coffee, rose, and stuck a hand out across the table at Barlow, who shook it.

"I'll be seeing you, Joshua."

"Take care, Charles."

Summerhayes followed Crook out, and Short Britches started for the door too.

"Hold it," said Barlow.

The old scout turned, his features an inscrutable mask.

"What the hell are you doing?"

Short Britches shrugged. "I'm just getting tired of being the one who's left behind to mind the store, while you go off and have all the fun. It's my turn for a change."

"No," said Barlow, shaking his head. "No, that's not it at all. You've never been interested at all in the fight against the Apaches, except when it hits us right here at home. You're doing this for me—or for Oulay and the vaqueros. Or maybe for all of us, because you're wondering if the Coyoteros would hit us again once they found out I was going against them."

Short Britches just looked at him, with a blank expression on his face. "You didn't trust me at all when we first met. Now you have a high opinion of me. You were wrong then—and you're wrong now. The fact is, I'm more qualified than you are for this job, and we both know it. I'm a better tracker than you ever will be. And I'm a born killer. You're not. So what are we arguing about? It didn't take General Crook long to figure out that he would be better off with me as his chief of scouts. You just don't want to admit this is so."

"Well, I don't believe you, not for a minute. And I don't think you should go. But you're going to do what you want. You always have."

"That's right."

"Just don't get yourself killed."

"I never have."

Chapter 20

Kiannatah reasoned that to brazenly enter the encampment of the Coyoteros and to present himself to Valerio as a volunteer who could help him and his people in their war against the White Eyes would probably not work. For one thing, it would quickly become apparent to Valerio, even if Kiannatah made no mention of it, that he was Netdahe. An outcast. And once this was determined, the Coyoteros might take offense, as though his very presence was an indication that he did not think they would fare as well against the Pinda Lickoyi if they sent him away. Of course, Kiannatah believed this was true, but to convince the Coyoteros of this truth, which would wound their pride, was something else. No, he had to earn his way into the confidence of Valerio. And the only way he could see to do that was to await an opportunity to show the Coyoteros what an asset he could be in battle.

To do this he had to be in the right place at the right time, and that meant he had to shadow the Coyotero war parties as they left the encampment—which itself had been easy enough to locate, high up in the Mogollon Mountains. Shadowing a group of bronchos going off to war was no easy thing, but Kiannatah wasn't worried. He was confident he could do it. And he did—for weeks.

The Coyoteros launched numerous raids from their mountain stronghold. For the most part, they attacked easy targets—isolated ranches, a party of gold hunters who, though alerted to the fact that there was an Apache war going on, had allowed their hunger for the yellow ore to blind them to the risks involved in continuing their search for the mother lode. One of the war parties that Kiannatah followed attacked a Butterfield Stage route way station. They wanted the horses held in the station's corrals. But the stage company had taken precautions, fortifying the stations along the route, and making sure that no coach rolled without the protection of an army detail or a squad of the hired guns it had hired. The way station attacked by the Coyoteros was manned by a dozen well-armed men, and they not only saved themselves but prevented the bronchos from making off with a single horse.

Win or lose, the Coyoteros always returned to the Mogollons, moving quickly but always careful to watch out for army pursuit. Kiannatah watched out for the yellow-legs too. But he never saw any. That puzzled him. Where was the United States Army? Surely it had been charged with the task of protecting civilians from the Coyotero threat.

Eventually, Kiannatah solved the mystery. Following the Coyoteros back to the mountains in the aftermath of the disastrous raid on the stage station, he discovered that he was not the only lone Apache shadowing the war party.

In the foothills of the Mogollons, he crossed the track of a lone Apache, who seemed to have come from the north, cut the fresh trail of the Coyoteros, and then turned to follow them. This placed him be-

hind the war party and in front of Kiannatah, who
quickened his pace, hoping to catch a glimpse of the
stranger. It occurred to him that this might be a broncho from another band, who, like himself, had come
to offer his services to Valerio. But the stranger made
no attempt to catch up with the Coyoteros. He merely
followed them for several miles, before breaking off
and heading north again. Curious, Kiannatah followed him.

Late that day, he caught his first glimpse of the
broncho. The man seemed to be in a great hurry, and
paid only cursory attention to the trail behind him.
Kiannatah got close enough, before darkness fell, to
determine that the broncho was Mescalero. When
night came, Kiannatah had another decision to make.
If he pressed on in pursuit, he might stumble into a
trap. The risks of continuing to follow the lone Mescalero were greatly enhanced now. But he pressed on,
and was soon rewarded. The Mescalero led him down
into a creek bottom, where Kiannatah could see the
light of a campfire under the willows and alders. In
the camp were four other Mescalero bronchos. Kiannatah was still thinking that these men had come to
join the Coyoteros in their war—until he saw the fifth
man in the camp.

The bent stovepipe hat aside, he recognized this
man immediately. It was the same man who, accompanied by several White Mountain Apaches and a
yellow-leg sergeant, had pursued Kiannatah from the
ranch of John Ward to the Mexican border in order
to rescue the Chiricahua maiden named Oulay. Kiannatah had killed two of the White Mountains, but he
had not known about this man until the man's bullet
had struck him. And that had been the difference—
he'd barely escaped with his life, while this man and

the bluecoated sergeant and the last remaining White
Mountain had taken Oulay from him.

Bitter hatred surged through Kiannatah at the sight
of this man, and it was all he could do to refrain from
aiming his besh-e-ger—his rifle—at the scrawny figure,
well illuminated by the firelight, and squeezing the
trigger. But he came to his senses in time. He could
kill the man in the stovepipe hat, but at the sound of
his rifle the five Mescaleros would scatter, disap-
pearing into the darkness. And then he would have to
deal with them. Under these conditions, the odds were
stacked too high for even him to overcome. So he
tamped down his anger and resentment, and found
solace in the thought that he would soon have another
opportunity to kill his enemy.

The question remained—what were the man in the
stovepipe hat and his Mescalero companions doing in
the Mogollon foothills? Kiannatah had always assumed that the man in the stovepipe hat had some
association with the army officer who had taken
Oulay, with the permission of Cochise, as his woman.
But he did not know this for sure. The best thing to
do, he decided, was to follow this group tomorrow;
perhaps their actions would enlighten him as to their
purpose.

Before dawn the next day, the camp was astir. The
man in the stovepipe hat dispatched the Mescalero
bronchos. Two headed south, two headed north. The
man in the stovepipe hat, accompanied by the fifth
broncho, also went south. Kiannatah followed this pair,
which stopped at the place where the last Coyotero
war party had entered the mountains. The other two
Mescaleros who had come this way continued south-
ward, but the man in the stovepipe hat and the Mescalero with him found a vantage point on high ground

and settled down to wait. Not far away, Kiannatah did the same.

The man in the stovepipe hat and his broncho companion remained on the lookout the rest of the day—and all of the next. Kiannatah was ill prepared for a long vigil; he had very little water and no food. But he dared not leave, even for a short time, to find sustenance. Instead, he remained in hiding, watching the others. Sometimes he held a pebble in his mouth. This was an old desert dweller trick—the pebble caused him to produce additional saliva, which kept his mouth and throat wet, which in turn allowed him to go longer without a drink. As for the hunger gnawing at his stomach, he simply chose to ignore the discomfort.

As he lay, scarcely daring to move, in the hot sun for hours and days on end, Kiannatah went over and over all the possible scenarios that might explain the actions of the man in the stovepipe hat and his Mescalero friends. He was pretty sure that they had not come to the Mogollons to join the Coyoteros. But if they were enemies of the Coyoteros, why did they not venture deeper into the mountains in an effort to discover Valerio's hideout? Kiannatah couldn't figure that part out. But he was confident that if he waited long enough, and watched closely enough, he would learn the truth.

In the morning of the third day, a Coyotero war party came down the canyon beneath the vantage point held by the man in the stovepipe hat and his Mescalero companion. There were sixteen bronchos in the party. Their faces and their horses were painted for war. There could be no doubt as to their intentions. Kiannatah was more interested in what the man in the stovepipe hat would do. He did nothing, save watch the Coyoteros file down the canyon, and out into the foothills. Once they were gone, the Mescalero went down to where his horse was hidden and rode south. The man in the stovepipe hat remained above the canyon for about an hour. Then he too went down to his horse, and rode back in the direction of the tree-lined creek, where he and the other Mescaleros had last congregated.

Puzzled, Kiannatah followed the man in the stovepipe hat. He realized that this was a perfect opportunity to kill the man. But he wanted to know what the old scout was up to.

The man in the stovepipe hat reached his old campsite and settled in to wait. At some distance, Kiannatah did likewise. A few hours later, one of the other Mescaleros showed up. Then another rode in. By the end of the day, two more had arrived. The only Mescalero missing was the one who had ridden south after the appearance of the Coyotero war party.

Kiannatah was growing weary of the game. That night he seriously considered slipping into the camp and abducting one of the Mescaleros. Perhaps, under the knife, the man would explain what he and his companions were doing. Kiannatah doubted that the old scout would talk under torture, but maybe one of the others would. He decided that he would watch for one more day before taking drastic action.

But with the next day came answers, for in midmorning the old scout and the Mescaleros had a visitor—a young yellow-leg officer, escorted by the missing Mescalero, the one who had ridden south twenty-four hours earlier. Kiannatah decided that if the soldier left alone, he would follow and, when the time was right, capture the man and torture him until he talked. His contempt for the Pinda Lickoyi was such that Kiannatah confidently believed that none of them could withstand pain the way an Apache could. He watched as the officer and the old scout spoke for a long time. But when the soldier finally left the grove of willows and alders, he was accompanied by all of the others. Kiannatah resigned himself to carrying on with the task of shadowing these men. At least now he knew with certainty that the old scout and the Mescaleros were not here to join the Coyoteros. They were spies, working for the United States Army. And they were up to something. Kiannatah needed to know what that something was.

The officer and his escort traveled for several hours in a southerly direction, leaving the foothills of the Mogollon Mountains and venturing out onto the desert plain. They then rendezvoused with a strong contingent of soldiers. In no time at all the entire contingent was on the move, returning to the mountains in a northwesterly direction. By sundown they were approaching the canyon where Kiannatah had last seen the Coyoteros. Before full darkness had fallen upon the land, the officer and the old scout had dispersed the troopers on the slopes on either side of the canyon. Seeing this, Kiannatah finally had the answers he needed. The yellow-legs were setting a trap for the Coyoteros.

Now he understood the actions of the old scout and the Mescaleros. After one of the Mescaleros had reported the return of the Coyoteros following the raid on the stage station, the man in the stovepipe hat had staked out the canyon they'd used to slip deeper into the mountains. The old scout had surmised that the Coyoteros would use the same route for inress and egress as long as it remained undiscovered. And he'd been right. The next raiding party had emerged from the same canyon. It was entirely likely that they would return, once more, by the same route. And this time they would be struck down by the concealed cavalrymen.

Thinking it over, Kiannatah grudgingly acknowledged the wisdom of the cavalry's strategy. To plunge into the Mogollons in hopes of finding the Coyotero hideout would likely end in one of two ways—either the soldiers would exhaust themselves in a futile search or they would fall prey to Coyotero ambush. Instead, the yellow-legs intended to strike at the raiding parties. Rather than attacking the head of the scorpion, they were targeting the stinger. By killing the bronchos who conducted the raids, they would go far in rendering the Coyoteros harmless. Without warriors, Valerio would have no choice but to stop the raids or surrender.

This result might not be realized after the ambush of a single war party. But following the planned ambush, the soldiers would fade back into the desert. The old scout and his Mescaleros would remain. Eventually they would detect another Coyotero raiding party emerging by some new route from the mountains. Then, the same thing would happen again—the cavalrymen would be alerted, and another ambush would be set.

All of this was perfectly clear to Kiannatah. All that remained for him was to decide how to react. He concluded that the situation might provide him with the opportunity he had been looking for. If he could somehow save the Coyotero war party from being wiped out, he would prove his worth to Valerio. How, then, could the Coyotero leader deny that the skills of an Avowed Killer were a real asset to his cause? Kiannatah wasn't naive—he didn't expect to be hailed as a hero by the Coyoteros. Some of the bronchos would resent his presence. That was inevitable. But he didn't care; he wasn't seeking friendship.

His mind made up, Kiannatah decided that his best course of action was to remain in the vicinity of the canyon. If he ventured out into the desert plain, in hopes of finding the Coyoteros returning from their raid, he might miss them. Besides, his scheme would be far more effective if by deed rather than merely by word he rescued the war party from destruction. True, some of the Coyoteros might die, but that was no concern of his; he would wait until they had fallen into the cavalry trap, and then he would save them.

He didn't have long to wait. Late in the afternoon of the following day, the Coyoteros returned. This time their raid had, apparently, met with success, for they brought with them a dozen fine horses, and some of them wore the clothing of the Pinda Lickoyi; most bizarre of all was the young broncho who had donned a calico dress over his himper and loincloth. Reaching the mountains, they began to let their guard down, and they were talking and laughing among themselves as they entered the canyon, blissfully ignorant of the fact that death awaited them there.

Suddenly, a shot rang out. Then another. And then an entire fusillade, as the cavalrymen rose up from their places of concealment on both sides of the canyon and began blazing away with their carbines. Several of the Coyotero were killed instantly. Others made a break for it, galloping deeper into the canyon—only to find that escape route blocked by the Mescalero scouts led by the man in the stovepipe hat. A few more of the Coyotero raiders toppled from their horses, cut down by the withering fire. Some of the survivors thought to flee back whence they'd come, but the yellow-leg officer had placed a detail of sharpshooters at the entrance to the canyon, and they blocked that route too. The Coyoteros were well and truly hemmed in on all sides. Seeing that their prey was doomed, several of the soldiers began shouting gleeful aspersions at the bronchos in the canyon bot-

tom. Within the span of a minute, half of the raiding
party was dead or dying; the rest had leaped from
their horses and sought cover behind rocks. Dust and
powder smoke half obscured the scene—this, in fact,
was the only reason the entire Apache party wasn't
instantly wiped out.

Kiannatah chose his moment well. He waited until
the soldiers began to grow careless in their overconfi-
dence. The Coyoteros weren't able to put up more
than a tepid defense; only occasionally did one of the
bronchos get off a shot. So the cavalrymen left their
cover and began to work their way, slowly, down the
slopes, firing as they moved. Only then did Kiannatah act.

During the previous night he had made his way to
the rim of the west canyon wall. This placed him
above the cavalrymen who had been posted on that
side, with the nearest being less than thirty yards
away. He had the advantage of knowing where all of
the soldiers had been hidden. They, on the other hand,
had no inkling of his presence, until he began to shoot
them from his vantage point.

With each shot, one soldier fell. Kiannatah got off
several rounds before some of the troopers realized
what was happening. Only then did Kiannatah move,
laterally across the rim, keeping behind the rocks, and
never exposing himself to enemy fire. From a new
position he fired several more times, killing two more
of the soldiers, and when the bullets began to sing off
the rocks that protected him, he moved again. The
troopers continued to fire at his previous position even
as he took up a new one and fired once, twice, three
times. The soldiers on the other side of the canyon
were now shooting in his direction too, but the distance was too great for any accuracy on their part,
and Kiannatah didn't worry about them. He moved

and fired so quickly and efficiently that the soldiers on the slope below—those left alive, anyway—began to panic, thinking they had been outflanked by a large enemy force. Instead of forging back up the slope to flush Kiannatah from the rimrock, they broke and scattered like quail. Several of them fell prey to the remaining Coyoteros.

The tide of battle turned, Kiannatah found a place from which he could clearly see up-canyon, in the direction of the place where the Mescalero scouts had appeared a few minutes earlier. He was hoping for a shot at the man in the stovepipe hat. But the man, and his Mescalero companions, had vanished. Kiannatah had to be satisfied with knowing that he'd turned the tables on his nemesis by using the same tactics the old scout had used against him years earlier, on the day he and the White Mountain Apaches had taken Oulay. Killing the old scout would have to wait for another day.

The canyon battle lasted less than ten minutes. Seeing that his ambush had turned into a death trap for his own soldiers, the yellow-leg officer made an orderly retreat, and before long the shooting had stopped altogether. For a while there was no sound in the canyon save the noises made by a dying horse in the canyon bottom. Kiannatah waited until all the smoke and dust had cleared before showing himself. Then he stood up in plain view of the surviving Coyoteros, and raised the rifle over his head.

"Do not shoot!" he shouted down at them. "I am Kiannatah, a Netdahe, and it is I who have saved you."

They didn't shoot. He ventured down the slope, and during the descent he passed by one of the soldiers he'd shot. The man wasn't quite dead; he crawled slowly, weakly, through the rocks, leaving a trail of bright red blood. Kiannatah drew his revolver and put a bullet into the base of the soldier's skull, hardly slowing his stride.

Once he reached the canyon bottom, where dead horses and Coyotero bronchos littered the pale sand, he saw the surviving warriors emerge from their hiding places. They looked at him with a mixture of wariness and curiosity.

"I wish to see Valerio," he said. "Take me to him."

Chapter 21

Deep in the Mogollon Mountains, the Coyotero stronghold was a collection of jacales on a high plateau from which lookouts could easily spot anyone approaching from three sides; the fourth was protected by a rugged peak. The inhabitants of the che-wa-ki were out in force as the Coyotero war party, accompanied by Kiannatah, rode in, and since the lookouts had also been able to see that the bronchos were bringing in their dead, there was great anxiety etched on the faces of the villagers. The wives and sisters and daughters of the slain warriors immediately launched into loud wailing when they saw the bodies; one woman proceeded to cut deep gashes into her arms and legs with a knife. Kiannatah observed this with indifference. He noted that, in spite of the attention paid to the corpses of the bronchos, his presence did not go unheeded. A number of the warriors watched him intently, and some with suspicion written across their features.

The leader of the war party dismounted and approached a stern, gray-haired man, launching into a narrative of the raid and the ambush in the canyon. As he spoke, most of the Coyotero men gathered round. He announced that the Netdahe who now rode with them had saved them from destruction. Single-handedly, the Netdahe had routed the yellow-leg soldiers, and then asked to meet with Valerio.

The gray-headed warrior brushed past the war party leader and approached Kiannatah, who had by this time dismounted, and was standing at his horse's head. Though he had never met the famous jefe of the Coyoteros, Kiannatah felt it was safe to assume that this was Valerio. The chief stood toe-to-toe with him for a moment, looking gravely into his eyes, as though he could see into Kiannatah's heart and know his true motives. Or perhaps, mused Kiannatah, he was just trying to intimidate. Kiannatah returned the gaze; he, who had stood up to Geronimo, was not one to be intimidated by the likes of Valerio.

"We are grateful for your help," said Valerio, begrudgingly. "In return, anything you ask, I will do, within reason."

"I ask for nothing—except to join you in your fight against the White Eyes."

Valerio looked at him for a moment more, then turned, making a curt gesture. "Come with me," he said, and led the way to a nearby jacal. At the entrance he stood to one side and motioned for Kiannatah to enter. This the Netdahe did, without hesitation, though, as always, he was wary. But only Valerio joined him inside the jacal. The Coyotero jefe sat cross-legged near the ashes of the fire in the center of the jacal. To show respect, Kiannatah stood until another gesture by Valerio invited him to sit, as well. Here, in private, hidden from the eyes of his people, the jefe dropped his guard, and Kiannatah watched the gray-haired man's shoulders slump, and his eyes fill with pain and regret.

"You have come too late," he said. "Our fight with the White Eyes is nearly over."

Kiannatah sat silent, waiting to hear more.

"I warned the Pinda Lickoyi that if they did not punish the scalphunters who had killed some of my people, they would pay a terrible price. But instead of punishing the scalphunters, they let them go free. And once free, these men murdered many Aravaipa, among them women and children. The Coyoteros went to war with the Pinda Lickoyi because of this. We thought that was the right thing to do. The Aravaipa are our brothers. Just as the Mimbrenos, the Mescaleros, the Bedonkohes, the Chiricahuas are all our brothers. But did our brothers join us in this war against the White Eyes? We thought surely they would. Yet even now the Coyotero stand alone. Just a few days ago word came from Mexico that Cochise had promised the White Eyes that he would not go to war against them." Valerio shook his head. "Even Cochise, after everything that has happened to his own people, has abandoned his brothers."

Valerio's lament left Kiannatah unmoved. "You do the right thing in fighting the White Eyes. So it does not matter if others fight with you."

Valerio fired an angry glance at his guest. "You are Netdahe. It does not matter to *you*. You are accustomed to fighting alone. And you do not have to concern yourself with the welfare of women and children. Without the other bands, the best we can do is hide out in these mountains, and send out raiding parties. Sometimes the men come back. Sometimes they do not. And even if they succeed, what good does that really do? They kill a few Pinda Lickoyi. They steal some horses. They are like mosquitoes stinging a great bear. Their efforts are hardly noticed at all."

"A few men can make a difference."

Valerio was silent for a moment. "Yes, sometimes that is true. You made a difference today, and you are but one man. But you fight the way you do because you have nothing to lose."

"Neither do you. None of us do. Sooner or later, all Apaches will know that what I say is true. Even Cochise will realize that he has been wrong to seek peace with the White Eyes. But then it may be too late."

"Too late?" echoed Valerio bitterly. "Too late for what? To defeat our enemies? This we can never do. They are too many, and we are too few."

"If you believe that, why have you gone to war?"

"To force the Pinda Lickoyi to treat us with more respect."

Kiannatah scoffed. "Are we the slaves of the Pinda Lickoyi, that we *hope* to be treated better?"

Valerio was resentful. "It is easy for you to speak so boldly. Again, you have only yourself to look out for. All of the people you saw out there depend on me to do what is best for them. I went to war to protect them from the scalphunters—to force the yellow-leg soldiers to do the right thing themselves, and kill the scalphunters, or drive them away forever. But if no others will join us in our fight, I must consider surrender. Soon, all of our young men will die. And when that happens, the Coyoteros will die."

"You forget, I have come to join you. Let me lead your young men, and soon we will sting the White Eyes like the scorpion, not the mosquito. And then, who knows?" Kiannatah shrugged. "Maybe the other bands will see that the Coyoteros are winning their war, and they will change their minds, and come to join you."

Valerio's eyes narrowed as he gazed for a moment at the Avowed Killer. He did not doubt that Kiannatah was genuinely interested in instigating a full-scale Apache war against the white interlopers. But he was

suspicious of this man's true motives. The survival of
the Chi-hinne, The People, had never been a priority
among the Netdahe. They wanted only to kill their
enemies, and a full-scale war would give Kiannatah
and his ilk plenty of opportunities for killing. But, ultimately, the Netdahe expected to die, and since they
did not expect to live, they didn't care if anyone else
did, either.

Even though he was suspicious of Kiannatah, Valerio thought that the Netdahe warrior might be useful
to him, in the short term. If the Coyoteros *did* win a
few significant victories, he might yet earn some consideration from the Pinda Lickoyi when the time came
to seek a peaceful resolution to the current conflict.
Of course, he could never tell Kiannatah that he ever
intended to seek such a resolution; the Netdahe
wouldn't stand for that.

But the Netdahe might not live to see that day. He
might die in battle. And if he didn't, Valerio was fully
capable of killing him, once he was no longer useful.

"You may lead the next raid," said the Coyotero
jefe. "But there are conditions. You will not take on
the yellow-leg soldiers unless you have no other
choice. And you will not attack the ranchero of the
man named Barlow, which lies to the east of the
mountains."

"Why not?"

"He is not our enemy. He tried to stop the
scalphunters. Before, he allowed us to kill some of his
cattle for meat, and he said nothing of it."

"I see," said Kiannatah.

"Some of the men here do not agree with me on
this matter," conceded Valerio. "A few months ago,
they attacked the ranchero, and were driven away.
The vaqueros who work for Barlow are good fighters.

But as long as they do not ride against us, I will not make war against them."

Kiannatah shrugged again, feigning indifference. He knew now that this man of whom Valerio spoke, the one called Barlow, had to be the officer who had taken Oulay away from the Chiricahuas—and away from him. The ranchero had to be the very one he had attacked years earlier. He had killed three of these vaqueros Valerio feared so greatly, and made off with Oulay. Only because of the efforts of the man in the stovepipe hat and his White Mountain scouts had he lost her.

He began to think about trying again.

For now, though, he would pretend to go along with Valerio.

"It will be as you say," he replied. "I will not lead your men against the ranchero, or against the yellow-legs. But I must at least take away their eyes. The soldiers are not alone. They are helped by Mescalero scouts. If I kill them, the soldiers will be blind, and we will be have more success. Besides, Apaches who turn against their own kind do not deserve to live."

As he spoke, he thought of Nachita, the Chiricahua he had murdered, out of nothing more than spite. That, more than his desire for Oulay, was what had turned Cochise against him. He told himself that he'd done the deed because of his anger—he'd just learned that Oulay had been taken away by a white man, with her father's blessing.

Valerio nodded wearily. When he spoke, it was without enthusiasm. "Do what you wish where the Mescalero are concerned."

He rose, and stepped out of the jacal. Kiannatah followed. Many of the Coyotero were still gathered outside, waiting to find out what would come of the meeting between their jefe and the lone Netdahe. Valerio informed them that Kiannatah had come to join in their fight against the White Eyes, and that he would be given the honor of leading the next raid.

Kiannatah only half listened to Valerio's speech, and paid no attention to the crowd. Their reaction to this news didn't matter to him. What mattered was that he had arrived in the nick of time. Valerio had lost his taste for war. He'd been on the verge of giving up the fight. But now he, Kiannatah, would carry on. And if he succeeded, the Coyoteros would win great victories—so great, in fact, that perhaps the other bands of the Chi-hinne would reconsider, and join in the effort. But no matter how it ended, Kiannatah would at least have another chance to kill the man in the stovepipe hat. And perhaps even another chance to take Oulay for his own.

Chapter 22

"It was my fault," said Charles Summerhayes. "I take full responsibility."

General Crook was pacing the length of the porch that fronted the Fort Union headquarters building. His movements, his expression—even his grim silence in the aftermath of the lieutenant's words—projected his aggravation. All Summerhayes could do was stand there and watch as the general continued pacing for a full minute—a full minute of exquisite torture for the lieutenant. It was bad enough that he'd disappointed Crook, a man he so greatly admired. Worse than that, he'd lost a third of his command. There were dead men on his conscience.

Cronin stood nearby. Short Britches was also present. He and his Mescalero scouts had returned to the fort with Summerhayes and the shot-up contingent of cavalrymen.

"The plan was unworkable, in my opinion," said Cronin, finally. "General, give me two full companies and I'll go straight into the Mogollons and flush those Coyoteros out. Or kill them all."

Crook stopped pacing. He glowered at Cronin, then at Summerhayes.

"Well, Lieutenant, perhaps Captain Cronin has the

right idea." That kind of thinking was exactly why he had deserved the promotion from major. "We tried your plan, Summerhayes. It didn't work."

Summerhayes didn't bother explaining to Crook that it hadn't really been his plan at all. Short Britches was the one who'd come up with the scheme to hit the Coyotero raiding parties as they came out of, or returned into, the mountains. If they struck at several such raiding parties, and were able to inflict significant casualties upon the bronchos, Valerio would probably give up the fight. This had been the old scout's assessment, and Summerhayes had agreed wholeheartedly. But he wasn't about to shift the blame to someone else. He'd been the one who had sold General Crook on the plan, and he was willing to pay the piper for its failure.

"No, sir," he said, "it didn't work. This time. But I still believe it's the right way to go about this."

"Do you now," said Crook dryly.

"The captain's plan won't work," remarked Short Britches.

Crook fixed his glower on the old scout—who seemed completely oblivious to it. Short Britches sat on the porch steps, carving a chew off a twist of tobacco that he'd gotten from the Fort Union store.

"And why not?" asked Crook.

"Because you'll lose a lot more men that way. Maybe two companies worth. They'll ride straight into an ambush. And they won't get anywhere near the Coyotero camp."

"We might," said Cronin coldly, "if you and your scouts do your jobs."

Short Britches shook his head. "The Mescaleros wouldn't go."

"The hell they won't," said Cronin. "They're in the

employ of the United States Army, and they'll go where we send them, and do what we tell them to do."

"No, they won't, because it would be suicide. To attack the Coyoteros when they are out of the mountains is the way to do this. We would have succeeded two days ago, except for one rifle. And I do not think it was a Coyotero rifle. I think it was Netdahe."

"Netdahe!" exclaimed Crook. "I thought they were all supposed to be down in Mexico."

"It's hard to say where a Netdahe will be," replied Short Britches. "But I think one of them was at that canyon the other day. I think this way because we did not know he was there until he started shooting. That is just like a Netdahe. They move like the wind—and cannot be seen."

"If he's right," said Cronin, "and the Avowed Killers have joined forces with Valerio, then we've got a much bigger problem, sir."

"Could be just one," said Short Britches. "They do not owe allegiance to any band, or even to one another. They are outlaws. They come and go as they please."

Crook proceeded to pace again. A moment later he stopped and turned to face the others. His mind was made up. "I'm inclined to agree with the scout, Captain. I think it would be foolhardy, if not disastrous, to venture deeper into the mountains. So we will give the lieutenant's scheme another try. Only this time, Captain, you will take your two full companies. The raids must be stopped. I do not have the manpower necessary to adequately protect every possible target of the renegades."

"Yes, sir," said Cronin, with smug satisfaction that he could not entirely conceal. It had rankled him that Crook had sent Summerhayes out against the Coyoteros, while he languished here at the fort. Even if he lacked faith in the plan, at least he would be in the field, where he belonged, leading men into battle against the enemy.

"And you'll be taking Lieutenant Summerhayes and the Mescalero scouts with you, Captain."

"But, sir—"

Crook held up a hand to silence Cronin. "I know how you feel about using native scouts, Captain. You've made those feelings very clear. But I know from experience that they can be very useful."

"They weren't very useful on the day that the lieutenant lost half of his command, sir."

Crook looked at Summerhayes. "Do you still have faith in your man over there? And the Mescalero scouts?"

Summerhayes glanced across at Short Britches— then nodded. "Yes, sir."

"Good. Because this time around I want you to stick with them."

Summerhayes opened his mouth to protest—and shut it without saying a word.

"What is it, Lieutenant?" asked Crook. "You don't look too happy about my decision."

"I would be honored to ride with Short Britches and the Mescaleros," replied Summerhayes. "But I doubt they want me along. I would just slow them down. I lack the skills they possess."

"Well, I hope you're a fast learner." The general turned on Cronin. "Captain, are you still here? You had better get started seeing to it that your men are fully equipped for the campaign, because you will be leaving in the morning."

"Yes, sir." Cronin snapped off a brisk salute and started off across the parade ground. Crook watched him go, and shook his head. Then he glanced at Summerhayes and, gesturing curtly for the lieutenant to follow, preceded to one end of the long porch. Only when he was certain that they were out of earshot of Short Britches did Crook face Summerhayes again.

"I'll be perfectly honest with you, Lieutenant. I think I might have made a mistake agreeing to let that man lead our scouts."

Summerhayes glanced over his shoulder at Short Britches, who wasn't paying them the least attention. "Why do you say that, General?"

"I get the sense he doesn't really care whether we win or lose."

"Well, sir, I don't know. All I can tell you is that I trust him."

"You trust him because your friend Barlow relies on him."

"Yes, sir, I admit that has a lot to do with it. He did get us some good scouts. Those Mescaleros are dependable men."

"I hope your instincts are correct, Lieutenant, for your sake—since you'll be riding with them."

"I'm not worried."

"Well, that makes one of us," said Crook dryly. He glanced across the sun-hammered parade ground in the direction taken by Captain Cronin. "Make your plan work. Because if it doesn't, we'll have no choice but to go into the Mogollons after Valerio. And if that happens, a lot of good men, on both sides, won't be coming back out."

"I'll do my best, sir."

Crook went inside the headquarters building, and Summerhayes returned to the porch steps, where he sat down alongside Short Britches and heaved a sigh.

"So if you're right, and it was the Netdahe, or even just one of them, how bad is it going to get?"

"Very bad," said Short Britches.

"And how do we stop him?"

"Only one way to stop a Netdahe. A bullet right here." The old scout pressed the tip of a crooked finger to his forehead.

"Will our plan still work if a Netdahe is riding with the Coyoteros?"

"I doubt it."

"So what do you suggest we do?"

"Come up with a new plan."

Summerhayes pondered that for a moment, then said, "You happen to have come up with one?"

Short Britches spat a stream of brown tobacco juice. "Nope. But I'm working on it."

They rode out of Fort Union at sunrise the next morning, with Cronin at the head of two full companies of men. Behind the column came a long wagon train of supplies. Ahead of it rode the Mescalero scouts, with Short Britches and Summerhayes. The latter had exchanged his uniform for civilian clothes—a buckskin shirt and stroud trousers, clothing he hoped would make it easier for him to blend into the desert environment. He was worried. Not about his own safety. He just didn't want to let Short Britches and the Mescaleros down. Or worse, make a mistake that would get one or more of them killed. The fundamental problem was that, though he had taken to the field against the Apaches on numerous occasions, and so could be counted as one of the army's most qualified officers where campaigning against the Indians was concerned, he had never felt quite up to the job, and still didn't. The Apaches were experts at guerrilla warfare. And the Netdahe were the most skilled of all. He knew with absolute certainty that he was no match for an Avowed Killer. And so he could only hope that his faith in Short Britches wasn't misplaced, and that the old scout would come through. For all their sakes.

Cronin's command encamped in the same location that Summerhayes had previously selected for his detachment, a willow-shaded depression about five miles south of the Mogollon mountains, where several springs bubbled up through limestone to provide plenty of water, and which nourished good graze for many horses. The tan peaks that loomed over them looked as grim and forbidding as massive, weathered tombstones in an old cemetery, and Summerhayes couldn't help but wonder if they marked his own final resting place. He couldn't shake the feeling that disaster loomed over them just like those mountains.

He envied Cronin, who appeared to be completely unafflicted by doubts or fears. The captain briskly went about directing his men in the details of making the camp. He took special care of determining where the horses would be picketed, and how the sentries would be arrayed on the perimeter of the camp. He was aching for a fight—you could just look at him and see that this was so.

That night, Summerhayes was welcomed at the fire of Short Britches and the Mescalero scouts. He was honored to be among men he perceived to be so brave and self-reliant and trustworthy. And yet here they were fighting against their own kind. Was that an honorable thing to do? Short Britches had explained to him that for centuries the bands of the Chi-hinne had waged war against one another. War was a way of life for the Apaches, and it had always been so. These Mescaleros had blood feuds against the Coyoteros, and the hate in their hearts was so strong that they were now willing to ally themselves with the hated Pinda Lickoyi, when anyone could see that it would be in their best interests—and the best interests of their band as a whole—to fight *with* the Coyoteros. Here, mused Summerhayes, as he ate a dinner of hot beans and hotter coffee, and listened to the Mescaleros talk softly and solemnly among themselves, not knowing what was being said and not really caring to know, was the reason the Apache would ultimately lose everything to the white man, despite their proficiency at desert combat—because they could not set aside their generations-old animosities long enough to cooperate against a common enemy. So, while proud to be allowed to ride with them, Summerhayes also experienced a certain degree of shame at playing a key role in the Apaches' self-destruction.

The next morning, long before sunrise, Short Britches and the Mescalero bronchos were ready to move out. Summerhayes, having slept very little the night before, was sluggish and bleary-eyed as Captain Cronin approached with brisk strides.

"You know what you have to do, Lieutenant," said Cronin.

Summerhayes sighed. He was happy to be spared the ordeal of spending any more time with the officious captain. "Yes, sir," he said.

"I'll expect to hear from you in a couple of days."

"We'll send a scout back when the Coyoteros make their move, sir. But there's no telling when that will be. Might be tomorrow, might be next week."

"I do not intend to sit around here and twiddle my thumbs for a week," said Cronin curtly.

Summerhayes just stared at him, not certain how to respond. The captain had express orders from General Crook himself to do just that, so Cronin was, in effect, announcing his intention to defy the general's orders, if need be. The lieutenant wondered what Cronin had in mind, but he didn't ask. Turning to his saddle horse, Summerhayes wearily climbed into the saddle, and without another look at the captain, followed Short Britches and the Mescaleros north toward the Mogollons.

Chapter 23

Kiannatah thought he had a pretty good idea of what the Pinda Lickoyi soldiers had in mind where dealing with the Coyotero threat was concerned. The yellow-legs did not dare venture too deeply into the mountains, knowing that to do so would expose them to ambush—and possible disaster. Instead, they were waiting in the foothills, hoping to catch the raiding parties as they either left the shelter of the Mogollons or returned to it. To this end, the man in the stovepipe hat and his Mescalero companions were being used to watch the routes the Coyoteros were most likely to take.

Knowing this, it would have been a relatively easy matter to devise alternate routes for egress from the mountains. This would improve the Coyoteros' chances of escaping the notice of the soldiers. But since Kiannatah's primary goal at this stage was to destroy the Mescaleros—and the old scout who led them—he did not want to escape their notice.

He had been in the Coyotero hideout only a few days when he approached Valerio with a plan. The jefe listened intently, and when Kiannatah was done, he nodded approval, and proceeded to summon the Coyotero bronchos. Standing in front of his jacal, he asked

the warriors for a dozen volunteers to ride with the
Netdahe in an effort to destroy the Mescaleros who
dared join the Pinda Lickoyi against their own kind. He
suspected, as Kiannatah did, that there would be some
who would not follow the Avowed Killer. Kiannatah
was, after all, an outcast, so it was a matter of honor
with them. But there were more than enough volunteers. Kiannatah allowed Valerio to chose twelve men
from those who offered their services. He noticed that
several of the twelve had been members of the raiding
party he had saved from the yellow-legs a few days
earlier. One of these was named Talpute, the broncho
who had led the previous raiding party—the one who
had readily admitted to Valerio that without the assistance of the Netdahe they would all have been killed.
Kiannatah decided that Talpute would be his lieutenant.

Later that same day, Kiannatah huddled with the
twelve bronchos and explained his plan to them in
detail. Its success depended largely on him alone; if
he failed to carry out his part of the plan, they would
all probably be killed. When he had finished going
over the details, he gave the men one last opportunity
to back out. No one did.

Talpute looked at the other Coyoteros, and asked
what was on everyone's mind. "If the goal is to trap
the Mescalero scouts, why are we using the same canyon that we used before? Surely the Mescaleros will
be watching other trails out of the mountains. They
will not expect us to use the same way, for fear that
we will ride into another trap."

"I have seen how the old scout works. He will be
watching the canyon."

Kiannatah sounded supremely confident. Talpute
shrugged, not quite certain that the Netdahe was correct, but unwilling to dispute him.

For his part, Kiannatah was well aware that if he

was wrong, it would prove difficult in the future to find even one Coyotero broncho willing to follow him. But he had no intention of failing.

He left the Coyotero encampment less than an hour later—alone. Knowing the Mogollons as well as the Coyoteros and Chiricahuas, he made a quick exit from the high country using a route other than the canyon where the yellow-legs had sprung their trap on the raiding party. Once in the sagebrush flats, he rode south and, a few hours later, cut the sign of a lone rider on an unshod horse. This he assumed was the trail left by the Mescalero scout who had been sent to bring the yellow-legs after the Coyotero raiding party had been seen leaving the mountains via the canyon. He made another assumption: The soldiers were still in the vicinity. After all, they had not yet achieved their objective of stopping the Coyotero raids.

It was easy enough to find the yellow-legs. They weren't trying to conceal their presence. Kiannatah did not venture too close. He didn't bother trying to discover just how many soldiers there were in the camp. That didn't matter. If he could destroy the Mescalero scouts, the yellow-legs would be blinded, and it wouldn't matter if they numbered ten or one hundred after that.

As the day waned, Kiannatah rode back toward the Mogollons. Before night fell, he had located a low rocky spine that twisted like a snake in a north-south configuration. Hiding his horse in one of the bends of the spine, he climbed to the rim and explored it from one end to the other, finding that there were only a few places where he was exposed to the view of anyone who might be on the desert floor. And from the top he could see miles to the east and to the west. It was a perfect vantage point for what he had in mind.

Kiannatah spent the night on the rim of the rocky spine. Sunrise found him alertly watching the flatland to the west, using field glasses he had taken from a Mexican officer, one of his victims from years before. In the direction in which he was looking was the days-old trail of the Mescalero scout who had brought the yellow-legs to the canyon ambush. Now all he could do was wait—and hope that the assumptions he had made about the old scout and his Mescaleros were correct, and that the twelve Coyoteros led by Talpute would do the job he had assigned to them. That job was simple enough—they were to be passing through the canyon this morning, as though leaving the mountains on another raid. Hopefully, the old scout or one of the Mescaleros would be watching the canyon. Seeing the Coyoteros depart, the old scout would send a rider to the soldiers camped a few hours away. And if that scout took the most direct route, Kiannatah would see him sometime today.

Kiannatah was accustomed to waiting for long periods of time. He did not allow himself to become impatient, and he was impervious to the discomfort of crouching in the rocks under the hot spine for hours on end. He remained continually vigilant.

His vigilance paid off. Early in the afternoon he spotted a ribbon of dust far to the north. That dust marked the progress of a horseman across the desert. Kiannatah's spirits rose as the rider came within view. With the aid of the field glasses, the Netdahe confirmed that it was a single Apache, and he concluded that the rider must be one of the Mescalero scouts. The Netdahe allowed himself a moment of triumphant self-satisfaction. He had been right, and his plan was working.

Descending to where his horse was waiting, Kiannatah put away the field glasses and vaulted onto the

animal's back. Kicking his heels into the pony's rib
cage, he urged it into a gallop. Circling the spine of
rocks, he headed across the flats on a course to intercept the lone Mescalero, who was already to the south
of him. Kiannatah didn't expect to get close enough
for killing before being found out. But the closer he
could get, the easier the task would be.

As it turned out, he closed the gap to within a few
hundred yards before the Mescalero happened to
glance behind him and see his pursuer. Unsure
whether the rider following him was friend or foe, the
Mescalero slowed his horse. As a precaution, he un-
slung the rifle that he carried on his back. At a hundred yards, Kiannatah did likewise. Seeing this, the
Mescalero realized that he was in for a fight. Lifting
the rifle to his shoulder, he took aim at the oncoming
Netdahe. Kiannatah abruptly steered his horse to the
right. Clinging to the horse's mane with his left hand,
his left leg hooked over the animal's back, he used
the horse's bulk to shield his body, and at the same
time slid the rifle under the galloping pony's neck.
Taken aback by this tactic, the Mescalero hesitated
for a few precious seconds, allowing the Netdahe to
trigger the first shot. One was all he needed. Kiannatah had two possible targets—the smaller was the Mescalero himself, and the larger was the Mescalero's
horse. He opted for the latter, knowing how difficult
it was to hit one's mark from the back—or, in his case,
the side—of a running horse. The bullet entered the
horse's body just back of the Mescalero's leg; the animal screamed in agony, half reared, and then started
to fall sideways. The Mescalero scrambled to jump
clear. He rolled and came up in a crouch, unhurt, and
still gripping his rifle. The horse lay on its side, thrashing helplessly. Grimly, the Mescalero moved forward
and with a quick slash of his knife put the horse out

of its misery. A bullet burned the air inches from his head, and he ducked down, using the carcass for cover.

Seeing his prey go down, Kiannatah got back astride his own horse, slowed it, and executed an agile running dismount, letting the pony continue on a new course that would take it well past the Mescalero's position, which he could not at the moment see, thanks to the contour of the land. Spinning, Kiannatah ran in a crouch back in the direction he'd come. The Mescalero heard the horse coming to his left. When it hove into view he was ready—but held his fire again, for the horse was riderless. He had just enough time to realize that he'd been fooled a second time. Then Kiannatah's bullet struck him high in the back. The impact hurled him forward. He sprawled facedown in the sand, stunned and gasping for air. Momentarily paralyzed and unable to lift his head, the Mescalero nonetheless could hear the approach of the Netdahe. Then he saw Kiannatah's n'deh b'ken, as the Avowed Killer stood over him. Though he knew he was doomed, the Mescalero tried to reach out for the rifle that lay in the sand beside him. Kiannatah waited until the Mescalero's fingertips could brush the rifle stock— and then he kicked the weapon out of his reach. The Mescalero lay still then, calmly waiting for the end. The Netdahe knelt beside him and, drawing his knife, lifted the Mescalero's head and cut his throat. He waited another moment, impassively watching his victim fight for life. When he was certain the Mescalero was dead, he turned and whistled. His horse responded, trotting toward him, pausing twenty paces away and snorting worriedly at the stench of death.

Well-satisfied with his handiwork, Kiannatah mounted and rode north, back toward the Mogollons, and a rendezvous with Talpute and the Coyoteros. Now that the Mescalero scout was dead, they would not have to worry about the yellow-legs, who would remain in their camp, blissfully ignorant of the fact that their scouts were about to be destroyed. *And in the process,* thought Kiannatah eagerly, *I will finally have my revenge on the man in the stovepipe hat.* That was one throat he very much looked forward to cutting.

Chapter 24

Charles Summerhayes was impressed. Short Britches had said that there was a possibility the Coyoteros would use the same canyon as before. And he'd been right. So far, at least, the old scout was one step ahead of the Netdahe who now rode with Valerio's bronchos and who, it was assumed, was now going to be leading the raiding parties. So Short Britches had sent two Mescaleros to watch the canyon. The other three had been dispatched elsewhere. Meanwhile, the old scout and the young lieutenant waited in the creek bottom shaded by willows and alders. It was, thought Summerhayes, a pleasant oasis in a land of sand and rock and cactus. But he wasn't afforded much time to enjoy it; the very next day one of the Mescaleros returned, to inform Short Britches that, indeed, a Coyotero war party had left the mountains by way of the canyon. As per the old scout's instructions, the Mescalero's companion had left immediately to return to Captain Cronin's camp.

Short Britches and Summerhayes saddled up and, accompanied by the Mescalero, rode out immediately. By midafternoon they had arrived at the canyon. Summerhayes calculated that Cronin and his detachment would show up before nightfall. Then, as before, they

would make preparations to spring a trap on the Coyoteros, who, it was hoped, would return this way.

But nightfall came, and there was no sign of Cronin.
Summerhayes started to worry, and though the old
scout's creased and weathered face was an inscrutable
mask, the lieutenant thought that he was more than a
little perplexed himself. What had happened to the
Mescalero rider sent to fetch the soldiers? Any one
of a dozen mishaps could have befallen him. As far
as Summerhayes could see, there was only one thing
to do.

"I'll go," he told Short Britches.

The old scout wanted to send the Mescalero instead;
his inclination was to keep the young lieutenant close
by so that he could look after him. He liked Summerhayes, and didn't want to see harm come to him.
And he believed that the Mescalero would be better
able to handle any problems that might arise en route
to the soldiers' camp. But he didn't argue. The lieutenant had something to prove. His self-confidence would
be seriously eroded if Short Britches objected.

Summerhayes went down to where they had left
their horses, and rode south of the foothills. The night
was cool and clear, and the stars would guide him to
Cronin's camp. With any luck he could be back at the
canyon with the soldiers by dawn. He had to remind
himself not to hurry, though—traveling at night in the
desert called for caution.

Because he traveled at an easy pace, he was still in
the foothills of the Mogollon—and therefore able to
hear the gunfire behind him. He was instantly certain
that the shooting came from the vicinity of the canyon.
And there was a lot of shooting. Checking his horse,
Summerhayes listened a moment, perplexed. What
was happening? The only scenario that made sense
was that the Coyoteros had returned, and Short

Britches and the Mescalero scout were trying to stop
them. But why would the old scout take such a
chance? The odds were stacked too heavily against
him. And Short Britches wasn't the type to take on
odds like that. Summerhayes would have expected him
to sit back and let the Coyoteros pass and hope that
the odds were better the next time.

Whatever the truth of it, the sustained and heavy
gunfire ringing down out of the mountains was a clear
indication that Short Britches was in trouble. Summerhayes spun his horse around and returned whence
he had come. To ride to Cronin's camp to fetch the
two companies of troopers would take hours—more
time than the old scout might have. The lieutenant
wasn't sure what good he could do by himself. But he
had to try.

As he drew near the canyon, Summerhayes began
to see muzzle flashes. The shooting wasn't as furious
as it had been previously. Up in the rocks where he'd
left Short Britches, the lieutenant could see at least
one rifle spewing flame. And all around that position,
both above it and below it, were more rifles. The
Coyoteros—who else could it be?—had the old scout
and the Mescalero surrounded.

Summerhayes pondered his next move. The Mescalero had said that the raiding party he'd seen the day
before consisted of a dozen bronchos. The lieutenant
knew his own limitations; he wasn't nearly skilled
enough in the art of desert warfare to get the drop on
a dozen Coyotero warriors. He had to do something,
though, and in a hurry. He couldn't be sure just how
long Short Britches and the Mescalero could hold out.
But what could he do?

Dismounting, he drew the carbine from its saddle
boot and ventured up the slope, moving as quietly as
possible through the rocks, trying to avoid skylining

himself against a sky so bright with stars. He came to
the rim of a depression and saw, much to his surprise,
a bunch of horses down below. These had to be the
Coyotero's ponies. And that meant there had to
be . . .

He flung himself to the ground just seconds before
the bullet ricocheted off a boulder's face, so close that
splinters of rock peppered his face. Summerhayes
scrambled on hands and knees laterally along the rim,
until he found good cover, which also afforded him a
clean shot down into the depression. He saw the shape
of a man moving through the horses. It was the Coyotero horse guard. Apaches never left their ponies un-
tended. Summerhayes could only hope that the single
shot fired at him by the guard hadn't alarmed the
other bronchos, that they couldn't distinguish it from
the firing they themselves were doing.

Sooner or later, though, they would realize he was
there. He had the element of surprise on his side—
now he had to do something to keep the momentum.
There was only one thing to do, and he didn't like it.
Being a cavalryman, and a horse lover, it was difficult
for him to raise the carbine and begin to shoot down
into the Coyotero ponies. But he'd seen this same
tactic used by Apaches to immobilize or, at least, dis-
concert their enemies. Good horses weren't easy to
come by in the desert. He tried to close his ears to the
screams of pain coming from the ponies down below.
Several went down, and the rest scattered. The horse
guard disappeared into the darkness. His carbine
empty now, Summerhayes decided it was time to
move, and he withdrew to the place where he had left
his own horse. Once there he reloaded the carbine, his
ears attuned to any telltale noise that would warn him
of an adversary's approach. Instead, he heard the
shooting diminish substantially. Were the bronchos

pulling out? Hearing his carbine, had they mistaken him for an entire cavalry unit? He waited, not certain what to do next, and half expecting to be jumped by a Coyotero broncho. Eventually the gunfire ceased altogether. Still he waited. When a half hour had passed without any further shooting, he headed up the rocky slopes, staying on foot and leading his horse. As he got closer to the position he believed to be held by Short Britches and the Mescalero, and being more confident now that the Coyoteros were gone, he began to whistle the "Battle Hymn of the Republic." When, a few minutes later, the Mescalero popped up out of nowhere directly in front of him, Summerhayes nearly jumped out of his skin.

The Mescalero made a curt gesture. "Come," he said gruffly. As he turned, Summerhayes noticed how he held his left arm stiffly against his side. The scout had been wounded, but in the darkness the lieutenant could not determine the extent of the injury.

Summerhayes followed the Mescalero another hundred yards up a steepening slope. They arrived at an overhang, beneath which sat Short Britches. The old scout was propped up against the back of the shallow cavity in the rock. His head was tilted to one side, his eyes closed, and Summerhayes had a bad moment when at first glance he thought the man was dead. Sitting on his heels in front of Short Britches, the lieutenant reached out and tentatively touched the old scout's leg. Short Britches flinched as though he'd been startled awake, and Summerhayes found himself looking down the barrel of a revolver. He gently pushed the gun aside, and his hand came away sticky with blood.

"It's me. Summerhayes."

Short Britches was surprised. When he spoke, his voice was reedy and weak, the words hesitant. His breathing was labored. "How did you . . . get there and back so fast?"

"I didn't get there at all."

"But all the shooting we heard—"

"I'm afraid that was just me. I stumbled upon their horses. Traded some lead with one of the bronchos, and then killed some of the horses. The rest scattered."

Short Britches grunted. "We thought it was Cronin. Guess the Coyoteros thought so too. They made for the tall timber after that. Good thing too." He thumbed back the hammer of his revolver, pulled the trigger. The hammer fell on an empty chamber. He didn't need to say more—Summerhayes realized that the scouts were out of ammunition, or very nearly so. He'd been right to hurry back, and was relieved to have made that decision.

"How badly are you hurt?" he asked. In the darkness of the cave he couldn't discern anything about the old scout's condition.

"I've been better," gasped Short Britches.

"That doesn't tell me much."

"I'm hit twice. The one in the shoulder doesn't amount to much. It's the one in my belly that might do me in."

Summerhayes felt a cold chill down his spine. Short Britches had been gutshot. The lieutenant knew that such a wound almost always meant death.

"I've got to get you to Captain Cronin," said Summerhayes.

"No."

"We might be able to get you back to the surgeon at Fort Union."

Short Britches scoffed. "Would you let that old butcher work on you, Lieutenant? No. Take me home."

"Home," said Summerhayes, momentarily confused. "You mean the ranch?"

"Yes." The old scout seemed to be drifting off again. Summerhayes feared that one time he would drift away and never come back. The idea that Short Britches was mortally wounded—that he might die— shook the young lieutenant. For some reason he'd always thought of the old scout as someone who was indestructible.

Summerhayes turned to the Mescalero. "Where are your horses?"

The Mescalero shook his head. "Gone. Coyotero take them."

"Damn it." Summerhayes realized the futility of trying to track down some of the Coyotero ponies that might still be running loose in the vicinity, especially at night. That would take time, and time was a luxury they didn't enjoy. "Okay," he said. "Help me put him on my horse."

The Mescalero helped him. Short Britches slumped forward over the horse's neck, but he had a good grip of the saddle, and Summerhayes could only hope he would manage to hold on. The ranch was at least a two-day walk to the east—the lieutenant wasn't even sure if he could make it, much less the old scout. But he was determined to try. Short Britches wanted to go "home," and since that could well be his dying wish, Summerhayes would do everything in his power to make it happen.

Before leaving, he turned once more to the wounded Mescalero scout, and told him to find the other scouts and then to ride to Cronin to inform the captain of what had transpired here. Summerhayes wasn't sure if he would be considered derelict in his duty by not reporting to Cronin himself, and then to be engaging in what the captain would undoubtedly call a quixotic attempt to honor a wounded man's request. But he didn't think Cronin and his troopers were in any immediate danger, as long as they stayed out of the Mogollons. He suspected that the raiding party was on its way back to Coyotero hideout. At least he hoped they were.

The Mescalero listened intently, nodded curtly, and then vanished into the night, still holding his left arm against his side. Summerhayes admired the man's stamina. Though wounded, he would carry out his orders. Of that, the lieutenant could be sure. In fact, it was just about the only thing Summerhayes was sure of. And the biggest question mark of all was whether he and Short Britches would make it to Joshua Barlow's ranch.

Chapter 25

"I don't know how he made it," said Summerhayes, sitting in a chair in a corner of the adobe ranch house's single bedroom, watching morosely as a stone-faced Joshua Barlow stood beside the iron four-poster bed, where Short Britches lay. He was struck by how small and gaunt the old scout looked under the covers—somehow he'd seemed much larger in life.

Barlow reached over and reverently closed the dead man's sightless eyes. Summerhayes stood up, not knowing what to say at a moment like this, and somewhat ashamed to feel his eyes burning with tears, especially in the presence of Barlow, who had known the old scout longer, and who had been closer to him. And Barlow seemed to be made of sterner stuff—there were no tears in his eyes. Still, Summerhayes knew his friend had to be hurting terribly inside.

For long, silent moments Barlow stood there, gazing at the old scout's face. Finally, he turned, and looked with gratitude at the lieutenant.

"I'll always be grateful to you," he said.

"For what?" asked Summerhayes.

"For bringing him back so he could die here."

Summerhayes shook his head. "I didn't do anything."

"You walked sixty miles through hostile country. You kept him alive somehow."

"No. He kept himself alive. How, I don't know. He lost more blood than I thought a human body could contain."

"He was the toughest hombre I ever met," acknowledged Barlow. "Funny thing is, after spending years with him, I don't know where he came from, or what he did before I met him, when he was working for John Ward. He never spoke of the past. Or the future, for that matter. And maybe that's the way to be in this country. Living one day at a time."

Summerhayes didn't respond, and a moment later Barlow heaved a sigh and turned to the young lieutenant. "You said there was a Netdahe with the Coyoteros."

"That's what *he* said," corrected Summerhayes, nodding at Short Britches. "I never saw him, myself. I don't think anybody did."

"The Coyoteros were after the scouts all along," mused Barlow. "That's why they used the same canyon as before. They must have had someone waiting to waylay the rider sent to Cronin. Then they turned on Short Britches. That's just the sort of thing a Netdahe will do. When on the defensive, attack. And attack the enemy's weakest point. Always do the unexpected."

"Can one Netdahe make that much difference?" Although he'd lived through the recent setbacks, Summerhayes wasn't quite ready to lay the blame on the doorstep of a single man. Even one of the notorious Avowed Killers.

"Sometimes. Depends on which one it is." Barlow went to the room's single window, looked out at the desert flats. Though he had no real reason to do so, he believed he knew the identity of the Netdahe in

question. It was just a hunch. And if he was right, it
was just as serious a development as if Geronimo himself had showed up in the Coyotero stronghold. For
himself—and for Oulay—perhaps even worse than
that.

"Well," said Summerhayes, "I'd like to hang around
for the burying. Then I have to get back to Fort
Union."

"Of course."

Barlow left the room. He went outside, and found
some of the vaqueros lingering in front of the adobe,
awaiting the news they'd all been dreading. He gave
it to them. Though they tried to mask their grief, he
could tell that the death of Short Britches affected
them deeply. Not one of them could honestly call himself a friend of the old scout. Not even Barlow could
do that. Short Britches hadn't been that kind of man.
He didn't make friends. But, like Barlow, the vaqueros
had valued him nonetheless. They'd felt safer just
knowing he was around. Because if you had to pick
one man to side with you in a scrape, it would have
been the old scout.

Mendez and two of the others began to dig a grave
out behind the adobe a ways, near where five other
graves were located. One was the final resting place
of Manolo. Three others belonged to the vaqueros
who had died on the night, long ago, when the Netdahe named Kiannatah had come to steal Oulay. The
other was occupied by yet another vaquero, one who
had died a year ago from snakebite. Watching Mendez
and the others work, and thinking of the others buried
in this place, Barlow wondered if anybody actually
lived long enough to die of natural causes in the Arizona Territory. It made you wonder why people even
bothered coming here at all, or why some, like the
Apaches, were willing to die to hold on to this land.

But then, all Barlow had to do was raise his eyes from the tombstones and look out across the vast desert plain, to the jagged blue line of mountains rising so majestically in the distance—and he knew why. Because even if you didn't live to a ripe old age, the years that you were fortunate enough to reside in this country were the best of your life, in the sense that those years were the ones that you lived to the fullest.

They laid Short Britches to rest late that afternoon, as the sun turned the clouds that streaked the western sky into broad bold strokes of orange and yellow and pink, and a wind kicked down off the Mogollons and began to cool the lowlands. All of the vaqueros were present. One of them had brought the mule that Short Britches always rode. Barlow opened a Bible and read a few lines of Scripture, realizing somewhat ashamedly that the only time he'd ever opened the Good Book was to read over someone who had died. When he was finished, some of the vaqueros spoke the Lord's Prayer together. As they spoke, Barlow glanced at Oulay. She stood across the gravesite from him, her back to the mountains, and he thought again of the lone Netdahe who now rode with the Coyoteros, and wondered if it was Kiannatah. The mountains had always been a menace, but never more so than now, because the one man Barlow had trusted in his absence to protect the woman he loved was gone. With Short Britches in the ground, Oulay was much more vulnerable.

When the vaqueros were done, all but Mendez and the other two gravediggers walked away. Oulay returned to the adobe. She had not wept in front of the others, but Barlow figured she was going to once she was inside. So he lingered at the gravesite, watching the vaqueros work, with Summerhayes beside him.

"Like I said, I'd better be starting back," murmured

the lieutenant. He didn't sound enthusiastic. "Believe it or not, General Crook assigned me to the scouts. I wonder what he'll do now. Probably make me chief of scouts." Summerhayes laughed softly, but it was a hollow laugh. He'd been trying to make a joke, but it wasn't at all funny, least of all to himself.

"I'll be coming with you," said Barlow grimly.

"You will?" Summerhayes was surprised— pleasantly so. Then he thought about Short Britches, and his joy was short-lived. "But, Joshua, Short Britches rode against the Coyoteros so *you* wouldn't have to. So that you could stay here, with Oulay. . . ."

"Yes, that's right. He died for my sake."

"Then stay," said Summerhayes somberly. "I can handle the Coyoteros."

"Oh you can, eh?" Barlow was amused.

"Sure."

"You never even wanted to be in the army, Charles. Remember?"

"That was then. This is now. I made the choice. Now I'm going to try to make the best of it."

Barlow nodded. "That's all any of us can do. But I'm going with you. Not because of Short Britches. Not really. I'm not seeking vengeance, and I'm not trying to lay to rest any guilt I feel about why he died."

"Then why?"

Barlow nodded at the mountains. "Because I've been wrong. I can't just hide here like a rabbit in its hole and hope the world will forget I exist. As long as there are Apaches up there, Oulay won't be safe. And especially if a Netdahe is one of them. So"—he turned and shrugged, smiling wanly at his friend— "I've made a choice. I'm going to eliminate the threat. Or rather, I'm going to help you and Crook eliminate it. I can't keep living like this. Every day I wonder if they're coming."

Summerhayes nodded. "I think I understand. But . . . what about Oulay?"

"Right. Now that Short Britches isn't here to protect her, what do we do?"

Summerhayes looked at Mendez and the other vaqueros. "You've got ten good men here. They're loyal to you, and to your wife. Are ten good men enough?"

"Maybe. They'd die to protect her, no question. Three of them died some years back doing just that."

"But that didn't make her safe," said Summerhayes.

"No, it didn't. So I'll take her to Fort Union. Giving her shelter—and protection—will be the price Crook will have to pay to get me to sign on." Barlow glanced again at his friend. "Think he'll pay it?"

"Without hesitation. But you know, I have a feeling Oulay won't be too fond of the arrangement."

"Right again." Barlow chuckled ruefully. "But at least I'll know she's safe. And that will make doing what I have to do a lot easier."

"Then that's what you should tell her."

A mile away, on high ground, hidden behind rocks so as not to silhouette himself against the setting sun, Kiannatah watched the burial of Short Britches through his Mexican field glasses.

He was jubilant. The old scout was dead. And Oulay was still here.

Following the night battle at the canyon, Kiannatah had slipped away from the Coyoteros in the darkness and confusion. Believing that a large force of yellow-legs was closing in, Talpute and the others had stopped fighting and drifted away into the high country. Kiannatah had whistled his horse to him, and waited. He thought, as the other bronchos did, that maybe the soldiers had come, but that didn't really matter—he was confident he could elude them, no matter how many there were.

At first light he had studied the ground carefully, and found the tracks made by Summerhayes, leading his horse with the wounded Short Britches in the saddle. Kiannatah had seen the blood. He wasn't sure of the wounded man's identity, but he knew that there was a good chance it was the old scout. He had followed the tracks. They had led him here. And now he was sure. The old scout was dead.

He was still at his vantage point when he saw eight riders leave the ranch. There was the yellow-leg officer, the rancher named Barlow, and Oulay, accompanied by five heavily armed vaqueros. Where were they bound? Kiannatah went down to where his horse was hidden, and mounted up. He would shadow the eight riders until he knew the answer. And sometime, somewhere, he would take Oulay again. This time he would not give her up.

Chapter 26

Upon arrival at Fort Union, Barlow asked for and immediately received an audience with General Crook. Captain Cronin had returned to the fort with his contingent; three of the Mescalero scouts had deserted, and one was dead, leaving only one other, and with but one scout Cronin could not carry out his orders. He was furious at Charles Summerhayes, and insisted on being present at the meeting between Crook and Barlow. For his part, Barlow insisted that Summerhayes be present as well. Crook acceded to all the demands. His first concern was the welfare of Short Britches.

"He's dead," said Barlow bluntly. "That's why I'm here."

"I'm truly sorry. Are you intending to take his place?"

"That's right."

"Unfortunately, we have only one Apache scout left to us."

"Under the circumstances, one will be enough. Besides, I have five vaqueros with me. They're all good trackers, good fighters. They've all fought the Apaches before."

Crook thought it over—and nodded his approval.

"That suits me. I won't ask for the reasons you've changed your mind. I have a pretty good idea. And that doesn't really matter. The main thing is, as it always has been, to stop the raids."

"Right," said Barlow. "I have two more conditions, General."

"Let's hear them."

"The first is that you allow my wife to remain here in the fort until the troubles are over."

"That can be arranged, certainly. I personally will vouch for her safety. Your second condition?"

"That Lieutenant Summerhayes be assigned to me."

"I protest!" exclaimed Cronin. "The lieutenant should be brought up on charges for gross dereliction of duty."

Crook fastened a steely gaze upon Summerhayes. "I must admit, the captain has a point. Your first responsibility was to the captain and the troops under his command."

"I know," said an unflinching Summerhayes. "But I had a dying man's last wish to consider. That's why I sent the Mescalero to inform Captain Cronin of the situation."

"He might never have gotten through," said Cronin. "The first one didn't."

"The Coyoteros had no desire to attack you or your command, Captain," said Barlow.

"Oh, so now you know what the Coyoteros are thinking?" asked Cronin tersely.

"I know what they were doing. They were after the scouts all along, which is why the first Mescalero was waylaid—to keep you out of the game."

"This is ridiculous, General," protested Cronin. "They can make all the excuses in the world, but the fact remains that Lieutenant Summerhayes did not do his duty."

Crook exhaled heavily through his nostrils. He was clearly perturbed. He glowered at Cronin, then at Summerhayes, and finally swung his gaze in Barlow's direction.

"The lieutenant deserves a medal, if you ask me," said the latter. "When Short Britches and the Mescalero with him were attacked by the Coyoteros, Lieutenant Summerhayes was on his way out of the canyon, heading for Captain Cronin's command. Most men would have kept going. But he put his life on the line to go back, and he sent the Coyoteros packing. As it turned out, he couldn't save Short Britches. But at least he tried."

"I will leave a final decision on this matter to another day," said Crook. "For now, we must concentrate our energies on defeating the Coyoteros. The lieutenant will be assigned to you, Mr. Barlow."

But Cronin wasn't inclined to let it go. "General, I . . . ."

Crook held up a hand, cutting the captain short. "I've made up my mind. Besides, it's entirely possible that Mr. Summerhayes will be killed before this war is over. And then the problem will have resolved itself." He glanced at Summerhayes, with the faintest of smiles tugging at the corner of his mouth.

Summerhayes nodded slightly. The general was right. His logic was unassailable, and Summerhayes wasn't the least bit offended.

"Very well, then," said Crook, turning briskly to Barlow. "Your conditions will be met. As the new head of scouts, I would be interested to hear what you have in mind."

"Do you have a map of the Mogollons?"

Crook turned to his desk, where several maps lay among an assortment of papers. He unrolled one of them, holding down one side with his scabbarded saber, the other with a heavy leather-bound book. Barlow bent over the map, studying it.

"I can't vouch for it's accuracy," admitted Crook. "This map was not produced by a survey team, but rather, I'm told, by prospectors over two decades ago."

"It's accurate enough," said Barlow. He pointed to a spot on the map. "See here—three canyons, extending deep into the mountains. Though it isn't shown, they converge—right about here. The most likely place for the Coyotero camp is here, maybe three miles from the convergence."

"How can you know this?" protested Cronin. "You're just guessing, Barlow."

"I know the Mogollons like the back of my hand," replied Barlow. "Back when Cochise and the Chiricahuas called those mountains home, I went up there quite bit."

"So what are you suggesting?" asked Crook.

"That you gather up as many troopers as you can muster, and that we push straight up these three canyons. The Coyoteros will come down to stop us. They'll have no choice."

"I thought you were opposed to a straightforward approach," said the general. "That you thought driving deep into the Mogollons would be a bloody business."

"Oh, it will be," replied Barlow bleakly. "A lot of men will die. But we will prevail. It's simply a matter of superior numbers."

"To divide our force into three parts, one for each of those canyons, is reckless," said Cronin.

"No, it isn't. Valerio has, at most, seventy to eighty bronchos. And he will have to split *his* forces if he intends to stop all three of our columns. Any one of the contingents should have a better than fair chance of whipping twenty to thirty bronchos. And by pressing on as quickly as possible to where the canyons converge, it supports the other columns, because it threatens to outflank the Coyoteros in the other canyons."

As the full scope of Barlow's plan became clear to him, General Crook's eyes gleamed with excitement. "Yes. Yes, of course. Well done, Mr. Barlow. I see your years at West Point weren't wasted. This is strategically and tactically sound. Captain?"

"What happens if Valerio concentrates his bronchos against only one of the columns?"

"Then that column must hold out as long as possible," replied Barlow, "giving the other two time enough to get behind the Coyoteros. When that happens, Valerio has only two choices—surrender, or withdraw to his camp and defend it to the death."

Cronin nodded, begrudging in his acceptance of the scheme. He didn't like the fact that Barlow had come up with it, but he couldn't very well complain too much, since his had always been the voice for taking the fight directly to the enemy, and damn the costs. "I have only one question," he said. "Where will Mr. Barlow and his men be?"

"When the Coyoteros come down to stop you," said Barlow, "we'll let them pass right by us. And then we'll move against their camp. Once they find out we're behind them, and threatening their hideout, the bronchos may scatter. They may even give up the fight."

Crook was solemn. "I don't want the Coyotero women and children harmed. I know I don't have to worry about you on that score, Mr. Barlow. But what about your vaqueros? Can you control them? I understand there's much bad blood between Mexican and Apache."

"Yes, there is. But they'll do what I tell them."

"Very well, then. I will send riders to summon Lieutenants Embrey and Walker back here immediately. With their companies we will be able to put nearly a hundred men into each of the three canyons. Embrey will command one column, Walker another, and you, Captain Cronin, will command the third. I will accompany you, Captain. We should be able to set out within the week."

Thanks to Crook, Oulay was provided with quarters at the end of Officers' Row, which just happened to be adjacent to the room that, years before, Barlow had shared with Lieutenants Summerhayes, Trotter and Hammond. Barlow had to wonder how the garrison—particularly the handful of wives who lived within the fort—would respond to Oulay's presence. She was, after all, an Apache. He didn't expect them to befriend Oulay, but he *did* hope they would not treat her badly. At least he would have a few days, maybe as long as a week, to spend with her—and he intended, by his presence, to ensure that the garrison wives, not to mention the soldiers themselves, remained on their best behavior.

She was worried, of course, knowing what he intended to do. He'd told her everything, even the details of his plan to end the Coyotero war. She had no illusions about the perils involved—to plunge into the Mogollons looking for a fight with Apache bronchos was a dangerous business, no matter how many troopers were involved. Though she didn't speak of her feelings, Barlow surmised that Oulay wasn't happy being in the fort, yet she understood perfectly why he'd brought her here, and she wasn't about to complain. Her duty, as she saw it, was to suffer through, to remain where he put her, so that he wouldn't have to worry about her while he was taking on the Coyoteros. Still, she had grown to love the little adobe house that had been their home these past few years—growing up a Chiricahua at a time when the Apaches were having troubles with the Pinda-Lickoyi, she had never before lived in one place for so long a time. She was terribly homesick, but tried to conceal that fact from her husband.

In the days they spent together at Fort Union, waiting for the army to prepare itself for the campaign into the Mogollons, they spoke only once of their greatest fears and what the future might hold for them. It was late into the night, when they lay awake, in each other's arms. During the daylight hours, Barlow was usually able to occupy his mind with making sure he and his vaqueros and the single remaining Mescalero scout would receive their fair portion of ammunition and provisions. And during the evening hours he could distract himself by joining the vaqueros around a campfire, where, usually these days, the conversation dwelled on Short Britches, not so much on his death, but rather on the remarkable abilities he had displayed while alive. But late into the night, when Oulay lay beside him, Barlow was no longer able to divert his thoughts from the very real possibility that these might be their last hours together.

"We might be moving out tomorrow," he said, abruptly. Although her eyes were closed, and she hadn't moved for a long while, he knew by the rate of her breathing that she was awake. "I won't be gone long, though."

She was silent a moment—then her eyes opened, and she gazed at him, and said, "They may be Coyoteros, but they are still Apaches. They are my people."

Barlow was surprised. He hadn't expected this to be

a concern of hers—he'd thought she would be worried about him, about when or whether they would be together again. But he told himself he shouldn't be surprised; leave it to Oulay to be worried about others beside herself, to see things in a larger perspective than he was usually able to.

"I'm sorry," he said, lamely. "But now all bets are off. Now the Netdahe are involved."

Her body was pressed against his beneath the counterpane, and he felt her shudder involuntarily; he suspected that she was wondering now whether the Netdahe who rode with the Coyoteros was the one who had kidnapped her. For her, there were many potential dangers out there, considering the circumstances. But the greatest danger to her was the Avowed Killer called Kiannatah. As long as he lived, she wasn't safe, regardless of whether all the rest of the Apaches laid down their arms and never again went to war against the White Eyes or the Mexicans.

"They said you were a friend to the Apache," she whispered. "From now on, they will not say that anymore."

"This has got to end," he said, exasperated—not with her, but with the fact that there was no happy resolution to the dilemma that confronted him. "We've got to have peace, and I've begun to think there's only one way to achieve it."

Her head propped up on one hand, she looked thoughtfully down into his eyes, her own dark gaze indecipherable. "By killing all the Chi-hinne?"

"No. But I may have to kill some of them. Even if they *are* your people. And *were* my friends."

With a sigh, she laid her head back down on his chest, and for a long while neither spoke; during this time Barlow let his senses record the experience of lying beside her, thinking the memory would help him get through the nights to come, when he would be without her. And then she showed him that she had an even better way to render this night a memorable one, that she wanted something more than just the memory of a moment to cling to. She whispered in his ear that she loved him, and followed this with a series of featherlight kisses that started at his earlobe and traveled along his jawbone to the corner of his mouth. She straddled him; aroused, he slipped inside her, and marveled at how perfectly they seemed to fit together, and how unself-consciously they made love. When they were done they lay with arms and legs entwined, and spoke no more of the uncertain future, but reveled in this intimate interlude that, while fleeting, was unforgettable.

Chapter 27

Early the next morning, Barlow emerged into the slanting sunlight and squinted at two men approaching across the parade ground from the general direction of the headquarters building. One of them was Summerhayes. The other was a civilian, clad in a travel-worn tweed suit. He was short, slight, balding. Strands of mouse brown hair were plastered to his sweat-glistening pate. His suit had large dark patches of perspiration. Here was a man unaccustomed to the harsh climate of the Arizona Territory. Barlow didn't hold that against him. The weather took a lot of getting used to. It could easily kill a man—just like everything else around here.

Summerhayes introduced the civilian as a Mr. Boswell, who proclaimed himself an attorney from Tucson. Even though Summerhayes had just performed the introductions, Boswell requested that Barlow identify himself. Barlow complied, somewhat indifferently. He had no idea what Boswell wanted from him, and he didn't really care. He could glance over the shining head of the attorney and see that there was a great deal of hustle and bustle on the other side of the parade ground; it looked very much like the campaign against the Coyoteros was finally about to get under way.

"What do you want, Mr. Boswell?" he asked, impatiently. "I don't have a lot of time this morning."

"You will want to make the time, I believe, Mr. Barlow, once you find out why I am here."

"I'm listening."

Boswell opened a well-worn leather pouch and dug around inside of it as he spoke. "I recently received some documents from an attorney in Athens, Georgia, a Mr. Jonah Cambreleng."

"Never heard of him."

"Apparently, Mr. Cambreleng was made executor of your parents' estate." Boswell brandished a thick sheaf of papers. "He has retained me to locate you and to present you with these documents, which include an inventory of your holdings, and of course, the last will and testament of both Timothy Barlow and his wife, Rose."

He offered the papers to Barlow, who took them, but hardly glanced at them.

"I need you to sign the top document, Mr. Barlow, and return it to me. Simply a precaution—proof that I delivered the documents to you, as I was charged to do by Mr. Cambreleng." He produced a quill pen and ink bottle. Barlow sat down on the steps of the barracks. Balancing the sheaf of papers on his knee, he signed the top document, and returned it to Boswell, as requested.

"Okay," he said, mildly exasperated. He was annoyed at Boswell for reminding him of his deceased parents at this particular time, when, in his opinion, he had enough to brood about. "Fine. You've done your job, Mr. Boswell. Now you can go home."

Boswell looked somewhat flustered. "Well, I, um, I

wanted to offer my services to you, sir, if, at any time, you find yourself in need of legal representation."

"I don't see why I would ever need a lawyer, but thanks all the same."

Boswell tilted his head to one side. "Perhaps you should find the time to read through the inventory of holdings, Mr. Barlow. You'll find that you are quite a wealthy man. And wealthy men tend to need legal representation from time to time. Hence my offer."

"He's a rich man?" asked Summerhayes, slightly amused and giving Barlow a funny look, as though he were trying to imagine his friend in such a role and was having a hard time doing it.

"Certainly. Even by Georgia standards, I'm sure. He owns several hundred acres of what has been represented to me as some of the finest land in the state. He owns a magnificent home, a couple of mills, and part interest in a number of business concerns, including a store in Athens and a hotel in Atlanta."

"I find that hard to believe," said Barlow. "The way I remember it, few people would have gone into business with my mother and father. He was a Yankee, and she, though Southern-born, was a Yankee's wife."

"Well," said Boswell, "I don't know anything about that sort of thing, but I did briefly skim the inventory, and noticed that your father's business partners seemed to be what they now call carpetbaggers."

Barlow nodded. That made sense. Carpetbaggers were Northerners who had gone south following the war's end to buy up Southern land and businesses. They were generally despised by the native-born population, because they took advantage of the wrecked Southern economy and offered bargain-basement prices for the property they sought. The Southern owners of these properties often could not afford to hold out for a better price. He was a little surprised that his parents had agreed to go into business with such men. But maybe they hadn't had much in the way of choices; Southern-born entrepreneurs had usually spurned them.

"Well, Joshua," said Summerhayes, as amazed as was Barlow by this turn of events, "looks like you don't have to expend any more blood and sweat trying to make that ranch a successful proposition. You've got everything a man could want—and more—waiting for you back east."

Barlow looked at him askance. "Who says I want to live back east?" He shook his head. "No. I have no desire to go back there."

"Then what will you do with it all?"

Boswell discreetly cleared his throat. "There's a subject worthy of careful consideration, if I may be so bold. Mr. Barlow, do you have a last will and testament?"

"Well, no, I don't."

"You possess an estate of great value now. You might want to consider having one drawn up."

Barlow smiled. "And you could do that."

"Why, yes, of course. I'd be happy to."

"For a modest fee."

"My rates are very reasonable. I might add that if you die intestate—that is to say, without a written will—your holdings in Georgia will go to the state itself."

"How long would it take you to draw one up? A will, I mean."

"A day—or two at the most."

Barlow shook his head. "I'm riding out in an hour. I may or may not come back. Give me another piece of paper."

Boswell searched his pouch, found a sheet of vel-

lum, and handed it over. Barlow dipped the quill in
the ink bottle and scratched out his signature on the
piece of paper. This he handed back to Boswell.

"Draw up a will, attach this to it. Would that be
legal?"

"Well, yes, I suppose so, though it's somewhat irreg-
ular. Still, I witnessed it."

"I'll sign on as a witness," offered Summerhayes.

Barlow handed him the pen. Boswell produced the
paper with Barlow's signature, and Summerhayes
signed below it.

"But . . . to whom do I leave your estate, Mr. Barlow?" asked the lawyer.

"My wife. Her name is Oulay."

"But can she own property in Georgia?" asked
Summerhayes. "She's full-blooded Apache."

Barlow looked at him. They both looked at Boswell.

"Well, I . . . I don't know," admitted the lawyer,
tugging self-consciously at the soggy collar of his shirt.
"But I will most certainly find out. You can rely on
me, Mr. Barlow."

"If she can't, or if she dies without a will of her
own," said Barlow, "I want you to be the executor of
the estate, Mr. Boswell. In that event, you will get the
best possible price for all my property, and you will
arrange for the proceeds to be spent to provide for
the Chiricahua Apaches." He noticed the funny look
that Summerhayes gave him, and added, "Those people are her family, Charles."

"Of course," said Summerhayes.

"I'm not sure . . . ." began Boswell.

"Just do it," said Barlow. "And made it ironclad
legal. One of these days, the Chiricahuas are going to
be dependent on the government of the United States.
And when that happens, they may not always get what
they need to survive. The trust you will create, Mr.

Boswell, if you sell my property, will be there to make sure that they do. Understand?"

"Perfectly," said Boswell. "I assure you, Mr. Barlow—"

"I know. And I *am* relying on you."

"Though I must say, I'm a bit confused." Boswell gestured broadly at the activity on the parade ground. "I take it that you are embarking with those men on a campaign against Apaches. And yet here you are, willing, in the event of your death, and the death of your wife, to liquidate your estate and provide for the Apaches with the profits."

"Yeah," said Barlow, with a crooked smile. "It's hard to explain."

And he didn't bother to try; he brusquely shook Boswell's hand and, accompanied by Summerhayes, headed across the dusty parade ground to join the other cavalrymen.

"There's something I want to tell you, Charles," he said, as they walked side by side. "It's about Captain Cronin."

"What about him?"

Barlow proceeded to tell how he had turned a pair of captured scalphunters over to Cronin, who, at the time, was Fort Union's commandant, and how those very same scalphunters had later been involved in the Aravaipa massacre.

"I understand," said Barlow bitterly, "that the captain claims he had no evidence to hold those men. But he did. I gave him the evidence. A pouch filled with scalps."

Stunned, Summerhayes stopped dead in his tracks. "You're saying that the captain . . . let those men go?"

"Had to have happened," replied Barlow curtly.

"Who else have you told about this?"

"Nobody."

"Why not?"

"At the time I just wanted to stay out of it."

"You should tell General Crook at once."

"No. I just wanted you to know—in case something happened to me."

"But I . . ."

Barlow kept walking.

From his hiding place some distance from Fort Union, Kiannatah used the Mexican field glasses to watch the yellow-leg soldiers' departure. He didn't need to see them turning north to know where they were bound. The United States Army was going after Valerio's Coyoteros, and they were doing so in force. With the soldiers rode the man named Barlow—the man who, in Kiannatah's view of things, had stolen Oulay away from him. He rode with some of the vaqueros from his ranch, and one Mescalero scout. Oulay, however, did not ride with them. Kiannatah had had his revenge against the old scout who wore the stovepipe hat. He wanted revenge against Barlow too. But he wanted Oulay more. And for that reason, he watched the soldiers ride north and did not follow them. He owed no allegiance to Valerio. It did not matter to him that this was the moment when the Coyoteros most needed his services. All that mattered was having Oulay for his own. His war against the Pinda Lickoyi—and the Nakai-Ye, as well—had always been a personal one. He had used the Coyoteros to pursue his own objectives; now circumstances dictated that he abandon them, and this he did without compunction.

His only concern now was how to reach Oulay. Barlow had brought her here for safekeeping while he was away on the campaign against the Coyoteros. And even though most of the soldiers had gone off to fight

Valerio, there were still enough of them remaining behind to make the abduction of the Chiricahua woman a difficult and dangerous proposition. Most men would have calculated the odds against success— and given up. But Kiannatah had an advantage over most men. He wasn't afraid to die. He was willing to tackle impossible odds.

This did not mean, however, that he was going to commit suicide by venturing into the fort itself. No, he would wait. He was exceedingly good at waiting, and he devoutly believed that, sooner or later, an opportunity would present itself. And when it did, he would be ready to act. In the meanwhile, he experienced a strong sense of elation and excitement. The ultimate prize was finally, once again, within his grasp. And this time, when he had her, he would never let her go.

Chapter 28

When they reached the foothills of the Mogollons, the soldiers, numbering nearly three hundred, split into three roughly equal groups. Lieutenant Embrey's detachment branched off to proceed up the westernmost of the parallel canyons, while Lieutenant Walker took his contingent up the one to the east. Captain Cronin led his command up the center canyon. Barlow, accompanied by Charles Summerhayes, the Mescalero scout, and his five vaqueros, including Mendez and Rodrigo, preceded Cronin by several hours.

Barlow knew the Coyoteros would have scouts monitoring all the trails into the mountains that might provide an enemy with access to their stronghold. He also knew that there was no point in trying to locate and kill the scouts before word could be sent to Valerio of the yellow-leg invasion. Regardless of whether they might have succeeded—which Barlow doubted—to have made such an attempt wasn't in keeping with his plan, which was to engage the Coyotero bronchos in a fight they could not win. The only question was whether the bronchos, when they came, would attack his small party, or move against Cronin's column. He was betting on the latter. They would expect Barlow and the scouting party to rush back to the main group once the ambush was sprung; it wouldn't occur to them that this handful of scouts were a threat to their hideout. Even so, progress up the arid canyon was nerve-racking. Barlow and his men constantly scanned the rimrock high overhead, expecting an attack at any moment.

They spent the first night in the mountains encamped in the canyon bottom. It was a cold camp—no fire allowed. That meant no hot meal, and no coffee in the morning. But nobody complained. No one in the party was so naive as to think they were keeping their whereabouts a secret from the Coyoteros; all were painfully aware that the bronchos in all likelihood knew precisely where they were. Yet only a fool would silhouette himself against a fire under such circumstances. Barlow and the Mescalero scout took the first watch; the others, two at a time, would do their stint as night guards in two-hour increments. Though he encouraged the others to try to get some sleep, Barlow doubted that they would. He didn't.

The next morning, shortly before sunrise, they rolled out of their blankets, grabbed their rifles, and stood there, no one making a sound, to listen to the echo of distant gunfire rolling up the canyon.

Cronin and his troopers were under attack.

Barlow's initial impulse was to ride to the sound of the guns. One look at the grim faces of the men who rode with him was all he needed to affirm that they felt the same way. But he had to fight that urge—and make sure they did too.

"Okay," he said curtly, "time to find the Coyotero village. Let's ride."

They continued north up the canyon, and in two hours' time reached the convergence of the canyon with the other two. They could no longer hear shooting from the south; Barlow could only wonder if Cronin's fight with the Coyoteros was over, or if the contours of the land were blocking its sounds from his ears. They scoured the ground, and found no indication that either Embrey's or Walker's command had yet come this far. But there was sign of unshod ponies—plenty of them. Barlow told the Mescalero scout to take the lead in tracking the Coyotero sign back to its source. And he warned his companions to stay alert; Valerio wasn't so foolish that he would leave his hideout completely unprotected. His caveat was unnecessary—despite being tired and hungry and saddle sore, the others were alert.

The Mescalero led them up a steep draw, at the top of which they found a narrow trail that wound its way up the steep flank of a mountain. The ascent was tough for both men and horses, and the footing was precarious, so they led their mounts. They were nearly to the top when a shot rang out. Barlow dropped to one knee, drawing his pistol, and sweeping the rocks above for the telltale puff of powder smoke. Mendez, who was directly behind him, spotted it before he did, and began firing his repeating rifle. Barlow used the opportunity to begin scrambling directly up the slope, advancing on the enemy. To his left, he saw Rodrigo doing likewise. Up ahead, the Mescalero was laying down covering fire, as well. Barlow had climbed fifty yards when he saw a slender figure darting between the rocks. He raised the pistol and fired. He missed. The glimmer of sunlight on a rifle barrel gave him warning, and he dived to one side. The Apache—he assumed it was a Coyotero—got off one shot that sang off the stony ground too close for comfort; then either Mendez or the Mescalero gunned him down. The Apache's body slipped limply between two large boulders and slid down the steep slope, starting an avalanche of small rocks.

Barlow reached the body first. He turned it over, and sat on his heels to gaze down at the face of a Coyotero boy who could not have been more than thirteen years of age. Rodrigo and Mendez arrived; the features of the former displayed some regret for the death of one so young. Even an enemy. But Mendez looked impassively at the corpse, and then spat to one side. Barlow looked up at him sharply.

"That is for Manolo, my cousin," muttered Mendez. Barlow let it go.

"I think your friend was hit," Rodrigo told him.

Barlow stood up, peered downslope, and saw that the other vaqueros were gathered round Summerhayes, who was sitting on the ground, hunched over. Cursing under his breath, Barlow descended to the trail.

"It's just a flesh wound," said Summerhayes, through clenched teeth. Pale, he was clutching his left arm, and bright red blood leaked through white-knuckled fingers. Barlow knelt, pried the lieutenant's hand away from the wound, and was relieved to see that the patient's diagnosis was correct. At his direction, one of the vaqueros began to bind up the wound—later, when they had time, they would have to cauterize it to prevent infection.

Turning away, Barlow noticed the Mescalero was jogging back down the trail. The Apache scout pointed to the north, and Barlow saw the smoke.

"Valerio," he said grimly. "Calling the bronchos back. He knows we're coming."

Summerhayes stood. He swayed unsteadily, caught himself. "I can ride," he insisted.

They pressed on, leaving the young Coyotero where he lay. The trail led them higher, onto the rim, and then into a stand of pine that dotted a high plateau. Here, they were hit a second time. As before, they

didn't see their assailants until after the first shots
were fired. The Mescalero, ahead of the others, had
his horse killed under him. He jumped clear, and then
used the animal's carcass for cover. Barlow and the
others dismounted; he, Rodrigo, Mendez, and one
other vaquero left their horses in the keeping of Summerhayes and the fifth vaquero before scattering into
the trees. They moved forward. The vaquero on the
right flank, beyond Mendez and Rodrigo, was hit in
the chest and went down. Barlow was immediately
aware of this, but remained unmoved; there would be
time enough for sadness and regret after the fight—
assuming he survived. Using the trees for cover as
much as possible, Barlow fired at powder smoke
whenever he saw it. He figured there were no more
than three Coyoteros up ahead, but he never was sure,
because a few moments later they stopped firing and
just faded away. All Barlow saw of them was the
fleeting glimpse of one broncho.

"We've got to hurry," Barlow told the others. "Valerio doesn't have enough rifles left to make a stand.
His only chance is to move the women and children
out. And remember," he added, as an afterthought,
shooting a look in the direction of Mendez, "don't kill
anyone unless you have to."

They proceeded on foot, with Summerhayes and the
vaquero bringing the horses along behind. Beyond the
plateau, they crossed a boulder field, climbed to a
ledge, followed it laterally around the south flank of
a peak, and suddenly found themselves above a
horseshoe-shaped depression that held the jacales of
the Coyotero stronghold. They were immediately fired
upon by a single broncho high up on the mountain-
side. They scattered, finding cover. The sentry got off
several more shots, but everyone except Barlow was
shooting back, and one of them hit the mark—the

broncho's body came tumbling down a steep scree slope.

Barlow was more interested in what was happening in the Coyotero village. Pandemonium reigned among the Apaches. The women and children were running in every direction. A handful of men fired at Barlow's party, but they were exposed to withering return fire from the rifles of the vaqueros, and several died almost immediately. The village was surrounded on three sides by steep, rocky slopes; the fourth side was open ground for about seventy-five yards, a gentle slope leading down to a brush-choked ravine. The majority of Coyotero women and children was fleeing in that direction. Barlow shouted at his men, and began firing in that direction, making sure that he shot well in front of the Coyoteros. Mendez and the others began doing likewise. Their bullets kicked up puffs of dust in front of the Apaches who, realizing that avenue of escape was cut off, were turned back toward the che-wa-ki, where many of them took cover behind the jacales, fearing that if they tried to climb the slopes on the other three sides of the village they would expose their children to certain death.

A growing sense of urgency compelled Barlow to take a big chance. Valerio had sent up a smoke signal, and sooner rather than later his bronchos would show up. The issue was just how close behind them the soldiers would be.

So far, everything had gone more or less according to plan, and Barlow had come prepared for this moment. He brandished a strip of white cloth, tied it quickly to the barrel of his rifle. Mendez, hunkered down a stone's throw to his right, looked at him like he was crazy—Barlow ignored the vaquero and kept working. As soon as he was done, he shouted at Mendez to cover him, and rose to proceed down off the

ledge in the direction of the Coyotero village, holding
the rifle, transformed into a flag of truce, high overhead.

It was the most dangerous moment of all—he'd
known it would be all along, and had tried to prepare
for it, but his heart thundered like a triphammer in
his chest, and he expected at any instant to feel that
brief explosion of indescribable pain as the bullet
slammed into his body, and he wondered if he would
live long enough to hear the report of the gun from
which that bullet was fired. He recognized just how
optimistic—or perhaps naive—he was being, thinking
that the Coyoteros, under this set of circumstances,
would have the presence of mind to hold their fire.
Mendez would call him crazy. The vaquero, if given
the chance, would ask why he thought the Apaches,
who had always been deceived by the whites, would
trust the white flag that he was flying. And Barlow
would have had to answer that he didn't expect them
to, not really. All he had was a slender hope that he
could prevent a bloodbath. That was a cause worth
risking his life for.

So he headed down the steep, rocky slope, braced
for the bullet's impact, but hoping for the best, and
with each step his hope soared higher, because he was
still alive, because the handful of Coyotero men who
had been fighting back were holding their fire now.
Thankfully, so were the vaqueros up on the ledge.
Knowing that, if he fell, Mendez and the others would
kill every man, woman, and child in the che-wa-ki was
small comfort.

As he drew near the village, Valerio, flanked by two
bronchos, came into view around a jacal. Barlow
pulled up twenty paces away.

"You," said Valerio bitterly. "They told me you
were coming. I would not believe them."

"This has to stop," replied Barlow, speaking in the Apache tongue. "I figured I might be able to stop it."

"Some said you were a friend of the Apache. But no friend of the Apache would be here today, killing women and children."

"I see no women and children lying dead. But I *will* see that, if you don't give up. The soldiers are coming. And you know you can't stop them, Valerio. You have too few men. Now it's your choice how this will end. Either your people live, or they die. You can try to blame it on me, or on the yellow-legs, or on the sun and the wind, for that matter—but whatever happens is on *your* hands."

"I will surrender," said Valerio grimly, "on one condition. That my people are allowed to live in these mountains in peace."

Barlow shook his head. "That isn't up to me, jefe. General Crook is the one you'll have to deal with. I think he's a fair man."

"All we wanted," lamented the Coyotero chief, "was to be left alone."

"Yeah," said Barlow curtly. "Me too. Where is the Netdahe?"

"Gone, for many days now. Ever since the fight with the soldiers' scouts."

Barlow nodded. He realized that Valerio could be lying to him, but he could see no reason why he would. If the Avowed Killer happened to be among the bronchos who had ventured forth to take on the soldiers, he would be found out soon enough.

He told Valerio to send up a smoke signal that would instruct the returning bronchos to enter the village prepared to put down their weapons. Until such time as the soldiers arrived on the scene, his men would remain on the ledge that commanded the che-wa-ki, prepared to fire if the Coyoteros did not com-

ply. He prayed that Captain Cronin would hurry. He
was holding the lid down on a pot that threatened at
any moment to boil over—Valerio knew that he was
confronted by only a handful of men; the only thing
that deterred him from continuing the struggle was
concern for the welfare of the Coyotero women and
children. But even if Valerio stuck to his guns and
surrendered, that didn't mean one or more of the returning bronchos wasn't going to size up the situation,
realize the disadvantage Barlow was working under,
and start shooting. He expected there to be some who
would refuse to come in, but he was hoping that these
diehards would simply melt away into the mountains
rather than continue resisting.

Valerio complied with his request. The first few
bronchos who appeared went along with their jefe's
decision and put down their guns. Still, Barlow was
vastly relieved when Captain Cronin and his detachment showed up. Lieutenant Embrey and his column
arrived just a few minutes later. Barlow could tell that
both contingents had been in a fight. It wasn't just the
empty saddles on some of the horses, or the blood on
the wounded, but also the expressions in the eyes of
the survivors.

Barlow told Cronin that Valerio had agreed to surrender, and that with any luck the fighting was over,
and the balance of the Coyotero bronchos would give
themselves up.

"Well," said Cronin, "I concede that your plan
seems to have worked after all, Mr. Barlow."

"The credit's all yours, Captain," said Barlow wearily. "This was your command, after all. But now
comes the hard part."

Cronin nodded. "I want to talk to Valerio. You will
translate for me."

"Sure." Barlow was worried. Cronin seemed to be

quickly assuming the imperious air of a victorious Caesar—and that would not go over well with Valerio. He also wondered what would happen to Cronin if he mentioned to Valerio that the captain was responsible for the release of the scalphunters who had then proceeded to massacre the Aravaipa. He figured Valerio would take back the surrender—if only just long enough to kill the captain. Of course that would lead to further bloodshed, and while Barlow thought that if anyone deserved to perish in this war it was Cronin, the others who would also perish if the fighting resumed didn't deserve that.

Cronin informed the Coyotero leader that he and his people would be taken to Fort Union, where he would meet with General Crook. Valerio had heard of Crook, and called him "Red Beard," though why the blond-haired general had acquired such a nickname among the Apaches was a mystery to Barlow. Valerio again asked that his people be allowed to live in peace in the Mogollon.

"If I'm not mistaken," said Cronin frostily, "you were living here in peace—until you decided to commit the folly of making war against the United States of America." He glanced at Barlow. "Make sure you change nothing in the translation."

Barlow clamped down on a quick surge of anger; it irked him that the captain would feel it necessary to make such a comment.

Valerio then asked that his men be given until the morrow's sunrise to come in. But Cronin shook his head adamantly. He wanted to be out of the mountains by nightfall. They would wait only a few hours before leaving, and, he added, those bronchos who had not given up by then would be considered outlaws, and hunted down.

Finished with Valerio, and seeing that Lieutenant

Walker and his men were riding in, Cronin turned to
the task of securing the area. He formed a cordon
of men around the Coyotero village. In what Barlow
thought was an unorthodox but effective arrangement,
Cronin had half of the men in the cordon facing in-
ward, to keep those Coyoteros already in the village
from leaving, and the other half facing out, to keep
an eye out for the bronchos still extant. Squads of
troopers thoroughly searched the jacales; they collected any and all weapons and tossed them into two
large piles.

Barlow returned to the ledge, and his men. He sent
Summerhayes down into the village with Mendez, who
was instructed to clean and cauterize the lieutenant's
flesh wound. The vaquero would heat the blade of his
knife in the flame of an Apache fire, then lay the
white-hot steel against the wound. Meanwhile, Barlow
and Rodrigo went back into the trees to retrieve the
body of the vaquero who had been slain. Barlow felt
an emptiness deep inside as he and Rodrigo gently
draped the body over a saddle horse and lashed it
down for transport back to the ranch. He thought of
the dead man—and all the other vaqueros—as more
like family than employees. Outsiders were wont to
comment on the fierce loyalty the vaqueros showed
him; Barlow's loyalty to them was just as strong. He
asked Rodrigo if he would volunteer to take the body
home. Rodrigo readily agreed to do so.

"With any luck," said Barlow, "the rest of us will
be along in a few days. Wait as long as you can—
then, if we're still not back, bury him with the others."

"*Sí*, padrone."

In the time allotted by Cronin, more than two score
Coyotero bronchos returned to the che-wa-ki and laid
down their weapons. They were greatly relieved to
find their families unharmed, and were greeted by

loved ones with much joy. But other families grieved; as the afternoon progressed, more and more women began to wail in sorrow, as news of the death of a husband or brother or son reached them. It seemed more than twenty of the Coyoteros had perished earlier that day in the attacks on the army columns. Cronin counted his own losses as twenty-eight killed and half that many wounded.

When the captain's deadline arrived, the soldiers began to move the Coyoteros out. They had been allowed to gather a few belongings, which they either carried on their backs or on a travois pulled by dog or human—Cronin would not allow them to use their horses, which were moved out separately by a detail under the command of Lieutenant Embrey. Lieutenant Walker was charged with the responsibility of burning the jacales as soon as the column was under way; he and his men performed this duty with a good deal of enthusiasm, thought Barlow. This day the Coyoteros had lost loved ones; the troopers had lost friends. And they were not in a forgiving mood where Apaches were concerned. Barlow decided that there was a fair to middling chance that violence would break out between the Mogollons and Fort Union; it was just as likely that the cavalrymen would start something as the Coyoteros.

Cronin called upon Barlow and his scouts—now reduced to three vaqueros and the Mescalero Apache, to ride as flankers for the column. He had a hunch that there were at least a dozen bronchos who had not turned themselves in. Barlow thought that was a pretty good guess. He could only hope that the Coyotero warriors who'd eschewed surrender would at least refrain from shooting at a "yellow-leg"; hopefully they would keep in mind that their people were at the mercy of the soldiers.

The captain was of the opinion that yet another campaign into the Mogollons would be required to clean out the last of the renegades. Barlow disagreed. Most of the holdouts, he told Cronin, would give up. The few that remained would more than likely head south, to join the Netdahe in the Cima Silkq. Cronin didn't argue. He didn't particularly like Barlow, but he had to admit that the rancher knew the country and the Apaches as well as anyone he'd met during his time in the Arizona Territory.

As they proceeded out of the Mogollons, Barlow's spirits began to rise. It had been a bloody day. He had lost another friend. But at least now he could take heart. The Apache war was over. There would be another, eventually—of that he was sure. But maybe the next war would be fought far from his home. Maybe he could stay out of the next one. The most important thing at the moment was that he'd survived, and would soon be reunited with Oulay.

He didn't hear the shot. He was struck a terrible blow that numbed his entire body, and he was vaguely aware of falling. His last sensation was of lying on his back on the ground, staring up at a sky that quickly turned black.

Chapter 29

When Cronin crossed the encampment, making for the hospital tent, he noticed that Barlow's three vaqueros, along with the Mescalero scout, were gathered out front. They sat on the ground, or on their heels, waiting for the same thing the captain had come for. As Cronin drew near, the vaquero named Mendez looked up at him. The Mexican's coal black eyes were impassive; his attitude was neither friendly nor hostile. He didn't say anything to Cronin, and the captain didn't speak to him, either. These men, he knew, were waiting to take Joshua Barlow home, and Cronin was ready for them to go. He wouldn't deny that they had performed a valuable service for the United States Army, and performed it valiantly. But they were Barlow's men, not his. He had no control over them.

As he was about to enter the hospital tent, Cronin was met by Fort Union's surgeon, Abraham Lee, a tall, cadaverous man wearing a blood-smeared apron over his uniform. His cheeks were gaunt and grizzled. Cronin knew Lee as a capable doctor. He'd known plenty, during the war, who hadn't been capable at all. In fact, they'd been little better than butchers or novices, which was sometimes even worse. Lee had been practicing medicine for about thirty years, or so

Cronin had been told, and he'd spent much of it in the employ of the army. So he had seen all manner of injuries, and Cronin counted on him for an accurate prognosis. Not just on Barlow, but on the other wounded men he'd brought back from the Mogollons.

Lee spared Cronin the merest glance, then stepped aside, to allow two orderlies to carry a blanket-covered body out of the tent on a stretcher. The vaqueros stood up, but Lee looked at them and shook his head.

"Easy there," he said, his voice hoarse and full of weariness. "Not your man." He turned to Cronin. "It's Jepsen. I couldn't save him. He'd lost too much blood."

Cronin nodded. He noticed that Lee was wiping his hands with his apron—in fact, he kept wiping them long after he'd gotten all the blood off of them, as though he were trying to wipe away the failure too. As an army surgeon, he had failed many times to save an ill or injured man. Nonetheless, he was still bothered when a patient died.

"What about the rest?" asked the captain.

"I'm pretty sure most will pull through. But I've got a half dozen men in there who can't be moved for a while."

"I understand. But I have to transport the Apaches to Fort Union. I'm leaving Lieutenant Embrey and a company of men here with you. The rest of us are pulling out in an hour."

"Send wagons back."

The vaquero named Rodrigo stepped forward. He alone among those who waited for word of Barlow spoke some English. "You said most?" he asked the surgeon.

Lee nodded. "Where your boss is concerned, I can't say with any certainty. Not right now. I got the bullet out. But the wound is deep, and a lot of damage was done. He also lost a lot of blood."

"He is a tough hombre," said Rodrigo. "He will live."

Lee grunted. "Sorry, but I don't indulge in wishful thinking. It's in God's hands now. I've done all I can."

Rodrigo turned to the others, and spoke to them in a muted voice, relaying to them what the surgeon had said. Cronin caught Lee's eye, nodded to one side, and they stepped out of earshot of the others.

"Tell me straight, Doc. Will Barlow live or die?"

Lee carefully considered his answer. "Let me put it this way," he said, at last. "I haven't seen very many men survive that kind of gunshot wound."

Cronin headed back for his tent. He was intercepted en route by Summerhayes. The lieutenant's arm was in a sling. The captain knew what he was after even before he spoke.

"The news isn't good," said Cronin, without breaking stride. "He might live and he might not."

"I want to return to Union with you, sir."

"All wounded men remain here."

"I'm fine, sir. I can ride."

Cronin turned on him. "You're forgetting something, Lieutenant. I didn't want you along in the first place. But General Crook overruled me. He assigned you to Barlow. Well, Barlow's here, and you'll stay here with him. I have nearly two hundred Apaches to transport to Fort Union, and I need men I can trust to do their duty. You have already proven that you cannot be counted on for that, Lieutenant."

Summerhayes bit down on his anger. "Maybe you're forgetting something, sir. Joshua Barlow's wife is at Fort Union. She'll have to be told. And it would be easier on her if the news came from a friend. From me."

"That Apache woman's feelings are of no concern to me."

"You don't care about the Apaches at all, do you, Captain? Not even the innocent ones. The women and children at the Aravaipa village, for instance."

Cronin's eyes narrowed. "I'm a soldier. I don't kill innocent women and children."

"Maybe they didn't die at your hand. But you were responsible."

"Watch your step, Lieutenant."

"If you hadn't let those scalphunters go," said Summerhayes bitterly, "all of this might have been avoided."

"You're staying here," rasped Cronin. "That's an order." He jabbed a finger in Summerhayes' face. "One you'd better obey."

"Miss? The general will see you now."

Oulay looked up numbly at the sergeant, who was leaning over her so that he could speak softly—he hadn't wanted to startle her, as she'd seemed lost in thought, sitting there on the narrow wooden bench in the broad central hall that split the headquarters building at Fort Union into halves. The sergeant had just emerged from the general's office, but she hadn't appeared to notice. Her eyes stared off into space. The sergeant thought he knew why. This was the Apache woman taken by Joshua Barlow as his wife. And Barlow hadn't returned from the campaign against the Coyoteros. The sergeant didn't know any more than that, but he could figure out the rest.

Rising, Oulay swallowed the lump in her throat, and fought down a rising panic. The soldiers had returned, captured Coyoteros in their keeping. But her husband had not. And no one would tell her anything. Not even the captain who led the trail-weary troops. Still, the way some of the soldiers turned away quickly when she looked at them told her plenty. She was afraid now that the man on the other side of that door would confirm her worst fears.

"Right this way, miss," said the sergeant, solicitously.

Oulay lifted her chin. She reminded herself that she was Chiricahua Apache. She had been taught, from an early age, to conceal her feelings. Her fears. And here, among strangers, she would even conceal her grief, when it came.

The sergeant opened the door for her, and she entered to find General Crook sitting behind the desk. It was getting dark outside—the purple shadow of twilight had fallen across the parade ground just outside the room's solitary window, and there was a single burning lamp on the desk, its yellow light casting the angles of Crook's face in sharp relief. Seeing her, Crook stood up. He was stiff, uncomfortable, but it wasn't a physical discomfort. He motioned to a chair facing the desk.

"Mrs. Barlow. Thank you for your patience. Please have a seat."

"I will stand."

"Please. I insist."

She complied, because she realized that if she didn't sit, Crook wouldn't—and he looked as though he needed to be sitting a lot worse than she.

With a sigh, Crook laced his fingers together on the desk in front of him, and looked at his clasped hands instead of at her as he said, "I have some bad news."

"Yes, I know." She was inwardly pleased that she sounded so calm and composed.

"Your husband was shot three days ago. It occurred while the troops were leaving the Mogollon. Most of the Coyoteros had surrendered. But apparently a few diehards remained. Captain Cronin speculates that it was one of those that shot your husband."

"Is he dead?"

"I . . . don't know. He wasn't two days ago, when the captain left him, and the other seriously wounded, at a camp just south of the mountains."

"He's not dead." She wanted to be sure she'd heard correctly.

"He wasn't two days ago. But I won't withhold anything from you. You have the right to know everything. According to Captain Cronin, he was in a very bad way. The post surgeon, Dr. Lee, did not hold out much hope, I'm afraid."

She stared at Crook, waiting for a flood of emotion to wash over her, threatening to sweep her away, and trying to brace herself for it. But nothing happened. She didn't feel any differently from how she had a moment before. All she could think about was that her husband had been alive two days ago—and he might still be alive. So there was hope. The general did not seem to have any. The doctor and the captain might not have had any. But she was going to cling to her hope until she knew for a fact that Joshua was dead.

"At any rate," said Crook, made more uncomfortable by her inscrutable silence, "I intend to leave first thing in the morning, with a contingent of troops, with wagons, to make for that encampment and to return the wounded here. Captain Cronin informs me that those soldiers who, um, who died have been buried in the field. But, um, if your husband has passed away, I will bring his remains back here to you, if that's your wish."

"Where are the men who rode with my husband?"

"They remained behind, at the encampment."

"Then I ask that you take me with you."

Crook was completely unprepared for that request. "Well, I . . . I don't know. Your husband's request was that you be kept safe here until he returned."

"But he may not return, General. If he is dying, I want to be with him in his last moments. And if he is dead, I want to be there to bury him."

"Of course." Crook thought it over. Her request was a legitimate one—and it was also one he could not bring himself to deny. "We leave in the morning, then."

She stood, thanked him from the bottom of her heart, and left the room. Somewhat in awe, Crook watched her go, thinking that she was one hell of a woman, and that Barlow had been one very lucky man.

Then he realized that he was thinking about Joshua Barlow in the past tense.

Chapter 30

He came out of nowhere, and in a split second had killed two men—one of them the trooper who'd been riding stirrup-to-stirrup alongside Summerhayes. Killed him with a bullet to the head, and the lieutenant suddenly found himself splattered with blood and brains. The corpse slid sideways out of the saddle, spooking the horse under Summerhayes, and for an instant it was all he could do to stay aboard. Then it registered that the killer was an Apache. And Summerhayes had been in enough scrapes with Apaches to know that he'd be better off fighting on foot. Yanking the carbine that rode in a scabbard under his right leg, he threw that leg over the horse's neck and slid to the ground on the left side.

It took him a moment to figure out what was happening. They had been riding north toward the Mogollons, having left Fort Union that morning, and had made good time, without problems of any kind. There was a storm brewing off to the west—angry black clouds and bolts of lightning accompanied by peals of thunder rolling across the desert plain—but Summerhayes thought the storm was moving north, and would pass them by. General Crook, himself, Oulay, and four troopers were on horseback. They were fol-

lowed by three wagons, each with a driver and a
trooper riding shotgun. They hadn't been expecting
trouble—the only renegade bronchos now remaining
on the loose in this part of the country were the Coyotero diehards, and they were holed up in the mountains. This particular Apache war was practically over.

Yet Summerhayes had no doubt that the man who
had literally risen up out of the ground was an
Apache. And the most remarkable aspect of the whole
business was that he was on his horse when he did it.
Both man and horse had been lying in a shallow hole
just a few yards away, covered by a thin film of sand.
Summerhayes knew that some Indians, and even a few
white men, were able to coax their mounts to stretch
out on their sides and lay relatively still; in a country
where quite often the only cover was a scattering of
sagebrush, this was a good way to stay out of sight, if
you could manage it. The lieutenant was also aware
that burying oneself in a shallow hole and covering up
with a layer of dirt was a common Apache ambush
tactic; in this way, they would wait until their prey
was almost upon them before springing the trap. But
he'd never heard nor seen of an Apache burying his
horse right along with himself.

The Apache and his horse had exploded out of the
ground not a stone's throw away, and the broncho
had immediately starting firing his rifle, killing the two
troopers nearest Summerhayes. Up ahead were Crook
and Oulay, riding side by side, preceded by two more
cavalrymen. The first of the three wagons, which followed single file, was no more than twenty yards behind Summerhayes. One of the troopers back there
was already shooting, and the lieutenant thought he
ought to do the same. He looked around for more
Apaches. But there weren't any more. At least none
that he could see. Just the one—and even as he swung

his rifle around to draw a bead on the broncho, he saw that the Apache had already reached Oulay and the general, and realized he had to hold his fire for fear of hitting either of them. Summerhayes assumed the Apache's target was Crook. Instinctively he began to run to the general's aid, hoping for a clear shot, and willing to take on the broncho hand-to-hand if necessary, regardless of the fact that his left arm was still in a sling.

But he didn't get the chance to tangle with the broncho. Seeing that the general, quick to recover from his surprise, was drawing a saber, the Apache struck him with the butt of his rifle, a blow delivered with such force that it sent Crook somersaulting backward out of the saddle. Then the Apache wrapped an arm around Oulay's waist and dragged her from her horse. Wheeling his pony around, he let out a wild shout of triumph and rode away.

It had all happened so quickly that the only trooper in the column who'd gotten off a shot was one of the men on the wagons. The two cavalrymen in the lead had just turned their horses as the broncho grabbed Oulay; now they brought their carbines up, about to fire at the fleeing enemy. But Summerhayes, concerned for Oulay, shouted at them to hold their fire. In that same instant, he reached Crook's side—and was relieved to see that the general was alive and conscious.

The wind knocked out of him, Crook clutched at his chest. "Don't worry about me," he wheezed. "Get after him, damn it!"

Summerhayes caught up the nearest horse—it happened to be Crook's—and leaped into the saddle. "Follow me!" he shouted at the two cavalrymen, and raked his spurs across the animal's flanks. It lunged into a gallop and he took off after the Apache with the pair of troopers right behind.

Kiannatah tried to guide his horse with one hand and hold on to Oulay with the other. But she was struggling to escape his grasp, and in exasperation he threw her across the horse's neck in front of him and struck her twice with his fist in the back of the head. This brutality knocked her senseless, and she lay limp, facedown.

A quick glance over the shoulder told him that the soldiers were in pursuit. He was surprised by this, thinking that the suddenness of his attack, and his killing of two cavalrymen, would have dissuaded the rest from wanting to continue the fight. Besides, it wasn't as though he had taken a white woman. Oulay was an Apache—so why were the yellow-legs chasing him?

He wasn't unduly alarmed by this development, however, being entirely confident that he could elude the soldiers and, failing that, kill them if he had to.

The situation could not quell the fierce elation swelling in his breast. He had Oulay once more in his possession! After days of watching the fort while avoiding discovery—no small feat—his chance had finally come. Having dismissed the option of trying to infiltrate the fort and take her out as one doomed to fail, he'd had no recourse but to wait until she emerged. And when she did emerge, he'd made his move, undeterred by the fact that she was accompanied by nearly a dozen soldiers.

Once he'd ascertained that they were traveling north, toward the mountains, he'd circled wide around to get in front of them. Then it was simply a matter of picking his spot. This had to be a place he could be sure the soldiers would pass close by. That the soldiers were traveling with wagons helped—they would choose the route that was easiest for these conveyances. He found his place soon enough—a narrow valley passing between a pair of low, rocky ridges beyond which, on either side, was rough ground. Kiannatah was confident the soldiers would pass through the valley, and there he set his trap.

Riding south by west, Kiannatah came to a shallow arroyo. His limber pony had no difficulty in negotiating it, even though there was a foot of fast-running water in the bottom. This was a development Kiannatah had not expected. It was raining hard just to the west of him—he could smell the rain on the still, lightning-charged air. In such a situation, the arroyos could become death traps, as they were prone to flooding. The horse beneath him struggled mightily to carry his double load up the steep embankment and, a moment later, was galloping across the flats again. Another glance revealed to Kiannatah that the soldiers were still a thousand yards behind him. Too far for an effective rifle shot, especially from the back of a hard-running horse.

The chase went on for several more miles. Kiannatah felt the pony beneath him begin to slow. It was barely perceptible, but he knew he wasn't imagining it. He could only hope that the cavalrymen's mounts were tiring even more quickly. Two more arroyos had blocked his path—in both cases there was hock-deep water in the bottoms. Both times his horse plunged down one embankment and struggled mightily up the other. And both times he looked back to see the three soldiers pursuing him successfully negotiate the arroyos.

He was beginning to think that he would have to turn and fight, when he came abruptly upon a fourth arroyo.

Just as he was about to kick his pony into a leap down the embankment, he saw out of the corner of his eye a raging flash flood—a wall of churning brown water, filled with debris, surging down the arroyo from the west. He checked the pony so sharply that it sat down on its haunches. The edge of the flood swept past him, instantly filling the arroyo completely. Making a snap decision, Kiannatah turned the horse and kicked it into a gallop, riding along the arroyo as though he were trying to get ahead of the fast-moving floodwaters.

He glanced left—and what he saw drew a curse from his lips. The three soldiers were gaining on him now, for they were angling across the flats to intercept him.

He looked right—and could see the edge of the flood tumbling down the arroyo. Could he get far enough ahead of the waters to actually make it across to the other side? If so, he would escape; the yellow-legs would have no choice but to call off the pursuit.

But then two things happened simultaneously that ruined any chance he might have had to outrace the flood. Oulay began to regain consciousness—and the soldiers began shooting at him.

Kiannatah could not shoot back. He had to prevent Oulay from throwing herself off the horse. He could only hope that the soldiers would be unable to hit their mark from atop galloping mounts.

His luck ran out.

He felt the pony shudder beneath him as the bullet struck, and in the next instant, he was flying through the air. The impact of the ground knocked the wind out of him. Landing on his side, he rolled, gasping for air. His horse was down, thrashing, and he knew it would never get up again. Oulay lay between him and the horse, some ten paces away. His rifle was with the horse—too far away for him to get to before the soldiers were upon him. All he had was a pistol stuck under his belt. The soldiers were still shooting at him. With bold contempt for the bullets burning the air around him, he stood up straight and started for Oulay, because she was beginning to stir.

Summerhayes saw this too. He and the troopers were no more than a hundred fifty yards away from their quarry now. The Netdahe's behavior alarmed him. Instead of shooting at them, or staying low to provide a smaller target, the Apache was walking toward Oulay. The lieutenant shouted at her to stay down. Perhaps she couldn't hear him over the roar of the floodwaters in the arroyo directly behind her. She straightened, saw the Netdahe's approach, and turned to run.

"Kill him!" Summerhayes shouted at the troopers, even as he levered another round into his repeater and fired at the broncho. The troopers with him fired almost simultaneously, and he experienced a brief surge of triumph as the Apache was spun around by the impact of at least one bullet. The Netdahe staggered, but didn't fall. He raised the pistol—and Summerhayes almost choked on the horror that filled him as he realized what the broncho was about to do. He shouted again—something incoherent—and watched helplessly as the Netdahe shot Oulay in the back. She was thrown forward, and in the next instant the broncho was gone, falling—or did he jump?—into the racing, churning brown water that filled the arroyo.

Chapter 31

When Manuel returned from the fields, he did so at a run, his face radiant with delight, for he had managed to snare a rabbit, and he was quite pleased with himself. It was not often that he managed to contribute to his mother's never-ending struggle to keep food on the table. But today was different, and he thought she would be very proud of him.

As he drew near his home, Manuel saw two saddle horses tied to the uprights of the ramada that stood adjacent to the adobe. He slowed to a walk—and then broke into a run again. This time, though, it was concern for his mother that prompted his haste. Reaching the doorway, he paused to let his eyes adjust from the brightness of the sun to the dimness of the interior. Two men sat at the table. His mother crossed the room quickly to put an arm around his shoulders.

"Manuel," she said softly, "your father has returned."

Manuel looked up into her face. He understood what she was saying, but the way she said it puzzled him. Often he had dreamed of this moment. But in those dreams it was a moment of intense joy. His mother seemed more apprehensive than joyful, however, and he wondered why.

He turned his attention to the two men. One of them was a gringo. A big, bearded man, wearing a soiled gray tunic and buckskin trousers. This was not his father. The second man, then, had to be the one. But Manuel did not recognize him. He was slender, with a dark, hawkish, even cruel face. The man—no, not just a man, his father, Manuel reminded himself—was peering at him with such intensity that the boy felt uncomfortable under the unblinking scrutiny. He wondered why his father did not say anything. Did not come to him with open arms. Yet Manuel was not hurt by this failure on his father's part to display the emotion one might expect from someone reunited with his family after many years' absence. In fact, he was relieved that the man—his father—was keeping his distance.

The other man, though, was a great deal more effusive. "Well I'll be damned, hombre," he said, staring at Manuel but addressing Manuel's father. "So this here is your rug rat." He grinned at Angeline. "You'll have to pardon me, ma'am. I'm just surprised as all get-out. I've done rode with this man for more'n two winters now, and not once did he see fit to tell me he had a wife and son."

"He did not see fit to tell us if he was alive or dead," said Angeline, and the anger underlining her words made Manuel glance up into her face again.

She spoke in Spanish, and Coughlin looked to his companion. "What did she say?"

The Mexican simply shook his head.

"Where have you been?" Angeline asked him. "What have you been doing all this time?"

"It is none of your business," he replied gruffly.

"I am your wife, so it *is* my business." She waited, watching him, expecting an answer—and getting none. "Then why have you come back now?"

Coughlin couldn't understand much of what was being said, but he could tell that the woman was agitated, and that his partner—though he didn't show it—was getting angry.

"Well," he said, "ain't this one big happy homecoming?"

Having spent most of her life in a border town, Angeline understood some English. She was also a very good judge of character. One had to be to survive in this country. There was something about the gringo that troubled her. That made her afraid for her son's welfare. And there was something about her husband that made her afraid too. He was not the same man who had left her years ago.

Abruptly, she turned and herded Manuel outside. She took his hand and started walking briskly away from the adobe.

"Mama, where are we going?" he asked.

She did not answer him, and it was all he could do to keep up with her as she strode down the single street of Santo Domingo.

Coughlin got up and went to the adobe's doorway, watched Angeline marching her son away down the dusty street.

"Not exactly the welcome you expected, I guess," he murmured. He didn't expect a response. "Still, I can see why you left this godforsaken place."

"Go, if you want," said the Mexican.

Coughlin grunted. "Go where? We don't have any money. In case you've forgotten, we spent every last peso we got for them scalps. Reckon this is as good a place as any to hole up until I can figure out what to do next." He was quiet a moment, scanning the sleepy town. "What we need," he added, finally, "is another good harvest of scalps. Only problem is, the nearest Apaches are up in the Arizona Territory, and that neck of the woods isn't healthy for us now. That leaves the heathens hiding out in the Sierra Madre. And even I'm not crazy enough to go up in there."

The Mexican was on his feet now, searching the adobe. Coughlin watched him for a while, mildly curious. Eventually the Mexican sat down again, looking disgusted.

"No pulque. Nothing."

"We can change that," said Coughlin, confidently.

"How?"

Leaning against the doorframe, Coughlin gazed out at Santo Domingo. "I have a few ideas," he said.

Leaving her son with friends, Angeline reluctantly returned to her home. She was confused. Having expected to be overwhelmed with joy on the occasion of her husband's return, she found herself, instead, wishing he had stayed away forever. And she was angry too—angry at him for being gone so long, and then returning without an explanation for his absence. As a border town resident, she had seen more than her share of bad men, and she could tell in a glance that the gringo fell into that category. Unfortunately, so did her husband.

In the days to come, it became evident that the people of Santo Domingo had the same impression about Angeline's husband and his Anglo companion. In the way of campesinos, they remained watchful while staying more or less out of sight. Those who spoke to Angeline—and most stayed away from her, as well—wanted to know just one thing. When would her husband and his companero leave? Angeline had no answer for them.

The gringo *did* leave a few days after his arrival, but he made it plain that he would not be away long. Angeline's husband remained behind. With the gringo

gone, he took the opportunity to make love to his
wife. Angeline wasn't interested, but she submitted.
He did not tell her that he loved her, or that he had
missed her during his absence; he simply used her, as
though it was his right, and without any regard for
her feelings. It was then that Angeline realized how
much she hated this man. Perhaps, she thought, she
had hated him even before his return. She wasn't
sure—for the longest time she had tried not to think
about him at all.

Eventually she worked up the nerve to ask him
what he intended to do. He would tell her nothing.
She wondered how long this situation could continue.
She missed Manuel, but did not dare let him come
home. Her husband did not seem to even notice that
his son was absent. He didn't ask after Manuel, and
while Angeline was relieved by his lack of interest in
their son, she was also angered by his indifference.

The gringo returned after nearly a week away. He
brought two jugs of pulque with him. That night, he
and Angeline's husband got drunk. They spent hours
in whispered conversation at the table, while she lay
in bed, pretending to sleep while straining to catch
any word or phrase. She heard the name of a village
that was located a day's ride to the west. But that was
all. The next morning, her husband and the gringo,
whose name she now knew as Coughlin, rode away,
without explanation. Watching them go, she hoped
that it was the last that she would see of either of
them. But she doubted it.

They were gone for more than a week, this time,
and as the days passed the other inhabitants of Santo
Domingo grew hopeful that they were gone for good.
But Angeline could not rid herself of the suspicion
that they would return. At least she had a respite—
and at least she was with her son again, for Manuel

could come home. He suggested that they go away.
The thought had crossed her mind. But where would
they go? She had no place to run to. Santo Domingo
was her home, and she knew next to nothing about
the world beyond the horizon—only that it was a dangerous place, where a woman alone with her young
son would likely not survive for very long.

Then her husband and his friend came back.
Angeline immediately sent Manuel away, with instructions to remain at the home of her friends until she
sent for him. The gringo had brought more pulque.
And pesos. A whole bag of money. In his drunkenness
that night, her husband promised to buy her a new
dress. Angeline knew this was a lie. She decided that
her husband and his friend were robbers. It was not
possible to earn so much money in so short a time
with honest work.

The soldiers came a few days later. The captain who
led the small detachment was someone she
recognized—Cordova, the one who had come here,
months before, with the French officer who was responsible for the deaths of several of her neighbors.

Watching the soldiers coming down the street of
Santo Domingo, Coughlin turned from the doorway
and, seeing that Angeline stood at the window, also
watching, went up to her and put the barrel of his
pistol to her temple. Her husband was sleeping off the
previous night's drunken binge, and did not stir. Not
that it would have mattered had he been awake,
thought Angeline. He would not have protested
Coughlin's actions. By now it had become clear to her
that the gringo was the one who made the decisions.

"I know you speak some English," murmured
Coughlin. "So you listen close. If they ask you about
us, you tell 'em we've been ridin' out lookin' for work.
Comprende?"

She nodded, trying to conceal her elation. The gringo was a fool, she thought. The captain would have to be an even bigger fool to believe such a story. Surely he would be able to take one look at Coughlin and know, as she had, that he was trouble.

After speaking to a handful of villagers farther down the street, Cordova turned and made for her adobe. Coughlin pushed her across the threshold. He brushed past her and sauntered over to the ramada, where he leaned against an upright and watched the captain while picking his teeth with a wood splinter. Angeline heard her husband move to the doorway behind her. Both her husband and Coughlin had their pistolas—they were always armed, day or night.

"Senora," said Cordova, bowing slightly at Angeline, an amiable smile on his face, "we meet again. I am pleased to see you well. How is your boy?"

"He is well, thank you, Captain."

Cordova glanced at the Mexican behind her, then at Coughlin. The smile remained fixed on his face, but it had lost much of its warmth. "I am told you have company. *Mucho gusto, señores*."

"Howdy," said Coughlin.

"This is my husband," said Angeline, gesturing behind her. "And that is his friend."

"Ah, I see," said Cordova. "Your husband has come home. *Bueno*. Where have you been all this time, senor?"

"North of the border," said the Mexican, "if it's any business of yours."

"That's fine," said Cordova. "Then you are not a Juárista, after all."

"No. Who said I was?"

Cordova shrugged. "It does not matter. I believe you. I am not here looking for Juáristas, anyway."

"Then why are you here, Captain?" asked Coughlin.

"Someone has been killing and robbing people in this area."

"There is killing and robbing everywhere in Mexico these days, I hear."

"Sadly, it is true. But these cases are different. The victims, most of them have been scalped."

"Now why would anybody scalp a Mexican?" asked Coughlin. "I thought there was only a bounty on Apache scalps. That's what I've been told, anyway."

"*Sí.* The people here, they say you have left the village a few times. Where do you go?"

"My pardner and I are looking for work," said Coughlin. "Not having much luck, I'm afraid."

"There is not much work to be found," said Cordova, as though he fully sympathized, "unless you are good with a gun. Maybe you should look north of the border, senor."

"There's a war goin' on with the Apaches north of the border. Me, I like to steer clear of that kind of thing."

"And there is a war going on down here too."

"Well, my saddle pard and I just want to stay out of trouble, Captain," said Coughlin. "We're what you might call a couple of peace-lovin' wayfarers."

Cordova nodded. "Yes, I can see that." He cast a long, speculative look at Angeline, then bowed again. "Senora, I wish you well."

"Thank you, Captain." She wanted to cry out to him, to tell him that her husband and the gringo were the men he was searching for. There wasn't a doubt in her mind that they were the ones who had committed the crimes Cordova had described. But she was afraid. Afraid mostly for Cordova, because she did not doubt that Coughlin or her husband would kill the captain without hesitation. Afraid too for her son, because they would probably kill her too. And what would become of Manuel with her gone?

So she did not cry out—instead, she watched the captain turn and return along the street to where his dragoons waited. Coughlin stayed where he was, and so did her husband, and together they watched until the soldiers were mounted and riding out of Santo Domingo. Seeing this, Angeline felt almost overcome with despair.

"Get inside," said the Mexican.

She turned on him, anger surging within her, overcoming the fear. "You bastard!" she said, nearly breathless with rage. "You are a thief and a murderer. You are a scalphunter!"

He grabbed her by the hair and pulled her across the threshold, and once inside the adobe, he threw her to the floor. She tried to crawl away but he reached down and yanked her to her feet—only to strike with a backhanded blow that sent her reeling.

Lounging in the doorway, Coughlin chuckled. "Better be careful there, missy. You go saying such things to other folks, you might end up eating dirt."

Again Angeline tried to crawl away. This time, her husband made no effort to stop her. She ended up with her back to a wall. Pulling her knees up, she wiped the blood from her lip and glared at the gringo, her eyes wide and bright like a hunted animal's.

"I know she's your wife and all, amigo," Coughlin, grinning, told the Mexican. "But if we have to kill her, I say we take her scalp. Nobody could tell it ain't an Apache topknot."

The Mexican simply grunted, and went in search of a pulque jug. Still grinning, Coughlin glanced at her, winked, and went back outside.

Chapter 32

When Barlow came to, he did so abruptly. His eyes snapped open and he inhaled sharply, like someone coming to the surface after too long underwater. Summerhayes, slack in a chair and dozing, nearly jumped out of his skin. As Barlow sat up in bed, Summerhayes shot to his feet. The effort to speak was painful for Barlow. He put a hand to his throat and Summerhayes took a cup of water from the bedside table and handed it to him. As he sipped from the cup, Barlow took in his surroundings. He was home.

"How did I get here?" he asked hoarsely.

"We brought you," said Summerhayes. "In an army wagon. Me and several of your vaqueros."

Barlow felt a constriction as he tried to draw a deep breath, and looked down to see the dressing that completely covered his upper torso. "What happened? Was I shot?"

"You don't remember?"

"Not really. Last thing I remember was riding in the Mogollons. We were bringing the Coyoteros out."

Summerhayes nodded. "That's right. And you got shot. Nobody ever saw who did it. Probably one of the Coyotero bronchos who refused to give up."

Barlow felt the dressing wrapped tightly around his chest. "It was bad."

"Very. There for a while, they weren't sure you would live."

Barlow started putting two and two together—realizing that it must have taken Summerhayes and the vaqueros several days to transport him here from the Mogollons if they'd put him in a wagon.

"How long ago did this happen?"

"Twelve days ago."

Barlow was shocked. He'd lost nearly two weeks of his life, lying unconscious from the gunshot wound. Hovering, apparently, between life and death.

"Where is Oulay?"

It was the question Summerhayes had been dreading. The one he'd been trying for days now to prepare for. He'd come up with a dozen ways to break the news to his friend, but there was no good way. Despite all the preparation, at this crucial moment, he failed miserably.

"She's . . . outside," he muttered.

Barlow swung his legs off the bed. He saw that he was wearing the bottom half of his long johns, and looked around for trousers.

"Don't get up," said Summerhayes, alarmed. "The doctor said you needed to stay down for at least a month."

"A month!" Barlow laughed—then winced, because it hurt too badly to laugh. "Not likely. Find me some pants."

"Joshua . . ."

"I'll find them myself, then."

"Be still," sighed Summerhayes. He dug in the trunk at the foot of the bed, found some trousers, and helped Barlow put them on. Amused, Barlow watched him work.

"You'd make a fine nurse, Charles."

Summerhayes didn't respond to the good-natured comment. He doubted that, after today, he'd find anything amusing ever again.

Once he had his pants on, Barlow stood up. The room tilted and began to spin, but he got a good grip on a bedpost and held on until the spinning stopped. His entire chest hurt like hell—he couldn't recall ever hurting quite this much. But he wasn't going to give in. He wanted to see Oulay, and he thought it would do them both a lot of good if he was standing when he did. Shaking off a solicitous hand from Summerhayes, he started for the door.

"Joshua . . ."

"What?"

Still, Summerhayes couldn't tell him—and cursed himself for a coward.

As soon as Barlow stepped out of the adobe, Mendez and another vaquero, who had been standing in front of the bunkhouse across the sun-hammered hardpack, saw him and started forward. Summerhayes motioned them off. Barlow saw none of this—he was momentarily blinded by the bright sun.

"Where is she?" he asked Summerhayes.

"In back," said the other, his tone dull and lifeless.

Barlow steeled himself, tried to forget the pain that every movement brought forth, and stepped around the adobe. Summerhayes followed, and noticed that Mendez and the other vaquero were just standing there in the middle of the hardpack, watching. They knew what was about to happen.

Leaning against the adobe at the back corner, trying to catch his breath, Barlow looked around. He didn't see Oulay, and turned to throw a quizzical glance at Summerhayes.

"Where?" he gasped.

Summerhayes bleakly pointed.

Barlow looked in the direction his friend was pointing—saw the fresh grave in the small cemetery where the vaqueros were buried. But it didn't register. He thought it was the grave of the vaquero who had been killed in the Mogollons.

"She's dead," said Summerhayes. "A Netdahe killed her."

All the life seemed to flood right out of Barlow. He sagged against the adobe as his knees almost gave out under him. "No," he said. "No."

"We thought you were dying. She asked General Crook to bring her to you. He agreed. We were less than a day out of Fort Union when the Netdahe came out of nowhere. He killed two troopers, and grabbed Oulay. We went after him. When we caught up with him, he . . . shot her."

"No," breathed Barlow, his tone one of pleading.

"I'm sorry, Joshua," said Summerhayes, nearly in tears. "I . . . I, for one, never thought he would do that. If it's any consolation, he's dead. Well, we shot him, and he fell into a flash flood that carried him away. We searched for the body, couldn't find it. But I'm sure he's dead."

Barlow seemed about to fall to the ground, and Summerhayes stepped forward quickly, reaching out to him, but Barlow savagely struck the helping hands away. "No," he sobbed and, through the exercise of supreme will over physical weakness, pushed away from the adobe and staggered like a drunken man toward the cemetery. Once there he fell to his knees beside the fresh grave.

As Summerhayes was about to go to him, Mendez and the other vaquero appeared. The former took one look at Barlow and laid a hand on the lieutenant's shoulder to stay him.

"Leave him be," said Mendez gruffly.

"I'm afraid," said Summerhayes, in a stricken voice, "afraid this will kill him."

"We will see, in time."

Summerhayes sat on his heels at the back corner of the adobe, prepared to watch over his friend for as long as it took. Mendez led the other vaquero away.

He returned several hours later, as the shadows of night began stretching across the desert, to find Summerhayes right where he'd left him. Barlow was sprawled across Oulay's grave, unmoving. Mendez handed the lieutenant a cup of steaming hot coffee, which Summerhayes gratefully accepted.

"He hasn't moved for a while," he said, agonized. "I don't know if he's still breathing."

Mendez sank down on his haunches alongside Summerhayes. "I have seen a loss like this kill a man. But the padrone, he is strong."

Summerhayes could tell that, in spite of his confident words, Mendez was worried too.

"I just wish there was something I could do," he said.

"Just be here. This is a fight the padrone must wage alone."

"I . . . I feel responsible."

"The Netdahe is the one who was responsible," said Mendez.

"But I keep thinking—if we hadn't given chase, maybe it wouldn't have turned out the way it did. Maybe he wouldn't have killed her."

"He would have. Because she would never have stayed with him. He would have *had* to kill her, sooner or later."

"Yes," said Summerhayes morosely. "I suppose you're right."

And so it went for the next twenty-four hours—

Barlow prostrate across Oulay's grave, and Summerhayes maintaining a vigil, sometimes with Mendez, sometimes with one or more of the other vaqueros. The loyalty to Barlow displayed by all the vaqueros did not escape the lieutenant's attention. They were as concerned for the padrone as if he were their blood kin.

That night a storm passed through, with plenty of thunder and lightning, and a hard downpour. Summerhayes wanted to try to coax Barlow inside or, at the very least, cover him with blankets or a tarpaulin. But once again Mendez restrained him. Solicitude would do more harm than good, he said. Draping a blanket over his head, Summerhayes stayed at the corner of the adobe, enduring the miserable night as best he could, but without a thought to his own comfort. To seek shelter would be akin to abandoning his friend, and this he would not do.

Somehow, he managed to doze off in the early-morning hours. The slanting sunlight of dawn brought him awake. He was surprised—pleasantly so—to see that Barlow was now sitting up. He remained beside the grave most of the day. Summerhayes considered this an improvement; at the very least he could see in a glance whether Barlow was still alive or not.

Then, abruptly, a couple of hours prior to sundown, Barlow got to his feet. A vaquero had just brought Summerhayes a cup of coffee, and was sitting on his heels beside the lieutenant to keep an eye on the padrone for a while. When Barlow stood the vaquero shot to his feet. Summerhayes tried to get up too but his legs were asleep, and the vaquero had to give him a hand. By this time Barlow was heading for them. Summerhayes was struck by how different Barlow's appearance was. His cheeks were gaunt, his eyes seemed sunk deep in their sockets. Worst of all, his eyes had lost their warmth. They were like chips of blue ice.

"I need a saddle horse. And load as many provisions as you can on a packhorse."

"*Sí*, Padrone." The vaquero was grinning. He was just happy to see Barlow back among the living. He took off at a run to comply with the padrone's commands.

"How about some coffee?" Summerhayes offered his cup.

"No."

"Food. then. You haven't eaten in a while."

"No."

Barlow continued around the side of the adobe, stopping at the wooden table, where a basin of water was kept. He washed the mud of the grave from his face. Leaning heavily on the table, he watched the mud blacken the water in the basin.

"I should change that dressing," said Summerhayes, concerned by the condition of Barlow's bandages, which were not only dirty, but soaking wet as well.

"Forget it." Barlow noticed that Mendez and Rodrigo and a few other vaqueros were coming across from the bunkhouse. He gazed blankly at them for a moment, then turned as though to enter the adobe. But he stopped well shy of the threshold. He could not bring himself to go inside.

With a sigh, Summerhayes asked him what he needed from inside. The answer—boots, a shirt, a rifle, and a pistol. The lieutenant went into the adobe, collected the items requested, and brought them out to Barlow. By this time the saddle horse had been delivered—a moment later another horse arrived, this one wearing a packsaddle laden with bags of coffee and flour and beans, and a pair of leather mochillas bulging with ammunition. Barlow donned the boots and the shirt, strapped on a gun belt, placed the rifle in a saddle scabbard.

"Where are you going, Joshua?" asked Summerhayes.

Barlow didn't answer. He didn't seem to hear.

"If you're going after the man who killed Oulay," continued Summerhayes, "I told you—he's dead."

Barlow looked at him. "You see the body?"

"No, but . . ."

"It doesn't matter anyway," said Barlow curtly. "There are more like him."

"So you plan to wage war against all the Netdahe renegades? You'll never make it back."

"I don't plan on coming back." Barlow stepped into the saddle, wincing at the pain in his chest. Once astride the horse, he took a moment to catch his breath, then bleakly scanned the faces of the vaqueros. "Take as many of the cattle as you want." He sat there, looking at them for a moment longer, and Summerhayes expected him to say something that spoke to his long association with these loyal and hardworking men. Instead, he nodded curtly, and turned his horse to ride away.

Summerhayes quickly stepped forward, grabbed the bridle on Barlow's horse. "I'll go along with you," he said.

"No. Get back to Fort Union before Cronin decides to court-martial you. So long, Charles."

Summerhayes let go of the bridle. As he watched Barlow ride south, Mendez came up to stand alongside him.

"That's the last we'll see of him," said the lieutenant sadly. "He'll never come back here. He's going to make war against the Netdahe. And sooner or later they'll kill him." He glanced at the vaquero. "Maybe I should have tried to stop him."

Mendez shook his head. He was trying very hard to mask his own sadness. "You could not stop him, senor. No one could."

"It killed him," murmured Summerhayes, more to himself than to Mendez. "I knew it would."

"No, senor," said the vaquero. "He lived for her. But now that she is gone, he has something else to live for. When the Netdahe killed her, he created another just like himself. Now the padrone is like the Netdahe."

Chapter 33

After two weeks Kiannatah thought that he might perhaps live.

When he'd stepped into the arroyo's floodwaters, he had been certain of death. Had welcomed the prospect. Now that Oulay was dead—dead by his own hand—he had lost the will to live. Momentarily, at least—not even his lifelong thirst for revenge against the enemies of the Chi-hinne was able to sustain him at that moment.

But Death would not take him. He had lost consciousness as the flood carried him away—and awakened to find that his body had been snagged by an ironwood tree that had fallen into the arroyo, its roots firmly anchored in the embankment. His body was entangled in such a way that his head and shoulders remained above the floodwaters. He used the tree to extricate himself, and lay there for the remainder of the day, oblivious to the lightning and the thunder and the sheets of cold rain that pelted him as the storm passed over.

Many hours later he moved again. It was night, and the storm was gone, and by moonlight he saw an outcropping of rock not far away. He tried to stand, but didn't have the strength, so he crawled, and while the distance was but a few hundred yards, the journey took him the whole night. He reached the outcropping as the eastern sky began to turn gray with the dawn; he climbed up into the rocks as the sun rose higher in the sky. In his vulnerable state he found its heat unbearable, and looked for shelter from it. Eventually he found a space, no more than a foot high, beneath a slab of stone. Into the shade of this crevice he crawled—and passed out.

When he came to, he checked his wound. The yellow-leg's bullet had caught him right below the rib cage on the right side. He coughed into his hand and saw no blood; the slug had missed vital organs. But he could already feel a fever. The bullet was still within him. He felt his back for an exit wound, and found none. He did, however, find an extremely painful, swollen spot, about two inches in diameter. He knew what that meant—the bullet might be right below the skin.

Kiannatah did not have the strength or resolve to deal with the bullet at that time. Instead, he slept, waking every now and then just long enough to take stock of his surroundings before going back to sleep. Several days passed. He had nothing to eat except a snake that happened into his grasp; like him, it explored the shadows of the crevice as a possible sanctuary from the heat of the midday sun. Instead of sanctuary, it found death. He killed it with one stroke of his besh, or knife, slicing off the serpent's head. He slit the snake's belly open from stem to stern and ravenously ate the raw flesh.

That same day he felt strong enough to cut his own flesh, making an incision with the point of his knife into the swelling on his back. The pain was excruciating, and he almost blacked out. The cut made, he used

both hands to squeeze the bullet out. There was a
great deal of bleeding, which he stanched with hand-
fuls of hot, sterile sand packed into the open wound.
That done, he allowed himself to pass out.

Eight days after crawling into the crevice, Kiannatah
emerged from the rock outcropping. He was able to
walk out. But he was still weak—and very thirsty. He
needed water desperately, and returned to the arroyo.
The floodwaters had long receded, and days of hot
sun had dried up what remained. But he climbed down
into the arroyo and found a low place where the sand
was still damp. He dug for hours, until he had a small
pool of brackish brown water from which to drink. He
stayed nearby the rest of the day, drinking his fill.
That night he left the arroyo and headed south. His
destination was the Sierra Madre. He had lost all his
weapons except a rifle and the knife. But for a Netdahe, that was enough.

Cochise awoke in his jacal, in the middle of the
night, with the blade of a knife at his throat, to see
the shadow of a man looming over him. The man had
an arm wrapped around his wife's neck, a hand
clasped tightly over her mouth. Her eyes were bright
with fear in the darkness. Initially Cochise thought it
had to be one of the Avowed Killers—perhaps even
Geronimo himself. Who else could slip unseen into
the Chiricahua village, and then into his jacal without
waking him? Cochise thought at that moment that he
was going to die; his one concern was that his woman's
life be spared. But he reminded himself that the Netdahe spared no one.

Then the shadow moved, and Cochise could see the
intruder's features by the faint light cast by the dying
fire's embers. It was Barlow.

"You!" he exclaimed, surprised.

"Be quiet," rasped Barlow. "I bring bad news. Your daughter, Oulay, is dead."

Cochise was stunned. At first he could not—would not—believe that he had heard correctly. But his wife knew the truth; one look at Barlow's face told her that it was. She began to wail, but the sound was muffled by his hand.

"Shut up," growled Barlow.

"Silence, woman!" growled Cochise. He thought he knew Barlow well. Until tonight, he wouldn't have believed that, under any circumstances, Barlow would have posed a threat to his wife. But now, looking at the man's face, he wasn't so sure.

She obeyed as best she could—her grief, too great to stifle altogether, now manifested itself into soft whimpering and crying. Barlow took his hand from her mouth, and the knife from the throat of Cochise, moving back out of the Chiricahua leader's reach. Cochise sat up, buffeted by a bewildering array of emotions—grief and anger chief among them.

"She was killed by a Netdahe," said Barlow, his voice pitched so low that Cochise could scarcely hear him.

"Kiannatah," breathed Cochise. It had to be Kiannatah.

"I don't know," said Barlow flatly. "I wasn't there. The soldiers say whoever it was is dead now. I'm not sure. But it doesn't matter. I'm going to kill them all."

Cochise stared at Barlow. This was not at all the man he had come to know. The death of his beloved daughter cut him deeply, but Cochise could tell that this was as nothing compared to what Oulay's death had done to her husband.

"They will kill you instead," observed the Chiricahua.

Barlow didn't respond. He didn't need to tell Cochise that for him death was no longer a concern. "Where are they to be found?" he asked.

"To the south," replied Cochise. "Scattered throughout the mountains. Some live alone. A dozen or so remain with Geronimo, but I do not know where his camp is."

Barlow nodded. "Fine. I wanted you to know about Oulay. And to tell you to keep your men away from me."

"That might not be possible. Besides, if what you say is true, I will help you fight the Netdahe."

"Fight them if you want," replied Barlow coldly. "Just stay out of my war. And tell your warriors to steer clear of me. I'll kill them too if they get in my way."

The warning issued, he rose and silently slipped out of the jacal.

Cochise could have followed—could have roused the entire camp in seconds. But he didn't. Instead, he put his arms around his wife, and tried to console her.

In the weeks that followed, Barlow killed several lone Apache renegades. Utilizing all the skills he had learned from years in Apacheria, he found the first two, and killed them before they even knew he was there. The first was a long rifle shot, bringing down a lone rider he had happened upon quite by accident. He picked up the second Apache's trail and followed it until, an hour or two after sunset, he happened upon the broncho's camp. The broncho's guard was down. He believed himself safe high up in the Cima Silkq, where no Mexican or White Eyes dared venture. For this reason he had allowed himself to indulge in a jug of tiswin, and so he was well on his way to being drunk when Barlow stepped out of the night shadows.

The broncho stared at the Pinda Lickoyi in disbelief, hesitating a fatal second before dropping the jug and lunging for his rifle. But his coordination and reflexes were fatally impaired by the strong spirits he'd imbibed; Barlow killed him with a single shot through the heart before the broncho could even bring the rifle to bear.

In both cases Barlow ran off the horses and left the corpses for the scavengers to feast on. He knew that sooner or later the tables would turn, and he, the hunter, would become the hunted. In fact, he took steps to hasten the day. He wanted the Netdahe to know that he was after them. Wanted them to come out in search of him. That was why he ran off the horses—in hopes they might return to a larger Netdahe encampment, a silent riderless warning to the other Avowed Killers that something was wrong. And it was why he left the dead exposed, instead of burying the evidence, as one intent on concealing his presence might have done. The circling swarm of buzzards, sure to gather over the death sites, might bring inquisitive Netdahe.

He got his wish. The next Apache he saw almost killed him.

The first warning that he had become the hunted came with a searing pain that took his breath away. He was riding through a steep-sided gulch when it happened, and he looked down to stare at the tip of an arrow jutting out of his shoulder. His right hand and arm were useless—to move them was too agonizing. He managed somehow to stay in the saddle and kicked his horse into a gallop, bending low over the animal's neck to present a smaller target.

He didn't go far. Where the gulch suddenly doglegged, he checked the horse and slid out of the saddle. Clenching his teeth, he grabbed the shaft of the

arrow just above the head with his left hand and
snapped it off. Carving a notch into the shaft at the
broken end, he pulled a .45 caliber shell apart and
poured the gunpowder it contained into the notch.
Setting this alight with a strike-anywhere match, he
drove the broken end of the shaft back through his
shoulder, using a large flat rock like a sledgehammer.
The blazing gunpowder cauterized the exit wound.
Barlow nearly passed out from the pain. When he was
able, he pulled the shaft out of his back. Blood was
pouring down his back, but there was nothing he could
do about that. He assumed the Netdahe would be
coming for him.

That he had been hit by an arrow rather than a
bullet didn't surprise him. Apaches usually did their
hunting with bow and arrow—with which they were
quite proficient, as a rule—in order to save on hard-
to-come-by ammunition. His assailant had probably
been a hunter; still, he couldn't assume the broncho
lacked a firearm. And whether he did or not, the
Apache would be after him. Barlow figured it would
be merely a matter of minutes before the broncho
tracked him down.

He moved quickly, taking off his hat and tossing it
out into the middle of the gulch. Then he shed both
his boots and his trousers. Shoving the top of one boot
into a trouser leg, he filled the leg with dirt and rocks
up to the knee before laying the trousers behind a
pile of rocks so that the trouser leg with the boot
fitted into it jutted out in plain sight. His horse stood
a few yards away, trailing rein leather, watching him.
Barlow went to the animal, but instead of mounting
up, drew the rifle from its scabbard and began to
climb. Sharp rock edges and small cacti cut at his feet.
Barlow's body was so racked with pain already from
his two recent serious wounds that what would other-

wise have been minor nuisance cuts and scrapes on
the soles of his feet were magnified, and stabbed at
his will to go on. He was tired of hurting. But he kept
climbing, despite the fact that he was quickly winded.
Finally he arrived near the rim and settled down in a
space between two boulders, whence he could clearly
see the gulch below. Now all he had to do was wait—
and hope his spur-of-the-moment trap lured the
Apache into the open. All he needed was one clear
shot.

And that was exactly what he got. First he saw an
arrow suddenly seem to sprout from the exposed trouser leg. A few minutes later, the broncho came into
view. He'd fired another arrow into what he'd thought
was his Pinda Lickoyi victim and, detecting no movement, assumed his prey was dead. Barlow waited until
the Apache had crept to within twenty paces of the
rocks that partially concealed the trousers—he dared
not wait until the broncho got closer, for fear his ruse
would be discovered. He drew a bead, squeezed off a
shot. The bullet hit the broncho squarely in the chest
and dropped him. He lay on his back, thrashing for a
moment, then died and was still.

Barlow didn't make the mistake of rushing down to
check his victim—he had no way of being sure that
the Apache had been hunting alone. So he waited for
more than an hour. But even waiting was dangerous.
He'd fired a shot, and a shot could be heard for many
miles in the mountains, and might bring unwanted attention. Eventually he left his place of concealment,
descended the slope, and checked the broncho to
make certain he was dead. Once sure of this, he got
dressed, caught up his horse, which by now had wandered nearly a hundred yards down the gulch, and
rode away.

Chapter 34

When Kiannatah reached the isolated jacal that had once been his home high up in the Cima Silkq, he was surprised at his reaction to seeing the horses in the corral he'd made, long ago, of cedar posts. Someone had moved in during his absence, and while he'd never put much stock in the idea of "home," and had never been possessive of anything save his weapons—and, of course, Oulay—he found himself angered by what he saw as a trespass. This was the place where he had intended to bring the Chiricahua woman he'd kidnapped. Here he had intended to keep her, and live with her; he'd even planned to eschew, at least for the time being, his involvement in raids against the Nakai-Ye and the Pinda Lickoyi. He had thought much of the time he would spend here with Oulay. But he'd never thought of it as something that would last forever. Only death was forever. Yet Oulay had tried to run away, at a moment when he could not have gone after her without being killed by the yellow-leg soldiers. So he'd killed her. It was the one killing he'd committed that he truly regretted. His dreams of the time he would spend with Oulay had included this place—and he resented the fact that an interloper had moved in.

He waited up in the rocks, watching the jacal, until
a man emerged. Kiannatah recognized him. He was
Netdahe—one of the bronchos who had followed Geronimo for a long while. The man collected some
wood from a pile at the side of the jacal, and took
this back inside. Kiannatah's instincts told him that
the man was not alone. So he continued to wait. The
afternoon waned, and the long blue shadows of the night
began to fill in the nooks and crannies of the high
country. Then a boy of about twelve years emerged
from the jacal; he went down to get some water in
a bucket.

Kiannatah waited until darkness had fallen before
moving in. Smoke was wafting from the jacal's smoke
hole; he could smell bread cooking. He was fairly certain that the Netdahe had a woman with him too, and
when he went through the doorway, he was prepared
for this. The Netdahe dived for his rifle, but Kiannatah
was quicker. As the other Apache brought the rifle
around, Kiannatah drove his knife into the man's
chest, turning the blade sideways so that it would pass
easily between the ribs and pierce the heart. The man
died instantly, and Kiannatah plucked the rifle from
his grasp as he fell. The woman—she was an Indian
woman, short and squat, and not Apache—lunged at
Kiannatah without hesitation, brandishing a large
knife. He could not get a shot off in time, so he swung
the butt of the rifle to block the knife stroke, and then
brought the barrel down across the woman's head.
Her knees buckled and she fell in a heap at his feet.
Kiannatah was short on ammunition, so he killed the
woman with a fierce blow to the top of her skull with
the base of the rifle.

Whirling, he saw the boy bolt out of the jacal. Kiannatah picked up the large knife that the woman had
dropped and stepped outside. The boy was quick; he

was already thirty feet away when Kiannatah hurled the knife. Pain from his yet-to-heal wound shot through him even as he threw, and he thought perhaps this was why his aim was off. The knife struck the boy in the back of the thigh. He went down silently; he did not cry out at the pain, and Kiannatah was impressed by that. When he reached the boy, he pulled the blade out, and still the boy did not make a sound. Kiannatah pinned him to the ground, placing the blade to his throat. He could feel the boy's body trembling. His eyes were wide with terror. Kiannatah considered letting him go. In doing so, he would be creating someone just like himself—someone who had watched his family killed before his eyes. Someone who would probably grow up with a thirst for vengeance that could never be slaked, and whose life would be ruled by and, ultimately, destroyed by that thirst. Kiannatah told himself that any hope that the boy might have had for a good life—if it had ever existed—was gone now. He, Kiannatah, had snatched it away. The least he could do was give something back in return.

"Do not be afraid," he said softly. Taking his hand from the boy's chest, he placed it over the frightened eyes. "Life is misery. In death you will have peace forever. Just close your eyes. You will not suffer long."

With a quick, deep stroke, he opened the boy's throat. The boy struggled briefly, clinging to life, and then died. Kiannatah stood up, wiped the blood from the knife on his himper, and walked back into the jacal.

As night fell, Barlow knew he was in trouble. He was suffering chills and fever, and began to think that perhaps the Apache hunter had dipped his arrows into poison. They did this to slow down their prey if the first shot wasn't mortal. Barlow figured that, if this was indeed the case, there would not be enough venom to kill him, but only to make him quite sick. He had been looking for a good place to hole up—not just for one night, but maybe a day or two—when daylight abandoned him. It was then that he saw the smoke. It came from somewhere up ahead, not far away. Proceeding with caution, he came to a ridge line from which he could look down and see a jacal. The moon was just now rising, and he could distinctly see a body lying on the ground some thirty or forty feet from the Apache hut.

There was no doubt in his mind that he had found the hideout of another Netdahe. The Avowed Killers lived like outlaws, isolated from the rest of their people, and often choosing even to spurn their own kind. But the body puzzled him. In this light and at this distance, he could not tell if it was male or female, young or old. He could smell wood smoke, but saw no firelight leaking around the edges of the blanket that draped the jacal's entrance. There were several horses in the corral. So it seemed likely that there was more than one person down there. The question was whether anyone was still alive.

Barlow recognized that the wisest course of action was to hide among the jumble of rocks on the ridge line and wait until morning to see if anyone emerged from the jacal. But he wasn't sure what his condition would be in the morning. He decided to press the issue; leaving his horse on the back side of the ridge, he took his rifle and proceeded down the other slope toward the jacal, intent on resolving the mystery now rather than later.

Reaching the body, he knelt beside it. An Apache boy, whose throat had been cut. Barlow peered at the jacal. He wasn't sure—but had the blanket covering the doorway moved, ever so slightly? Then the moon-

light glimmered off steel. He dived to one side as the
rifle in the doorway spat flame. Immediately he was
up and running, because he'd been caught out in the
open, and the nearest cover was a pile of rocks at the
base of the ridge, where it curved round to one side
of the jacal. The rifle spoke again, and a bullet burned
the air inches from his head. He dived into the rocks,
wincing at the pain that racked his body. Crouched
behind this cover, he fired three shots in quick succes-
sion through the jacal's doorway. The blanket danced
as his bullets tore through it. There was no answering
fire. Barlow waited, taking the opportunity to load the
rifle and to check his pistol to make certain every
chamber housed a bullet. With disgust he noticed that
he was trembling slightly. It was the adrenaline surging
through his body. There was only one way to find out
if the man inside the jacal was still above snakes. Barlow got up and raced for another pile of rocks some
twenty feet along the base of the ridge. No bullets
chased him. He began to think he'd gotten lucky—
that one of his shots had hit its mark.

Inside the jacal, Kiannatah had moved away from
the blanket-draped doorway seconds before the fusillade. In the dim half-light of the jacal's interior, he
checked the rifle. There was one round left. He
glanced at the dead Netdahe. The man might have
had more ammunition stashed somewhere in the jacal,
but Kiannatah sensed that he did not have time to
conduct a search. He had not been able to identify
the intruder in the darkness, but he was pretty sure
the man was a Pinda Lickoyi. He couldn't figure out
how a white man had survived venturing this deeply
into the Sierra Madre; like many other Apaches, Kiannatah had been lulled into believing that the Cima
Silkq was a safe haven that neither Mexican nor
American would dare try to penetrate. He had to as-

sume that there was more than one Pinda Lickoyi out there; no sane white man would come here alone. And sooner rather than later they would charge the jacal. With no ammunition, his chances of fending off an attack by even a few white men were slim.

He crawled to the back of the jacal, leaving the rifle, loaded with its single shell, beside the dead Netdahe, moving to the trap door that gave access to the tunnel that would take him far enough away from the hut so that he could slip into the rocks unseen. As he started to descend into the tunnel he had a thought, and went back to collect the body of the woman. This he dragged through the trap door after him. Leaving the corpse in the tunnel, he began to crawl. It was pitch-black, and the tunnel itself was barely wide enough for his broad shoulders, but Kiannatah wasn't bothered by the momentary sensation of being buried alive. It galled him that he as running away from a fight. This time, though, he had no choice. The one consolation was that, in all likelihood, the white men would assume that the Apache lying dead inside the jacal was the one who had been shooting at them. Thinking this, they would not search for or pursue him. The corpse of the woman, bludgeoned to death, did not fit into the scenario. Neither did the body of the boy he had left outside. But maybe the Pinda Lickoyi would overlook that. Two unexplained deaths would be more difficult to overlook.

Reaching the end of the tunnel, he climbed out and in a crouching run made for the nearest cover. There he paused only a moment, looking and listening, straining eyes and ears to detect any sound in the stillness of the desert night that might signify danger. But he heard nothing. Satisfied that he would make good his escape, Kiannatah disappeared like a wraith into the deeper darkness.

Back at the jacal, Barlow made his move, sprinting across open ground and boldly barging into the hut. He tripped over the body of the Netdahe and landed badly. Dazed and consumed by pain, he lay there a moment. Somehow he found the strength and the will to get back on his feet. He gazed for a moment at the corpse of the Apache. This, then, was the broncho who had fired at him. And he had killed him with a lucky shot through the doorway. The Apache looked like a Netdahe. That made four. It was odd, he thought, that he felt no diminution of the burning desire for revenge that had completely overcome him while he lay on Oulay's grave.

He remembered the body of the Apache boy that lay outside. That didn't make sense to him—he couldn't figure out why this Netdahe would have killed one of his own. But his head hurt, and he wasn't thinking clearly. All he wanted to do was lie down and sleep. The venom in his system was making him nauseous. He couldn't stay here. It wasn't safe.

Leaving the jacal, he returned to his horse, feeling a measure of remorse that he didn't have the time—or the strength—to bury the boy. It was a shame to leave him to the desert scavengers. But there was no help for it. He mounted up and let the horse have its head. After what seemed like an eternity in the saddle, wandering aimlessly through the night, he had the sensation of falling—and blacked out before he hit the ground.

Geronimo and the two Netdahe bronchos with him found the body of the Apache hunter the day after Barlow had killed him. The host of buzzards circling high in the morning sky had brought them, and when they arrived, they found several of the birds feasting on the corpse. They fanned out and checked the gulch for sign, putting the clues together for the complete story of what had happened here. After a few minutes of this, they reunited near the corpse, sitting on their haunches and impassively watching the buzzards pluck morsels of raw flesh from the body.

"It was a white man who killed him," muttered one of the bronchos.

Geronimo nodded. "Just like the others." He looked, thought the others, more somber than usual. "One White Eyes?" asked the third broncho. "He must be loco."

"At least this time he was wounded," said the first, hopefully. "I saw blood."

"That does not make him any less dangerous," said Geronimo.

"He is only one man," said the other broncho, his voice bitter with contempt. "We must hunt him down and kill him."

"Do what you will," said Geronimo, standing up. "I go north."

The third broncho was incredulous. Could it be possible that Geronimo was afraid of one white man? That seemed to be the only explanation. Yet the broncho was afraid too—afraid enough of Geronimo to keep his mouth shut.

Nor did Geronimo say anything further. He was a man who put great stock in dreams and visions. There were some among the Chi-hinne who believed him to be a prophet, a man who could see into the future, and he had used the superstitious natures of his people to good advantage on numerous occasions. But Geronimo was himself a creature of superstition. For some time now, he had suffered from an anxiety that he could not overcome. He had a feeling that the terror that he and the other Netdahe had spread across Apacheria would someday soon be turned upon him and his kind. There was always a price to pay. The White Eyes said that a man who lived by the sword would die by it. That a wrong done would come back to haunt the perpetrator. This notion was not alien to the Apache. Geronimo realized that some might say he had a guilty conscience. Whether it was a guilty conscience or a strongly developed sense for self-preservation, he knew that the deaths of three Netdahe in the past days—all clearly at the hands of a solitary white man—constituted a very strange set of events. No one had thought that such a thing was possible. The entire Mexican army was too fearful to enter the Cima Silkq. And now a single white man had entered the stronghold of the renegade Apaches, and had managed to slay three of the Avowed Killers? No, it was too strange. It made Geronimo uneasy. He took it as a sign that now was the time to make a change.

"I will go north, and live among the Bedonkohe who remain there," he told the others. "Come with me, or stay. It is up to you."

And with that he headed back down the gulch for the place where they had left their horses.

Barlow came to feeling a hand gently touching his face, and for an instant he thought he was back in his adobe home, with Oulay beside him, caressing him, and his heart sang with joy as he murmured her name.

Then he opened his eyes, and as his vision cleared, he saw the round, creased face of an elderly Indian woman, illuminated by flickering firelight, looming over him.

His left hand lashed out and closed around her throat.

"Who are you?" he hissed, speaking in her own tongue. "Where am I?"

Fear filled her eyes as she clawed at his hand. He

was too weak to maintain his grip, and when she broke free, she let out a shrill cry of alarm and fled.

Barlow realized that he was inside a jacal. A small fire burned in the ring of stones marking the center of the hut. He was alone, but could hear other voices—excited Apache voices—outside. He tried to sit up. That required supreme effort. He'd made it up on one elbow when the blanket covering the jacal's doorway was swept aside and Cochise entered.

The Chiricahua jefe settled cross-legged near the dying fire and looked gravely across the jacal at Barlow.

"Some of the men out there," said Cochise softly, "they say you are crazy, and that you should be killed before you hurt somebody."

"Most of them never liked me," said Barlow dryly.

"You were more dead than alive when they brought you in," continued the jefe. "I am told you've killed several Netdahe. If this is true, then I would say you have been fortunate."

"I'm not done killing Netdahe. Maybe my luck will hold out."

Cochise nodded, and Barlow saw the sadness flicker across his features, even though the Chiricahua leader was trying his best to conceal the grief he felt. "I have lost a daughter. But you have lost everything. You do not care if you live or die. You have replaced what you lost with a thirst for revenge. This makes you like the very Netdahe that you hunt. Maybe that is why you frighten Geronimo."

"Frighten?"

"The Netdahe are gone from the Cima Silkq."

Barlow didn't believe him. He thought Cochise was telling him this just so he would call off his crusade against the Avowed Killers.

"Really," he said, skeptically.

"Have you ever known me to lie?" asked Cochise sternly.

Barlow admitted that he had not.

"They are going north, to scatter and live among the bands up there. So they will be hard to find."

"You're sure all the Netdahe are gone."

"You have been here for three days. In that time we have been looking, and can find none of them."

"Hopefully, one day, you will find none of them left anywhere on the face of the earth."

Barlow spoke with such rancor that it gave Cochise pause. He gazed speculatively at the white man for a moment before speaking. "Even though the Netdahe have caused trouble for those of us who prefer to live in peace, I do not hate them. Most, including Geronimo, have good reason to want to kill their enemies— the same reason that has brought you here. They have seen their loved ones murdered, just like you. But there is the one called Kiannatah. . . ." Cochise looked away for a moment, trying to maintain his composure. "I hope that before they kill you, Barlow, you will kill him."

"If he as the one who took Oulay, he's already dead."

"Unless you saw his body with your own eyes, you cannot be sure of that."

"I've never seen this Kiannatah."

"If you ever meet him, you will know him."

"How?"

"He is the worst of them all. And the most dangerous." Cochise got to his feet. "I will go find your nurse, and send her back. Try not to scare her anymore. In a few days the poison will leave your body and your wounds will be well enough healed that you can be on your way."

"Trying to get rid of me?"

"Yes," admitted Cochise bluntly. "Seeing you re-
minds me too much of my daughter."

"I'm sorry. I promised I would keep her safe."

"No one is safe out here," replied Cochise, as he
left the jacal.

Chapter 35

He was five days north of the Sierra Madre when the dragoons struck. He had stopped for the night, and was brewing up some coffee over an outlaw oven—a small, smokeless fire built in a hole excavated about a foot deep—when he heard them coming, even though they were doing their best to approach stealthily. That in itself was alarming, but he decided he didn't want a war with the Mexican army, and since he had nothing against them, and nothing to hide, he did nothing. So when a dozen of them rode into his camp, surrounding him immediately, he just sat there, minding his coffee, and nodding pleasantly at his uninvited guests.

"If I'd known you were coming," he said, speaking in their tongue, "I would have made more java."

"Put your hands up," said an officer, a lieutenant—the man Barlow assumed was in charge of the patrol.

Barlow had not failed to notice that some of the dragoons were aiming their short-barreled carbines at him. And they were all looking fairly unfriendly.

He stood up, slowly raising his hands. "What's going on?"

The lieutenant glared at him, and ordered two of his men to search Barlow's belongings. Two more dragoons dismounted and moved closer to Barlow, one in front of him and one in back, both holding their carbines on him.

Barlow watched the dragoons rifling through his meager possessions, then turned to the lieutenant. "What are you looking for?"

"Scalps."

Barlow shook his head, wearing a crooked smile. "Indian scalps? Don't have any. But what if I did? It's your government that was foolish enough to offer the bounty on them."

The lieutenant spoke to the dragoon standing behind Barlow. The latter had an inkling of what was coming, and as he turned he threw up an arm in self-defense. The dragoon was swinging the butt of his carbine at Barlow's head, and the blow was deflected, but still it was delivered with enough force to knock Barlow off his feet. Landing on his back, Barlow snarled as curse at the dragoon. As he intended, this angered the Mexican, who stepped in to deliver another blow; Barlow kicked him right between the legs, and as the man doubled over in agony, lashed out with the other leg so that the tip of his boot caught him right below the chin. The dragoon's head snapped back, his helmet went flying, and he went down like a poleaxed steer.

The other dragoon was no fool; he stepped away from Barlow and aimed the carbine. But the lieutenant snapped an order, and the dragoon reluctantly lowered the weapon.

"We will take him to the captain—alive," the officer told his men.

Barlow was hustled to his feet, and his hand were tied behind his back. All the while, several of the dragoons kept him covered, and all of them were wary, treating him with respect. The man he'd kicked in the

head was still out cold; one of his companeros doused
him with water from a canteen to rouse him. The dragoon, still dazed, was loaded onto his horse, while
Barlow was helped into his saddle. Barlow consulted
the stars as they headed out; the Mexicans and he
were headed due north. At least, he thought, that was
something to be thankful for.

They reached an encampment a couple of hours
later; Barlow calculated that an entire company of dragoons was gathered around their fires. Though he had
long been out of the army, he studied the layout of
the camp with an experienced eye. There was water—
a small creek—nearby, and some good graze for the
horses, which were now picketed and under guard,
was to be had. And there were plenty of sentries
posted; whoever was in command wasn't taking any
chances.

A few moments later her was dragged off his horse
in front of a tent from which emerged Captain
Cordova.

"Senor!" exclaimed Cordova amiably. "What a
pleasant surprise to see you again."

"It's a surprise for me too. But not a pleasant one."

Cordova ordered his hands unbound. Barlow ruefully rubbed his wrists and took another look around.
"Where's your French counterpart, Captain?"

"Called back to Mexico City." Cordova leaned
closer, pitching his voice in a conspiratorial whisper.

"Rumor is that all the French are leaving now.
Whether the emperor stays behind or not . . ."

Cordova shrugged. "Who knows what Maximilian
will do?"

"Well, that's too bad about the French."

"Oh, yes." Cordova laughed derisively. "We are all
very sorry to see them go." He gestured toward his
tent. "Please be my guest." He turned to the lieuten-

ant. "Thank you, Ramirez, but I am afraid you captured the wrong man. Tomorrow you may have better luck. See to your men."

The crestfallen lieutenant snapped a brisk salute.

Once inside the tent, Cordova poured Barlow a brandy and offered an apology. "More than twenty people from villages in this vicinity have been murdered recently," he explained. "Most were women and girls, and most of them were scalped."

"You know what's going on, don't you?" Barlow sipped the brandy gratefully.

"I have a good idea. It would be difficult to distinguish between the scalps of an Apache woman and a Mexican woman, no?"

"Yes. Looks like your government's chickens have come home to roost, Captain."

"You say that with a great deal of satisfaction."

"I guess the scalphunters can't find enough Apache topknots."

Cordova poured himself a double shot of brandy and knocked it back. "Not far to the east is the village of Santo Domingo. Do you remember the young woman there? The one with the boy?"

"That your men were going to hurt, if not kill?"

Cordova winced. "Please. An unfortunate situation."

"Yeah, I remember. What about them?"

"The woman's husband has returned. With a friend. A gringo. Not long after they arrived, the murders began."

"I knew of a gringo and a Mexican riding together—and they happened to be scalphunters."

"It is as I thought," muttered Cordova. "But I had no proof. Will you ride into Santo Domingo with me tomorrow, senor, and identify the two men? If they are the ones you know, I will arrest them."

Barlow finished off his brandy. "No."

"But why not, senor?"

Barlow had to think first. "Because of the woman and her boy. I take it you've paid a call already. You go riding in there with your whole company, her husband and his gringo friend will try to shoot it out with you, for sure. Innocent people might get hurt."

"What do you suggest?"

"I'll go in alone. They won't be afraid of one man. With any luck, I'll get the drop on them. I'll need a change of clothes—and a couple of other things."

Cordova thought it over. "You understand, senor," he said, finally, "that we want to take them alive, if possible."

"Sure," said Barlow, with a straight face.

He had no intention of bringing anyone back alive.

When Coughlin came to, the early-morning sun was slanting straight into his eyes, burning like red-hot pokers through his eyelids. He groaned and scrunched his eyes more tightly shut and tried to turn his head away from the light, but the process of turning his head started the pain—a dull, insistent throbbing in his skull. He remembered what had happened the night before. He and the Mexican had drunk more than their usual evening allotment of pulque. He was suffering from a hangover to end all hangovers. And he had spent the night, passed out, sitting up against the front wall of the adobe where the Mexican's woman lived. Just to his right was the ramada, which offered at least a modicum of relief from the already-hot sun, but the prospect of standing up—or even crawling on hands and knees—to get into the shade of the ramada was more than he could face at the moment. So he just sat there, squinting against the relentless sunlight. His throat was parched. There was

an earthen jug lying on its side to his left. He groped
for it, picked it up, shook it. And mumbled a heartfelt
curse to find it empty.

Also to his left was the doorway into the adobe. He
noticed that the door was open, and heard movement
inside. He slid his back along the wall, caught himself
before he fell right over on his face, and peered round
the doorframe. The Mexican was seated at the trestle
table in the middle of the room, his head resting on
his arms. Coughlin thought that he was still sleeping.
The movement was being made by Angeline. She had
her back to him, and she as putting a pot of water on
the oven to boil. Coughlin indulged in a rare moment
of wistful melancholy, as he wondered what it would
have been like had he led an ordinary life, marrying
a good woman and settling down somewhere to raise
a family and make an honest living. All those things
he had spurned and spoken of with contempt, but
there was something to be said for having a woman
make you breakfast every morning. Maybe, he told
himself, maybe it wasn't too late for him to put down
roots. Maybe he could find some Mexican senorita
who would put up with him.

A sound drew his attention to the street of Santo
Domingo. As usual, the thoroughfare was nearly
empty. The inhabitants of the village generally stayed
out of sight of Coughlin and the Mexican. They remained virtual prisoners in their adobe huts, rarely
venturing outside. But this morning, there was one
man, on a horse, at the far end of the street. He was
coming into town from the west. He wore a sombrero
pulled down low so his face was concealed, and a
brown serape. Coughlin pegged him for a *bandolero*.
Or maybe he was a Juárista. Or maybe he was both.
The man was slumped in the saddle, as though he was
weary from a very long trail, and there was something

lethargic even in the shuffling walk of the horse beneath him. Both man and horse were covered with
trail dust.

The man rode on up the street to the well that
marked the center of Santo Domingo's square, less
than a hundred yards from where Coughlin sat. There
the newcomer dismounted, moving slowly, stiffly. He
dropped the well bucket and then cranked it back up
again, taking his time. He placed the bucket, now full
of brackish water, on the rim of the well so his horse
could drink its fill, and while the animal did so, the
man leaned against the wall of the well and gave the
town a long, slow survey. His gaze swept over Coughlin, paused for a second or two, and then moved on,
apparently uninterested.

Coughlin couldn't muster up much interest in the
newcomer, either. As long as the man watered his
horse and moved on, there wouldn't be any trouble.
And Coughlin figured that was just what the newcomer would do. What, after all, was there of interest
in Santo Domingo?

But when the horse drank its fill, and the man had
slaked his thirst from the bucket, Coughlin saw that
he took up the reins of the horse and began to lead
the animal on up the street—straight for the scalphunter. Coughlin sat up straighter, more alert. It was obvious, even at a distance, that the stranger was no
campesino, and that he as well-armed. There was a
rifle in a saddle scabbard, and no doubt a pistola or
two on his hip, though these were hidden by the folds
of the brown serape. And he probably had a knife
too. Coughlin had never known a Mexican who didn't
favor a knife.

For a moment Coughlin thought the man was coming straight for him. But instead, the stranger walked
right by him, stopping at the ramada, where he tied his

horse to one of the cedar uprights, and then settled down at the table that stood in the striped shade. He sat facing the street so he could lean against another of the uprights and prop his booted feet on top of the table. The sombrero was still pulled low over his face; even at fifteen paces, Coughlin still could not say what he looked like.

The scalphunter waited a minute or two, expecting the stranger to say something to him—to at least ask if it was permissible for him to partake of the comfort of the table in the shade of the ramada. But the man said nothing. He just made himself right at home, and that riled Coughlin a little. He'd come to think of Santo Domingo as his own little fiefdom—well, his and the Mexican's—and he wasn't about to let some pistolero saunter into his territory and start making claims.

The anger that rose up within Coughlin served to clear away some of the cobwebs from his brain, though it did nothing to alleviate his pounding head-ache and raging thirst. Still, he managed to get to his feet, relying greatly on the wall for support. He glanced inside the adobe again. The Mexican was still asleep—or, more likely, still passed out. Coughlin considered waking his partner so they could deal with the interloper together. But then the scalphunter reminded himself that the stranger was just another greaser, after all. He didn't need any help dealing with the likes of him.

"What in the hell do you think you're doing?" he asked, his words slurring over a thickened tongue.

The stranger's head moved only slightly, as he looked at Coughlin from beneath the brim of the sombrero.

"I am sitting in the shade, senor," he replied.

He spoke Mexican, and Coughlin's comprehension

of that language was, to say the least, indifferent. He was in no mood to try to carry on a conversation with the bean eater in the man's own language. His head hurt too badly for that. "Speak English, damn it," he growled.

"I sit in the shade, senor," said the stranger, in heavily accented English this time.

"Well that shade doesn't belong to you."

"No. But does it belong to you?"

"It belongs to my pardner. This is his house, and that's his table you're sittin' at. And you didn't even ask first. Now, where I come from, that just ain't polite."

The man looked at him for a moment from under the sombrero, and finally said, softly. "Then maybe, senor, you should go back where you came from."

Coughlin's breath gusted in a sharp exhalation as though the stranger had punched him in the solar plexus.

"What did you say?" His words dripped menace.

The man had his arms crossed as he sat back against the upright. Now he unfolded them, and held his hands out, palms up. "Senor, I did not come here looking for trouble."

"Then you'd better change your tune," growled Coughlin, with a good deal of bravado, since he thought he now had the stranger cowed.

"Sí," acknowledged the stranger. "My apologies. I tell you what, senor. I have a bottle of tequila in my saddlebags. I got it in a little cantina down in Monterey. It is the best tequila in all of Mexico. I would like to share it with you. Let's say it is payment for your allowing me to sit here in the shade for a moment."

"Tequila, you say," muttered Coughlin.

"Sí, senor."

"I could use a drink," allowed the scalphunter.

The stranger swung his legs off the table, stood up

slowly, and walked to the far side of the horse from
Coughlin. Belatedly, the scalphunter's instincts for
self-preservation—instincts honed razor-sharp after
four years of war and nearly as many plying a perilous
trade—kicked in. He felt for the holster at his side,
and was relieved to find his pistol there. Just to be on
the safe side, he drew the gun and laid it in his lap.

"Ah," said the stranger. "Here it is." He held up a
bottle so Coughlin could see it. Then he tossed the
bottle at the scalphunter. Coughlin watched the bottle
spinning in the air as it came toward him. He couldn't
help but do that. And in that instant the stranger took
off his sombrero and whacked the horse across the
haunches with it. The horse jumped forward, con-
strained by the fact that the reins were tied to the
upright. But it moved enough for Coughlin to see that
the stranger had a pistol in his hand.

With an incoherent curse, Coughlin moved, rattlesnake quick. The stranger's bullet smacked into the
adobe where his head had been a split second before.
Coughlin tossed off a shot as he dodged, hoping for no
more than to buy himself a second or two to find cover.
The short missed. Even so, the stranger didn't even
flinch. He stood there, legs planted wide apart, steady
as a rock, taking careful aim—and his second shot hit
the scalphunter in the hip and threw him violently
against the adobe. Coughlin managed to get off one
more shot, going down. And with his last glance at the
stranger, he realized that the man *wasn't* a stranger to
him, after all, and he experienced a sickening despair.

But only for an instant. Because Barlow's third shot
caught him in the forehead. The bullet slammed
Coughlin's head back against the adobe, exited the
back of the skull, and splattered the scalphunter's
brains all over the wall.

Staggering into the doorway of the adobe, the Mexican raised his pistol and fired. The bullet grazed Barlow's gun arm. He dived to one side, rolling, and as he came up, intent on returning fire, he saw a movement behind the Mexican.

It was the woman, Angeline.

And her presence made him hesitate, for fear that if he missed his mark he might hit her.

The Mexican grinned. He did not understand why his adversary wasn't shooting back, but the fact remained that he wasn't, and that gave the Mexican an edge he intended to exploit. He took more careful aim with his pistola. Then his mouth flew open in a silent scream, and his eyes widened with surprise, and he pitched forward suddenly, a knife buried to the hilt between his shoulder blades. His trigger finger convulsed, and the pistol went off, but the shot went wide, and he was dead before he hit the ground.

Barlow stared at Angeline. She was framed in the doorway now, staring in horror at her handiwork. He got to his feet, went to stand over Coughlin, and looked down at the scalphunter for a moment. This time he felt a sense of satisfaction. Because the scalphunter had started it all. He had been the catalyst, if not the cause, and because of his actions, so very many people had died. Barlow had promised Cordova that he would take this man alive. But he'd made that mistake once before.

He saw movement out of the corner of his eye, and noticed that the street was filling up with the campesinos of Santo Domingo. They were venturing closer, cautiously staring at the bodies of the two scalphunters, some daring to believe that their long ordeal was over. Then, through them came Manuel, who paused when he saw his father lying dead, but only for an instant, before running into his mother's welcoming arms.

Barlow looked at her, then, and saw that she was watching him, with an expression he did not understand. He didn't think he wanted to. So he turned to his horse. He had a foot in the stirrup when Manuel broke away from his mother and ran to him.

"Must you go, senor?"

"Yes," said Barlow, and climbed into the saddle, wincing slightly at the pain from his fresh wound. But what was one more wound? One more source of pain?

"Can't you stay, for a while?"

"Don't worry. You're safe now. You and your mother."

Manuel looked over his shoulder at his father, and when he turned back to Barlow, the latter thought that there was a very old soul lurking behind the young boy's eyes. An old soul filled with wisdom—and the melancholy that comes with wisdom.

"More like him are out there," said Manuel. It was more than a statement of fact. It was a lament, muttered with the world-weariness of one who had lived his whole life under the cloud of uncertainty and hardship and danger. "Please stay."

Barlow felt sorry for him. Not just because of what the boy had seen and endured, but because he thought he had finally found some measure of protection from a harsh and cruel and unpredictable world. And Barlow knew now that he could not protect anyone.

"I can't," he said. "I've got to go. I've . . . got some things I have to do, up north."

Manuel was grasping at straws. "Then maybe, senor, you will come back when you have done these things, yes?"

Until now, Angeline had watched this exchange from the adobe's doorway. She stepped forward, coming up behind her son to rest her hands on his shoulders. "Let him go, Manuel," she said softly.

Barlow nodded, turned his horse away.

"We will wait!" called Manuel.

He looked over his shoulder, and his gaze was captured by Angeline's, and in her eyes he could see what he thought was an echo.

And he rode on.

THE PRE-CIVIL WAR SERIES BY
JASON MANNING

WAR LOVERS

0-451-21173-1

Retired war hero Colonel Timothy Barlow returns as
right-hand man to President Jackson when there's
trouble brewing on the border—trouble called the
Mexican-American War.

APACHE STORM

0-451-21374-2

With Southern secession from the Union in the East,
the doomed Apaches in the West are determined to die
fighting. But Lt. Joshua Barlow is willing to defy the
entire U.S. Army to fight the Apaches on his own terms.

GRITTY HISTORICAL ACTION FROM
USA Today BESTSELLING AUTHOR

RALPH
COTTON

SIGNET BOOKS

"A writer in the tradition of Louis L'Amour and
Zane Grey!" —*Huntsville Times*

National Bestselling Author
RALPH COMPTON

**Available wherever books are sold or at
www.penguin.com**